BLACK SWAMP WOLF

LLOYD HARNISHFEGER

Pandora, Ohio

Order this book online at www.trafford.com
or email orders@trafford.com

Most Trafford titles are also available at major online book retailers.

Printed in the United States of America.

ISBN: 978-1-4669-7316-9 (sc)
ISBN: 978-1-4669-7315-2 (e)

Trafford rev. 01/09/2013

www.trafford.com

North America & international
toll-free: 1 888 232 4444 (USA & Canada)
phone: 250 383 6864 ♦ fax: 812 355 4082

The wolf backed slowly out of the tunnel. She turned, shaking fresh dirt from her muzzle, searching for scent. She stood perfectly still for several moments, her silver gray coat shining in the morning sun. She snapped her ears forward and listened. Slanted faintly golden eyes searched the surrounding thickets. Nothing moved.

Satisfied at last, she re-entered the den. Her three pups greeted her with yips and whining. Settling in the semi-darkness the mother allowed her growing brood to nurse.

Otah remained unmoving. From his vantage point fifty paces upwind of the den, he had watched his enemy. The sun had risen well above the willow scrub before he finally slid carefully back out of sight. His spear was gripped so tightly it was only with difficulty that he was able to flex his fingers. A quiet rage brought trembling.

"I will yet kill it," Otah vowed, half aloud. "Yes, the wolf and her pups as well. I shall take vengeance for the death of my mother by this hateful beast!"

Sliding back down the small knoll where he had been lying to spy on the wolf, Otah checked his weapons and headed back to his shelter. The day was as warm for this date in autumn as he had seen in all his nineteen years. Still the uneasy breeze held a hint of what would soon follow.

Otah had been preparing for the cold for some time, but it was a hard task for one alone. His father gone to the "Other Place", his mother torn to pieces and killed by the wolf pack, and his sister. . . Oh, his sister! How lovely she was, and only four summers younger than he. It was no surprise that the Mastodon Hunters had stolen her! He would deal with them too, but was unsure how.

The young man's memory was as clear as the noonday sun. After all, it had only been four winters since she had been taken. The scene replayed itself in his mind.

*   *   *

Life had been hard for the two of them alone along the river. Without parents, Otah had become like a father. It was he who must provide. Leaf, his sister, although very young, then had done her best to assume a woman's duties. It was fortunate for both of the young survivors that from her earliest days Leaf had been carefully taught by her mother. She knew how to gather seeds and crush them into meal. Roots and bulbs of the cattail plant were a chore, but these also she had managed. Nuts and berries were easier and more fun too, but they held little sustenance. Leaf worked hard. She seldom cried anymore.

Otah slumped to the ground as the memory of her loss seared his mind. He had told the girl that he was going on a hunt and might be gone for several days. Some of these words were true, but most were a lie. Actually he had planned to hunt west along the river in hopes of finding the camp of the Mastodon Hunters. If they still proved to be friendly he would ask that he and his sister might join with them.

The band he sought had not seemed unfriendly in the past. Otah and his father had met with them on one occasion long ago. There had been no trouble then, even though the Clan of some thirty members could have easily done them harm. The Hunters' weapons and tools were far superior to those Otah and his father could make. For this reason also, the two of them could have been overpowered. Still, Otah thought wryly, what did we have that they could possibly want? While not clear then, the answer was obvious now. They wanted his sister, Leaf.

After two days Otah had found the Clan. Once again they had welcomed him. Especially accommodating was a young man Otah remembered from the visit with his father some years before. Called Fox, he was a few years older than Otah, a fact he never let the young man forget. In some ways he resembled a fox.

Fox was handsome and vain. During the two days Otah visited, the arrogant young man had seemed intensely interested in Otah's family.

"Why is your father not with you?" he had asked. "Did he stay with your mother and sister?" He seemed very curious about the father.

When Otah explained that his father had gone away to the "Other Place" Fox seemed even more inquisitive. Otah thought that the man seemed pleased to hear that the father was dead.

"And your mother. Is she well?"

"Afraid of wolves," Otah replied.

Fox was astonished. "Wolves you say? Surely you could have killed them easily. While they appear to be fierce they are actually *cowards!* You should have killed them. I would have killed them."

Otah swallowed his anger. The words Fox used were true, but Otah already knew all of that. "It's easy," he thought "to make bold, bragging statements when you have good weapons. Weapons chipped from the finest flint and chert, crafted by an old man whose only duty was to produce them for the Clan. A different Elder made handles for axes and strong , straight shafts for spears. Also significant was the fact that this proud young man had the advantage of thirty Clansmen to back him up. Still Otah knew that he must not cause trouble if he and his sister were to be asked to join the Mastodon Hunters.

Having been gone for five suns, Otah knew he must return to the hut and his sister. The wolves were still a threat especially since they had dug a den not far from their home.

A terrible image of little Leaf in danger had been enough to cause Otah to gather his things and say goodbye to Fox and Chief Spotted Hand. He started east at a trot, anxious to be back to the hut.

While the young hunter had made several obvious hints, there had been no offer of acceptance into the Clan. Not long after this he had returned from a hunt to find his sister gone.

                    *   *   *

With such memories fresh in his thoughts Otah returned to his house. It was a lonely place now. No more was heard the jabber of mother and daughter at their tasks. No more did he hear the tapping of his father chipping flint. No more would games be played with the small rounded bones. It was now a place of silence.

Otah was terribly lonely.

He chewed a stringy piece of beaver meat as darkness filled the hut with gloom. He would have preferred to shed tears, but after nineteen winters he was now a man. Men did not cry! What sustained him now was hatred. Hatred of the mother wolf and her pups.

A mere half day's walk from the hut, they were not to be ignored. On several recent nights he had heard them outside. He knew which animals they were, since the pups, now more than half-grown, had not been as silent as the mother. By mid-winter these youngsters would be big enough and strong enough to add to the danger. All of the pack, mother and pups, must be destroyed, and soon. There was no time to lose.

With first light Otah carefully examined his two spears. The first, made by his father just a few moons before he had to go to the Other Place, was a thing of beauty. The shaft was of tough Osage orange wood. It had been straightened by hours of patient heat treating over a small fire. The true artistry, however, was revealed in the flint point. Many,many winters before, Otah's father and grandfather had traveled a very long distance beyond the southern edge of their home beside the Black Swamp to arrive at the source of the finest flint there was. Working together they had pried loose several blocks of the glistening stone. Otah's father and grandfather struck off many long thin flakes of the material. These they had secured in their packs. The twelve day trip north with their treasure had been one of the proudest and happiest times of their lives.

The grandfather had told the story of their trip on many nights, the family seated in the hut around a tiny fire. Both he and Otah's father had carefully described the route, even scratching a rough map in the dirt floor. "Some day," the grandfather had told Otah, "all this flint will be used up. You yourself will need to go when that time comes." Otah had paid little attention. What was a trip to the far off flint quarries to a happy boy of six? He would rather play along the river!

Otah ran a careful thumb along the cutting edge of the spear. The blade was thin toward the tip, and remained very sharp/ It would do.

The other weapon was a different matter. Otah glared at it in disgust. Despite the careful instructions by his father years before, Otah had never really practiced the technique of flint napping. The shaft was crooked and the point was thick and dull. Dangling threads of sinew binding added to a total picture of incompetence. He threw it against the wall of the hut. "More of a _club_ than a spear!" he growled.

Neither weapon was meant to be a projectile. A spear-thrower would have allowed Otah a much safer attack on the wolves or an enemy. He was, however unable to make the device or the thin, jointed arrows required for it. He had no choice. The two weapons he possessed were meant for stabbing. This required closing with an animal and fighting it hand to fang. It was fortunate that he did have his father's axe and fire-making kit. Also a knife and flint napping tools remained.

Otah picked up the ugly spear again. He balanced it at arm's length and made several Imaginary thrusts toward the hut wall. In disgust he threw it against the wall _again._ His father's spear felt much better when he experimented with it, but still provided little comfort as he considered the battle to come.

Otah was afraid. He feared the beasts he must attack and he had no confidence in his weapons. The mother wolf was his equal in body weight and far exceeded him in speed and cunning. Yes, he was very afraid, and he had good reason to be!

The following morning found him once again concealed at the brow of the hill overlooking the den. He clutched his only good spear as he watched and waited.

Evidently his enemy had left the den to hunt. The pups, three of them poked noses out from time to time but only one ventured beyond the hole. In his two previous observations of the den site, Otah had not failed to notice this particular cub. A male, somewhat larger than his siblings, he was unmistakable. He had given the animal the name "Sand", because of its distinctive yellow-brown coat. "That one," Otah thought, "could be danger! He will most certainly come to the aid of his mother when the attack comes!"

Otah realized that his continuing observations of the den were no longer necessary. By this time he was well aware that making these visits was merely a way of avoiding what must soon be done.

"So Fox says wolves are cowards," he grumbled as he headed back to his hut again. "Perhaps some are, but this one is *not!* She is a killer and I have observed no fear in her." This thought once again thrust into his mind the way of his mother's death.

*   *   *

Shortly after his father had gone to the "Other Place" Otah had returned from hunting to find Leaf cowering at the back of the hut.

"What is it?" He had had to shout to be heard above her sobs.

"She is gone to the "Other Place", Leaf screamed. For several minutes she continued to cry and wail in grief.

Otah shook her violently. "Tell me! Tell me *now!* He roared."

Trembling and crying, the young girl fought to control her fear and grief. "Mother Was digging roots and I . . . . ."

"Where? Where did this *happen* ?" Otah shouted . He shook her savagely once more. "I will go to her now. You must show me the way." He began to throw some dried meat into his pouch.

"No! *NO!*" She screamed. The wolves! The awful wolves!" She curled her small frame into a ball. Once more he could not understand what his sister was trying to say. He seized her roughly by the arm and dragged her to her feet.

"Stop this!" He hissed. "Stop it *now!* We must hurry. It may not be too late. Get ready to go."

"I . . . .I . . . . .No . . . .No, I cannot, " she quavered.

"Then you must tell me where this happened. Quickly! *Quickly!*" He demanded, shaking her once more. "Mother was digging roots, you said. Tell me the place exactly."

"M . . .mother was . . . d . . digging roots. I had gone near the river to gather . . .to . . . .to . . gather. . . a . . a. . . . acorns. Then . . . then . . "

Raging in frustration, Otah shouted at the girl again. "Where Leaf? *WHERE?*"

The girl hardly heard his demands. "I heard screaming! I ran. . . I lost . . . lost . . all my acorns . . and then no more screams."

"Leaf. Leaf! Look at me. Did you see mother then?"

"I saw . . I saw . . . blood all over. They were at her, biting, tearing . . Oh! . . .Ohhhh." She fell from his hands in a faint.

In desperation Otah pulled her to her fee. He locked his fingers in her hair and slapped her hard across the face. She blinked twice and would have fallen again had he not shaken her hard. "WHERE WAS MOTHER?" he shouted directly into her face.

"The family trees," Leaf managed to croak. "It was at the family trees. The wolves . . .two wolves. . . their teeth. . . . biting. . . biting. .. ."

Otah nearly threw the girl to the floor of the hut. He draped a sleeping robe over her and told her to stay inside until he returned.

The young hunter grabbed both spears. He made sure his flint knife was secure in its sheath, patted Leaf's head and dashed away. He finally had been told where the attack had happened.

The spot was vaguely familiar to him. Many winters before while his father was still with them, all four had been gathering nuts near the river. It was then that little Leaf had noticed four young cedar trees growing side by side among the stones. All in a row, there were two tall ones, one smaller, and one smallest of all.

"Look!" Leaf had cried, clapping her hands in glee. "It is our *family!* See, here is father and brother, then mother, then the tiny one is *me!*"

All had smiled at her imaginings. Over the years they had often stopped at the site to see how the "family trees" had grown.

Cramming a piece of tough, dried venison in his cheek, he was off at a fast trot. He remembered the place which he was to learn was very near the wolf den. With difficulty he forced a steady gait. It would be foolish to tire himself before he had covered the half day's journey ahead.

In his heart, Otah knew that speed was no longer important. The wolves would have done their grisly work long before he could arrive. Still he raced along, leaping over downed logs and bursting through clumps of brush.

As he ran he could imagine the horror of what had happened near the family trees. Fox had been partly right. In one way wolves might be considered cowardly. Any hunter with some experience would have seen a wolf pack stalking a moving herd. Deer, caribou, even buffalo, it made no difference. The wolves were patient and watchful. Too smart to risk injury in an attack on a healthy animal, they kept their distance until one of their targets began to show signs of weakness. Only then did they begin a serious stalk. Was this being cowardly or was it simply being smart?

Sick with dread at what he was soon to find, Otah could imagine the hidden wolves watching, watching, their yellow eyes always on his limping mother. Her swollen joints were so painful that she could hardly walk, much less run! Too many winters digging for bulbs in the cold swamp muck, too many hours kneeling to scrape at pegged-down hides, too many nights forming red clay into bowls, all had taken their toll.

As he continued to run, Otah tortured himself by imagining what the attack had been like. He could see it in his mind's eye. The beasts would have silently circled and circled, ever closer to the old woman. The female would have gone in first, fangs flashing as they tore the muscles in the woman's lower calf, further crippling her. As she struggled to remain standing, the heavier male would have launched himself at her head. Hardly would her body have struck the ground until the huge jaws would have clamped on her throat. Mercifully the end would have come in just a few minutes.

He assumed that growls and screams had brought Leaf to the horrible scene, too late to help their mother. This certainly was fortunate. Had the young girl arrived much sooner the animals would have killed her too.

Otah forced the awful images from his mind in order to concentrate on his route. Soon enough he began to recognize familiar landmarks. At last he flew past the family trees. Breathing hard, he slowed to a fast walk. His hunter's eyes scanned the ground. Every disturbed leaf and blade of grass showed the way. He forced himself to go on. He knew that the very next step might reveal the horror that he did not want to see.

The scene was eerily the same as he had imagined it. Trampled weeds and scraped patches of earth told their story. Her body, twisted and torn, lay half concealed in a clump of dying ferns. One glance was enough. It was *more* than enough!

Hardly more than a boy, he fell to his knees and wept. He cried for his mother and for his little sister. The only good thing he could think of was that his father had gone to the "Other Place" and would not have to know of this tragedy.

Now Otah must be a man. The wolves were nowhere to be seen, undoubtedly well fed and sleeping in the den. There was no way he could carry the body back to his hut. Even if he could he would not want Leaf to see their mother like this! It had been some time since death had taken her. There was no time to ponder.

His flint knife slashed into his carrying pouch. Opening it wide, he held his breath and secured it over his mother's face. Tearing some saplings from the soft ground nearby, he was able to make a primitive sled. More tears fell as he gently rolled what remained of the stiffened body onto the poles and began to pull.

Softened earth along a small creek which emptied into the river provided a burial site. He used the worthless spear he had built to loosen the soil enough to enable him to scoop it out with his hands. When the opening was deep enough he lined it with ferns and cedar boughs. The soft earth quickly did its work and the sad job was finished. The completed grave was covered with the largest boulders he could carry. By then twilight was upon him.

*   *   *

The memory of those terrible times and the recent disappearance of his sister had renewed his resolve. The wolf and her cubs must die! Thankfully the pups' father had left the den until the pups were grown. Attacking one adult wolf would be hard enough. Two would have been impossible. The question he wrestled with was the method of dealing with the mother wolf. At first he had proposed a simple headlong approach. "If," he told himself, "the minute she left the den I ran straight at her and threw my worst spear. . . .I could. . .it would. . . ." It was a fool's plan and he knew it. "There *would* be a killing," he said in disgust, "but the killing would be mine!"

A second idea merited more serious consideration. If he watched until she left to hunt, he might be able to enter the den and snatch one of the pups. Then he could tie the small creature to a tree. Hiding on a branch just above the pup he could wait until its cries brought the mother. When she was directly under him he could dive upon her, the spear aimed at her back.

Otah was almost ready to put this plan in motion but he did not. While two of the pups posed no real danger, except perhaps a few bites and scratches, the third one did. The one he had named "Sand" was growing fast. He bossed his littermates and snatched much more than his share of the meat his mother brought to the den. At times it even appeared ready to challenge its own mother! Undoubtedly this young wolf, bigger and stronger than the others, would someday become the leader of his own pack. "Yes," Otah thought, "Sand will fight!"

Twice more he spent precious time watching the den. The days were shorter, the nights growing cold. Finally he devised the only plan that he felt had even a slight chance of success. He would build a snare.

Otah had been using snares to capture birds and small animals since he was a boy of but a few summers. First learning the technique from his father, he had improved the method until even as youngster he was doing much to provide meat for the family. Alone now, he still depended upon such devices to keep himself alive and fed.

Snaring a rabbit or a grouse was one thing, but using this procedure to capture a mature wolf was something else again!

For two long evenings, seated by a small fire in the dark and lonely hut he had perfected his plan. Lengths of sinew, split and flattened were excellent for the deadly snares he set for small game. Sinew was thin but very strong. Almost scent-free, it did not alert the intended prey. Concealing a loop of sinew along a game path was a simple matter. The victim was often entangled before it even realized what had happened.

Sinew was fine for rabbits, but for a full-grown wolf it was laughable. The only material with any chance of success was rawhide. Otah knew he must get some and he must get it soon.

Making rawhide meant the fresh kill of a large animal. Otah wished Leaf were still with him. She could have helped in his quest of a deer. Not only the hide, but the venison itself was needed. Alone it would be a miracle if he could bring one down.

Faced again with the rapidly approaching winter, he was aware of the desperate need for a successful hunt. It would take time and care to butcher the meat, then cut it into thin strips for drying. He was not at all sure if he could make pemmican, even if he had the necessary intestines for stuffing. Also needed would be the nuts and berries to add to the pulverized meat. Leaf had learned the method from her mother, but that was of no help now. She was gone.

Otah examined the long-unused grinding stone and the smooth flat rock which accompanied it. He guessed that he could do the grinding of meat. He had no choice. The berries were no problem. Even though it was late in the season they were still plentiful on the nearby hillsides. All of this would make no difference until he had brought down a deer. Had the man the help of a bow and arrow his task would have been relatively simple. This marvelous device, however, was not to be invented for another thousand years. The spear-thrower [or atlatl] was second best, but Otah reminded himself that he was unskilled in the making of one.

What was it his father had so often told him?

"Patience,. . .patience. . . plan and wait!"

Well Otah would do just that. There was only one way for him to be successful hunting deer. He must be able to approach close enough to use the good stabbing spear.

In the night the plan came to him. He had not been asleep. He was frightened. Had the spirit of his "Gone Away" father visited him to tell him how this hunt might be accomplished? It seemed to be so! Otah had lain perfectly still and did not sleep until the dawn. He feared things he could not understand.

Otah had very little to work with. Several cured skins lined the hut, but none were large enough. The plan was to disguise himself as a coyote. He then could approach the deer on hands and knees until very close. At the right moment he would leap up and use the spear.

Finding deer would not be a problem. There had been a herd of some thirty animals foraging that fall on the far side of the river. Often he had watched them hungrily, but with no means of capture, their presence only led to frustration. They had little fear of humans. Except for Otah they had rarely encountered any. Coyotes posed no threat to the deer either, except in early spring when fawns were being born.

He pulled the skins down from the wall, and feeling rather foolish, attempted to drape them over his body. Had his mother or Leaf been present there would have been much laughter! He tried binding them under his arms and across his back but still he was not covered. Rabbit skins, of which he had plenty, were tied over his arms and legs. Dropping to all fours he hobbled around in the hut, loose skins flapping and swishing. The entire concoction was a disaster, but it was all he had.

"Tonight I must be near the meadow where they feed," he thought. "At dusk when they come out to graze, the darkness may help my disguise." Little did he know or consider the deers' ability to see in the darkness, and his lack of it.

That afternoon Otah was about to make ready for his hunt when once again his father's admonition came to him.

"Patience . . . . patience . . . . plan . . ."

The words from his past did their work once more. "What have I forgotten? Where will this plan fail?" he asked himself. In only a few minutes several problems appeared before him. First of all he had done nothing to disguise his scent, not to mention that of the skins. These had undoubtedly soaked up the smoke and cooking odors in the hut. Perhaps more serious was the wind. If the night proved to be still every sound he made by crawling would be sure to alert the herd. Also, without a breeze carrying his scent away his presence would never go unnoticed.

There was one more defect with his plan, but he was not to realize it until too late. Still he decided to take time to correct as many of the problems as possible. It would mean several more days before he could try his disguise.

He took the skins outside and considered what must be done. Once, hunting with his father, he had been shown a large red fox rolling over and over in some weeds. "See what he does?" the father had asked, smiling. "There is something decaying there. The fox is using that smell to hide his own."

"But why?" the young Otah had asked.

"So he can sneak up on whatever it is he wishes to catch. Maybe a rabbit or a goose. If they smelled a fox they would run off or fly away, but they would not fear the odor of something long dead!"

Knowing of no dead carcasses in the area, Otah simply buried the skin bundles in river muck. It would have to do. As for the wind, he would wait until the right breezes came, even if it meant the loss of more time. He was being patient. He was planning!

Two evenings later Otah stopped his work long enough to test the breeze against his cheek. The wind was light but steady from the west, flowing directly down the river valley. He took a deep breath, squared his shoulders and headed off to dig up his "costume". He shook off the dirt and straightened the messy hides and their pitiful lashings. They smelled very bad, but that was good. An inspiration came. He scooped up double handfuls of the reeking goo and smeared it liberally all over his body.

With only the good spear in hand he trotted away in the twilight. He reached the river at its shallowest point. This was where his family had always crossed. At that moment it struck him. The flowing water would soon wash away all his careful, stinking disguise! He was committed now however and no thought of turning back even entered his mind.

The water was as cold as he had ever felt it. He bundled the skins as best he could and steadied them on his head. Four steps later a slippery rock on the river bottom was his undoing. He fell completely under, but came up in time to rescue the bundle which was already on its way downstream.

Otah was furious with himself, for by the time he would have applied more muck to the skins and himself it would be fully dark. Dripping and raging he staggered back to his hut.

"Patience!" he screamed aloud to the watching trees. "I *have* patience, but how could I have known about all of *this?*"

The following evening found him on the far side of the river. Dry skin clothing kept him much warmer after his second icy crossing. The muck was harder to locate on the other river bank, but he finally found some. With the blackish concoction heavily applied to the pelts and his body, he started west to find the deer herd. The sodden earth-covered skins made hard going. The unfamiliar south bank slowed his progress too. Still he trudged on.

The first star was visible in the west when Otah at last saw the shadowy shapes of the feeding animals. As he had expected, they were scattered across a small meadow free of large trees. "At last!" he breathed. Clutching his only spear he dropped to all fours and began his stalk. While in this low position he soon realized that he was unable to see the deer. Every few feet it became necessary that he cautiously stand up to see over the bushes.

The animals were working their leisurely way toward the west. Otah's slow pursuit found him no closer than he had been at first. He was determined to keep on. Then the final blow fell. Heavy clouds that had been threatening all that day, moved in, completely blotting out the moonlight he had depended upon.

He did not scream his anger and frustration this time. He simply started back, staggering along in the darkness. It was late when he finally reached the hut. Too tired and too discouraged to make fire, he simply dropped to the sleeping skins and slept.

The morning brought cold, driving rain. This was good, since the hunter was forced to stay in the hut and make better plans. He had learned that crossing and re-crossing the frigid river was a mistake. He must prepare a temporary camp south of the river. From there he could make much easier stalks upon the deer he sought.

The foul weather continued for another day and night. Finally there was a bright autumn day. Otah set to work building a rude raft of fallen timbers. Hauling the windfalls, positioning them on the bank, and lashing them together with roots of the cedar tree was hard but rewarding work. He had wrapped all his food, weapons and fire-making material into a tidy bundle. With a long, heavy pole he shoved off into the river.

Another mistake!

Very soon the pole proved too short to reach bottom. With no means of guiding the awkward craft, Otah found himself speeding downstream, the raft slowly twisting in the current. The pole touched bottom at times. When it did he pushed with all his strength, attempting to guide the raft toward the south shore.

As the stream narrowed the current seemed to gather speed. Otah was by now wet to the knees. Keeping his balance on the shifting logs was ever more difficult. With sinking heart he finally felt one of the longest logs catch and hold. The raft swung slowly around and finally lodged against the muddy, gravel-filled bank.

He scrambled ashore and collapsed, sobbing. The raft had grounded back on the *north shore* again!

It was only by luck and sheer determination that he had kept his bundle dry. By this time heavy clouds were building in the west. There was nothing to do but make a temporary camp, spend the night, and attempt the crossing *again* on the day following.

Otah felt a little better when he had gathered brush and cedar boughs for shelter. Although his palms held blisters from spinning the fire stick he finally felt heat from a small fire. His freezing feet tingled pleasantly as he pushed them as close to the flames as possible.

Something was wrong! He had heard nothing. No unfamiliar scent was on the breeze. Nothing moved in the reeds along the river bank. He was not fooled. In the years since he had lost both father and mother his senses had sharpened. With only himself and his small sister, Leaf, to protect he had learned to trust his instincts.

There! On a fallen tree some sixty paces away she stood watching. The mother wolf. His hated enemy! Behind her he could barely make out a pair of pointed ears above a yellow-brown head. It was Sand! Almost as big as its mother, the cub watched, unmoving.

Frustration and rage were Otah's weapons. Gripping the good spear he leaped to his feet. Facing the wolves and brandishing the spear, he roared a challenge. They did not move, but even at that distance he fancied that he could see their hackles rising. He shouted again and slashed at the bushes. Still showing no fear, both animals slowly turned and melted away into the brush.

With his present distress in attempting the river crossings and his frustration with unsuccessful hunting escapades, he had almost forgotten his vow to kill the she wolf. This encounter had once again strengthened his determination. "I will soon take the skin off that thing which murdered my mother and terrified little Leaf!" he growled. He meant every word!

Otah kept careful watch as he hurried to gather large pieces of driftwood. The fire must be kept going all night if he were to keep the wolves from his camp. He wrapped all his cured venison in a small pouch and climbed with it into a tree far from his camp. He tied it to a limb well off the ground. No wolf could get it there!

Otah wrapped himself in his sleeping robe and sat against the back of the lean-to.

He dozed until the first drops of rain began to patter on his covering. Thankful for the large logs he had gathered, he felt sure that they would continue to burn so long as the rain did not increase. He slept then, even though cold rain found its way into his shelter and down his back!

It was almost dawn when he heard a commotion. It seemed to be coming from the tree which held his food bag. Snuffling and low growling noises could not be mistaken. A *bear!* Otah's shoulders slumped. He buried his face in his hands and groaned. His precious food, safe from wolves, had been no problem for the black bear. The animal was gone and so was the venison.

As soon as there was light enough to travel Otah gathered his bundles and ran west at the fastest pace he could maintain. Fear gripped him as he ran. The hut had been unprotected far too long, and he dreaded what he might find there. Seeing him by the river, the wolves may have decided to raid his hut.

Choking and gasping for breath he came sliding into the tiny clearing that surrounded his home. Before he even entered he was well aware of what he would find inside. The skin door flap was torn to shreds. Wolf tracks covered the still wet clay around the hut. With a sinking heart he crawled inside. *Destruction!* The few remaining strips of dried venison were gone. Wolf droppings were everywhere. Perhaps worst of all, the handle of his father's great stone axe had been gnawed almost in two. Otah sank to his knees in absolute despair. Now he was not only a poor hunter, but was in danger of starving as well.

Otah was ready to quit. "Just let me die and go to the 'Other Place'", he moaned. "Perhaps I will see father and mother there. Father told us it was a happy place where the hunting was always good. "Yes," he resolved. "I will simply stop trying. Without food I will 'go away' soon enough."

Then in the night as he shivered in sorrow and regret, a sudden vision filled his mind. "Leaf!" he cried aloud. "I must rescue my sister from the Mastodon Hunters! I dare not give up. I *will* kill a deer! I will dry the meat just as mother and Leaf used to do. Then . . . Then I will make rawhide thongs to capture my enemy and her pups. I will take *their* skins as well!"

*   *   *

Once *again* he braved the freezing water! Gaining the other bank he did not stop to make fire. Running would warm his legs soon enough. He would not slow his approach until he had finally found the deer herd.

The animals had moved further west. They had also been traveling southward away from the river. Otah was thankful he had started early, as it was late evening before he found them. They were grazing peacefully on the side of a gentle slope which rose above an area of swampy ground.

Despair nearly assailed him again as he attempted to drape himself with the pitiful coyote disguise. "Patience!" he reminded himself. "Well," he thought, "my patience is nearly gone and my planning has been pathetic, but as long as I have strength I will not *quit!"*

The brush and weeds were not so thick here. Crawling was easier too. He made steady progress. The deer were not spooked, but twice a young spike-horned buck threw up his head and stared in the hunter's direction for several moments. Otah froze and remained unmoving until the animal was feeding once more.

Suddenly Otah fell flat in terror. A terrible commotion was erupting just over the ridge top. Bushes were torn, large grunting sounds were heard, as were the snorts and growls of fighting animals. He eased himself over the hilltop. The deer nearest the hunter scattered as the reason for the commotion became apparent. In amazement Otah watched two bucks engaged in mortal combat. The smaller animal appeared to be injured. "Why doesn't he run away?" Otah marveled. "It is clear he can never win against the hooves and antlers of that magnificent animal he's fighting!"

Sometimes, for no apparent reason, fortune smiles on one. It often appears that luck, or whatever one may call it comes along at the precise moment it is needed most. This was the case for the young hunter now flattened in the grass some forty paces from the fighting bucks.

"They are *locked!*" He gasped in astonishment. He had heard of such a thing, and indeed Father had once found the remains of two deer whose antlers were still locked in the deadly embrace that had killed them.

The smaller, badly wounded animal kept falling, pulling the bigger buck's head almost to the ground. It struggled mightily, shaking and thrusting this way and that but the entwined antlers held. Four coyotes circled the contestants, ready to move in when it was safe. There was no time to lose. Otah leaped to his feet and ran shouting and screaming toward the struggling deer. The coyotes scattered. The herd flashed away over the hill, their flopping white tails spreading the alarm.

Darkness was nearly upon him as he followed the fight. The larger deer was tiring too. Evidently the contest had been going on for some time, perhaps for days. Otah was so excited he hardly knew what to do. "Fire!" he whispered urgently. "I must make fire as fast as I can. The coyotes will not be far away and will be watching for their chance, just as I am!"

It was more than coyotes that Otah must fear. The battered and bloody animals would be a magnet for every predator within hearing. Bears, wolves, even the occasional swamp panther would be attracted to such an easy kill. Twice and three times the fire-making spindle flipped away from his shaking fingers. He found it again each time. Twirling the blunt end of the fire wand into the piece of rotted wood for several minutes finally brought a curl of smoke. He kept the rhythm going until a tiny mound of black sawdust formed around the spindle. He bent low, and cupping his hands around the glowing spark, blew gently upon it. Adding tinder of dried moss from his kit finally produced a true, bright flame. He piled on ever larger twigs and sticks until the fire was burning steadily.

Otah dashed about gathering heavier sticks. The ends of these he placed in the fire. They must serve as torches to keep any predators at bay until morning.

The night seemed never to end, but Otah felt no need for sleep. He tended the fire carefully, adding even some heavy logs to the blaze. The recent rains had soaked the wood but once on the flames they soon began to smolder. When the fire was truly roaring he took the cool end of one burning stick and circled the two unfortunate deer. He could see shining eyes keeping watch just beyond the fire-lit clearing. Shouting and waving his burning brands kept them away at first, but as the hours passed they seemed to become bolder.

False dawn arrived. The antler-locked deer were a pitiful sight indeed. The challenger was being dragged about by the larger animals' struggles. It was obvious that death was near, for the smaller animal had ceased trying to fight or even to stand. The bigger buck was still moving, but the weight of the other kept his head and neck dragged almost to the ground.

Otah was ecstatic! As dawn broke before him he saw everything he needed for life and for all his further plans. Warily he moved closer to the pair of animals. Only one remained alive. It was fighting for breath in great ragged gasps. Summoning some impossible inner reserve of strength, it reared and bucked in a last effort to rid itself of the hated burden that was killing him. The stag's great hind legs were splayed as he tried vainly to back away from the carcass holding his head. The magnificent buck, leader of his herd and father of many fawns and yearlings, was dying too.

Otah gripped the good spear in both hands. Knuckles white with tension, he tried a false jab. The deer went wild! His flailing hooves tore the ground, but he backed only a few paces away from the hunter. Otah felt no sympathy for the terror the beast was feeling. The locked-together deer were a gift. The gift of *life!* He must take immediate advantage of this unbelievable stroke of good fortune. They would die anyway, he assured himself.

"Somehow," he told himself, "I must get behind the animal." The antlers were now no threat of course, but the thrashing hooves could cause a wound that might be his end!

Patience. . . patience. . . plan. . ."

The words came back to him and he saw the wisdom they held. He backed away from the very real danger, and instead began to build up the fire.

The coyotes were keeping their distance, displaying the same patience as the human they watched. He did not bother with them. If he was successful in bringing the buck to the ground, and would begin butchering, then the coyotes and possibly other predators would become bolder. Otah must be doubly alert then! He sat against a bush and waited.

The weak fall sun was nearly overhead before the larger deer finally fell to the ground. Its legs scrabbled weakly but he was unable to rise. Otah circled behind the stricken pair, but still he watched and waited. He wished to make sure the animal was unable to make a sudden lunge and slash with its hooves. He waited some more. Suddenly he noticed the big muscles in the buck's forelegs bunching and quivering. "I've been a *fool!*" he chided himself. "I've given the animal time to rest and recuperate." Now was the time!

The hunter moved closer. The deer was aware of him and was obviously preparing to strike out with his legs. Otah leaned in and drove the spear deep, just below the spine. Had young Otah been instructed by an experienced hunter he could not have struck a more killing blow. The chief of the deer herd shuddered a moment and died. It did not suffer as it certainly would have, locked together with its challenger. Predators

would have torn and savaged it for hours.

Once again Otah was thankful for the tools left to him by his father. It had been

another stroke of luck that he had had them with him when the wolves invaded his hut.

They could have chewed the handles to pieces as they had done to the axe. They might

have even carried the smaller ones off into the forest. He inspected each one carefully.

The pink flint skinning knife still held its serrated edge. It really needed some re-touch

sharpening. Each piece of the flint-knapping kit was intact in its small doeskin case.

Tears formed as Otah ran his fingers over the well-polished surfaces. Everything was in

its place. He made no attempt to re-sharpen the knife's edges, as he didn't have the skill.

One careless stroke could easily snap the brittle flint blade. That would be devastating!

He rolled both animals onto their backs. Their antlers still held their heads

together in their fatal embrace, but he paid no attention to them. The larger animal would

be attempted first. It was necessary to minimize the weight as soon as possible.

Removing the entrails would accomplish this. The offal could be dragged away from the

kill site where the coyotes could fight over them! The shiny blade, hardly as long as his

smallest finger, slipped easily through the hide of the underbelly.

Otah knew that he was doing a very poor job. Much of the meat would be wasted.

He did make sure, as he worked, to rip the slippery strands of sinew from the forelegs and

along the spine. These silken strings he tied loosely around his neck for safe carrying.

The largest intestine had to be cut loose from the stomach. Once it was free he stripped its contents with thumb and finger. This long tube he also draped around his neck. The smell was horrible, but it was proof that fresh venison would soon be roasting!

Otah took time to build up the fire, for it had almost gone out. It was becoming clear that another night and day would probably be necessary before he could head north with the meat and hides. He stopped butchering long enough to roll several large logs next to the fire, as they would need to dry out before they would burn well. He must attempt to stay awake again. This second night's vigil would be somewhat easier, since he could drag the carcasses very close to the fire where he would be sitting. Still, he was extremely tired now. The lurking predators, maddened by the smell of the meat, would naturally be more dangerous too. Otah's hardest hours lay just ahead but he was determined to save the venison and the hides.

His eyes were drooping as the sun began to set. He made himself perform one more task while the light still held. Raising a heavy rock as high as he could reach, he brought it down hard upon the larger deer's skull. It was essential that he extract and save the brains. These would be needed later when he attempted tanning the green hides. If this smelly mess was not worked well into the flesh side, within a few days the skins would become so stiff as to be practically useless.

Otah was so exhausted that it was becoming almost impossible to raise the boulder high enough. "That she-wolf!" he growled aloud. "Had she and her pups not chewed the handle nearly off Father's stone axe this job would be easy. But she will *pay!* I'm too tired," he admitted. "Tomorrow I'll try to split the skull of the smaller animal. Now I must sleep, but only for a few minutes."

"Patience . . . patience . . . plan! . . . . " echoed his father's voice from years past. "I'm too *tired,*" Otah moaned. But the words persisted. "I must sleep, but if I do the animals will slip in to steal the meat. How can I keep this from happening?" Almost by magic a two-fold plan took shape in his tired brain. First he made teetering piles of stones all around the carcasses. He hoped that any animal attempting to drag a portion away would knock over the stones. The noise should awaken him. Like many a good idea it did not work. The second phase of his plan was more drastic. He tied a long dry twig to his thumb, then placed the other end of it in the fire. As the stick burned, the flames would eventually reach his hand. No one, no matter how exhausted, can stay asleep with a blistered thumb!

He fought sleep for yet a moment. Several hunks of fresh liver had been roasting on a rock almost among the flames. It was burned black on the outside and almost raw within. He gobbled great chunks of it down, falling asleep almost between bites. His arms and hands were black with dried blood from the butchering

With food in his stomach nothing would be able to wake him now. Not the rattle of falling rocks, not lurking, hungry animals. *Nothing. . .* except. . .

He leaped up with a yowl and tore the blazing stick from his thumb. Ignoring the pain, he threw more brush on the fire. By its light he soon discovered that a sizable haunch from the larger buck was gone. Only the combined weight of the still-joined animals had saved most of the meat. He was not concerned. The loss had been small and there was no way he could transport all of it anyway.

Otah managed to stay awake the rest of the night. He kept the fire roaring, which kept the predators away.

Dawn found him hard at his tasks. He worked the smaller deer's hide free and spread it out, flesh side up. The rough chunks of meat he hacked off were far from the neat cuts his mother and sister would have made but he knew he must hurry. Bones and antlers were ignored. They would have been most useful but there was not enough time to save them. When the skin was piled with as much meat as he could handle he tied it up, leaving a flap of skin for a hand-hold. At the last minute he remembered to crack the smaller deer's skull and extract a double handful of dripping brains. He would need them!

Now a problem presented itself. If he dragged one load to the river the rest of the venison would be unprotected. There was no choice. Most of the meat must be abandoned. Otah took the larger skin and piled a much lighter load upon it. He planned to tie the two together and attempt to drag them, one behind the other. His tiny flake knife had made it possible to cut some ragged but serviceable thongs. These did the work very well but they were slippery and hard to tie. He smiled grimly as he thought of another purpose for the rawhide. "With this I'll snare that wolf and finish her forever!" he said.

Dragging the two loads across the wet meadow grass was not too hard. Trouble soon developed however. The grass disappeared on the rocky ridges and the packs snagged on everything. Rocks, brush, and roots, every obstacle seemed destined to slow Otah's progress. By mid-day he was barely beyond the kill site. He decided to cache half the meat. The tree he selected was far from ideal but he had no time to search for something better. One by one he hoisted the bloody sections to the highest limb he could safely reach. This time he selected a slender sapling for the cache. No bear would risk such flimsy branches. They would never support a large animal's weight. He was learning!

More rawhide strips secured the meat but it was not a tidy job. "Father would have scolded me for such poor work," he told himself. He was careful to strap down both hides. He had use for them!

The dragging went much better with half the load. Still it was late afternoon when the river finally appeared. He searched below the flood plain until he found a suitable log. Rolling and sliding it to the shallow water was difficult but he finally had it half in the current. The large bundle of meat and skins was not a concern, but his fire-making kit was. He tied it tightly around his neck, just under his long black hair. Also around his neck the sinew and intestine flopped around but remained in place.

Otah took three deep breaths, clutched the meat with one arm and pushed off. The shock of icy water brought a gasp. He kicked with both feet and paddled with his free arm. The river was taking him east but this was no problem since he had traveled westward on the hunt. By the time the log finally grounded on the north shore not far from his home he was barely able to scramble onto the sand. His legs were numb and he was having trouble breathing. As soon as the bundle was free of the log he pulled it to higher ground. With great relief he discovered that his fire-making kit was still dry. His hands were shaking so violently that it took far too long to kindle a blaze, but at last he could crouch before the flames.

By partly unrolling the precious bundle of meat and skins he was able to lie on one skin and cover himself with the hair side of the other. The fire burned itself out by midnight but Otah was unaware of it. Rolled up in the thick deerskin and clutching the meat next to his body, he had the best night's sleep he'd enjoyed since the hunt began. It would not have been so pleasant had he been aware of two pairs of slanted yellow eyes reflected in the dying fire! His enemy and her number one cub were watching. Watching and *waiting!*

*   *   *

The hut was very small for the work he was attempting but it was too cold outside. Otah had smoothed the smaller skin out as best he could, then pegged it down with a ring of sharpened stakes. Even with a tiny fire along the wall, scraping the fat and blood from the flesh brought the perspiration dripping off his chin. The tool he was using was not one from his father. It was a woman's knife, a fact of which Otah was becoming well aware! Of brown-gray flint, the scraper was crescent shaped and sharpened only on one edge. It had no handle, so a fold of skin was needed to keep it working. Even with the skin holder it soon became slippery with blood and grease. He sweated and grumbled but did not quit. "Women's work!" he growled as the tool slipped from his fingers yet again. He had no woman to help him. Mother, killed by the she-wolf and gone to the "other place", and Leaf, precious sweet little Leaf, undoubtedly carried off by the Mastodon Hunter Clan. "Fox . . . would be . . the one. . . to take her!" The words were grunted out in rhythm with the scraping. "Just before I left the Mastodon Hunters those years ago, Fox had told me he wanted to be called 'Kardo', which meant 'soon'. I wonder what he was hoping would happen 'soon'?"

"First the wolves, then I take the trail of revenge and rescue!" Bold words indeed! Had he known then of what lay in store for him, perhaps he would not have felt so brave!

It took three days to finish scraping the smaller skin. His arms were aching and his fingers stiff and sore from the unaccustomed work. "How do they do it?" he wondered. "I have seen mother and even Leaf, working at such tasks for days and days. Then they had to stop and prepare food, make pemmican, dry the meat, sew clothes and moccasins. . . On and on!"

He stuffed dry grass against the freshly scraped hide just as he had seen Leaf do it. It was then rolled as tightly as he could and secured with rawhide thongs. It would have to be washed and "brained" before long, but the larger pelt was rapidly stiffening. It must be scraped soon, then he could begin cutting the all-important heavy rawhide strips he planned to use to snare the hated wolf, and if possible her pups as well!

For the first time in months he hummed a little song that Leaf had made up when she was still very small. Her soft, child's voice singing happy, made-up songs was what he missed the most.

The larger skin was a problem. It had become so stiff that he was hardly able to handle it. Never had he seen this trouble when his mother was with them. Evidently she had made certain to work the hide very soon after butchering. Otah needed that leather!

"Patience. . . patience. . . plan…."

The words were like a singsong in his head. "It has hardened too much," he thought as he sat looking at the thing. "How can it be softened up again?" The rest of the

afternoon he studied the problem. All at once he thought of an answer. "What softens

leather?" he asked with growing excitement. "Water! Of course, the answer is *water!*"

Even though the day was nearly gone he wrestled the unwieldy hide through the

low door opening and headed for the river. The awkward burden bumped and jolted

along, catching on everything that protruded. Finally there he broke slivers of ice and

waded in as far as his waist. The cold shocked his system as yet again he had to brave the

terribly cold water. Several heavy rocks weighted the hide to the river bottom. He marked

the spot with a pile of flat rocks, then set off at a warming run back to his hut.

Entering the small clearing, he was horrified to see a commotion in the heavy

brush behind his home. The wolf and her two cubs must have entered the hut and were

just in the act of dragging the smaller skin away! Without spear or knife he was not ready

to fight them. Undaunted however, he grabbed up several blackened stones from the fire

pit and charged. Screaming and throwing, he did all he could to make them drop their

prize. Fortunately the roll of skin had caught on a jagged stump. The wolves were all

three tugging and worrying at it, but it held.

Otah's aim was not good, but one of his stones struck the largest pup, the one he

had named Sand, in the side. With a yelp, it and its sisters fled in panic. Not so with the

mother! She held her ground. Front legs astraddle the deerskin, her snarls proved she was

about to attack. He dropped his last rock and began backing toward the hut. The spear

was just inside. Easing his way around the house he slipped in and grabbed the spear. It

felt comforting in his hand. He peered out of the door opening, but the wolf was still out of sight behind the hut.

Otah rounded the edge of the house, roaring and stamping his feet. She eyed the hunter warily and at last released the deerskin. Neither moved. Again the great muscles in her chest bulged and quivered. He braced himself in a crouch, the spear extended at arm's length. Her white fangs glistened as her lips drew back and back in a vicious snarl. A low rumbling growl broke the stillness. Time seemed to stand still as neither made the first move. Then a remarkable thing happened. Otah heard nothing, but the she-wolf did. One ear flicked back slightly, but her eyes never left her enemy. Then Otah heard it too. A soft *"yip – yip" floated* from beyond the clearing. The frightened cubs were calling their mother. *"Yip – yip" came* again.

Visibly torn, she took a step backward. The stiff guard hairs on her neck and back were still standing like sentinels but the instincts of motherhood were winning the battle. She turned and loped away toward the cries of her pups.

Otah sank to his knees, trembling with relief. "I must prepare my snare!" he told himself. "I cannot hope to be so lucky another time. She will kill me or I will kill her. That is the way it is! I must act before the winter snows begin and make my task much more dangerous."

Next morning he arose to find an inch of snow covering the ground!

*　　　　　*　　　　　*

The river water had done much to soften the larger hide, so he dragged it back to the hut. As there was a sudden spell of warmer weather he staked it down in the clearing. Using the tiny, razor sharp knife of pink flint he began cutting rawhide strips. By carefully following the uneven contours of the skin he was able to create long, unbroken strands. The width of his little finger nail, the wet, slippery bands were the strongest thing he could make. They would certainly hold the wolf, at least until he could move in with the spear. He hummed Leaf's little song as he cut and cut, all the way around the edges of the hide in ever smaller circles.

Although he hated the thing that had killed his mother he also respected its strength and cunning.

Patience . . . patience. . . plan. . .

In his mind he pictured the wolf den, now probably dusted with snow. He intended to drape the snare over the entrance hole while she and her cubs were off hunting. This seemed simple enough, but there as no way it would work. Anything new around the den would cause suspicion. The smell of the rawhide would signal food as well, especially for the young. After a late meal of new, jerked meat he sat and pondered. "There must be a way," he mused, chewing on a long strip of the stringy meat. "There *has* to be a way, but I must spend more time watching."

Before first light he set out on the by now familiar path to the den. The smaller skin, wrapped fur side in around his body was almost too warm. He had fashioned a hood of sorts which protected his head from the cold while keeping both hands free.

Otah smiled to himself at the sight he must present. His mother and Leaf would have laughed at the clumsy, flapping buckskins he wore. They would have chewed the skin until it was soft and pliable. Next, careful cutting then sewing with the finest strands of sinew would have resulted in a soft, tight-fitting garment. Leaf might even have smoked the skin over a smoldering fire to lend a beautiful golden tint to the finished

product. With every passing day his appreciation for his mother and sister continued to

grow. "Well," he thought, "I am a man. What do I know of making clothes?"

Almost halfway to his observation knoll he noticed the wind, which had been

unsettled since dawn, was shifting to the west. This would never do! If the animals were

at the den or in its vicinity they would get his scent, no matter how far back he stayed.

Muttering angrily he turned and trotted back toward his home. Patience was paying off!

More snow fell during the night. The wind had swung back to the east however,

so he wrapped himself in his skins and left the hut. He was hardly well under way when

he noticed that his right foot felt wet and cold. A quick look was all he needed. A hole

was growing in one of his moccasins. They had been made by Leaf with instructions by

her mother, but finally they were wearing out! Back to the hut he went, considering how

he could renew his shoes. He would need boots soon too. Would the fight never come?

Another day was lost, but he was proud of his efforts. The new boots fitted

loosely over the thin moccasins. They were not only free of holes, but kept his feet

warmer too. Like his attempts at making clothing, the boots were a pitiful sight. Another

problem with them was their stiffness. He must remember to pull them off when the fight

took place, no matter how cold it might be.

Getting to the knoll beyond the wolf den the next day was a nightmare. New snow

had fallen and even though it was not deep it *was* slippery. He staggered over hidden

rocks and roots invisible in the snow. He fell twice but luckily was not injured. The wind was right however. Peeping over the brush on the crest of the knoll he had an excellent view of the den. He had used the site so often that there was real danger that his scent might linger there. Tracks going in and out clearly indicated that the wolf family was still using the den.

He watched eagerly as one of the smaller pups peered out of the tunnel. She looked this way and that as her pointed black muzzle tested the breeze. Satisfied, the small wolf moved a few feet from the entrance and began pawing at a slightly rounded hump under the snow. Otah was elated! The young female was preparing to feed on the body of a deer which the mother had dragged back from her kill. This was what he had been waiting for! The wolves, even the younger ones, now able to eat on their own, would gorge on the fresh meat, then creep back into the den to sleep.

He must move swiftly now. With three eating, the carcass could not last more than a few more days. He eased back down the hill and set off at a run. As soon as the wolves had eaten again and were sleeping in the den the snare must be in place.

At the hut he dug up the rawhide which he had buried in the ashes. The thin lasso was stretched to its full length. It was long enough. He braided three strands together, being careful to handle it as little as possible. He needed to avoid leaving much scent. The loop he fashioned was, he judged, just large enough to encircle the adult wolf's head and neck. The greasy slip knot moved freely. Excitement was building as he considered the steps that must now be taken.

Patience. . . patience. . . plan. . .

Otah was all for heading out the next morning but he forced himself to wait another day. "I'll let them feed again, then watch until I am sure they are all asleep inside." he mused.

The wind was wrong the next day! He paced angrily around in the hut. If everything was not right the following day he might miss this chance entirely. With great relief he awoke to blowing snow and a steady east wind. He dressed as warmly as his ragged clothing would allow and left. The good spear he kept in hand, the other thrust through a loop of sinew above his left shoulder. The length of braided rawhide rope he allowed to trail out behind him as he walked. This might, he felt, help further disguise his scent.

The familiar knoll was slippery with its covering of new snow. Otah was thankful for that, since it helped to deaden any slight sound his careful progress made. The snow was another bonus he had not counted on. Many tracks littered the area near the opening. As the falling snow tapered off he could plainly see that the animals had once again been tearing at the frozen carcass, the remains of which still lay close to the den. He strained his eyes in an attempt to see if a trail of tracks led away from the area. None was visible!

"I must *stand!*" he told himself. His legs were cramping from the hours he had lain curled under the sleeping robe. Any movement could, he knew, alert the wolves to his presence. Also, standing would expose his upper body. Until that moment only his snow-covered hood could be seen above the hill. Cautiously he moved his right leg. Extending it was agony. The ugly boot caught on a snow-covered vine. The scraping noise this made was loud, but Otah hoped the wind would carry the sound away. He lay perfectly still for as long as he could stand it, then extended the other leg. There was no sound or movement from the tunnel, but Otah did not move again for several moments.

"Now must my plan be set in motion," Otah told himself. Fear was his ally. His heart pounding, he inched his way backward down the hill, slipping out from under the snow-covered robe. This he left as it lay. For the present he no longer needed it. "And," he thought, "I may not need it or any other again!" He had no illusions regarding the outcome of the fight to come. The she-wolf was big, strong, and cunning. Only planning and deceit would win the day. "I have been patient and I have planned as well as I know how, perhaps the wolves will take me but I must avenge the death of my mother!"

Completely out of sight below the hill he circled far to the north until he judged that he was opposite the den. A dead branch twice as long as his body was exactly what Otah needed. Carrying it carefully lest it catch on the bushes, he crept up the bank which held the wolves' lair. He was now directly above the opening. With great caution he set one foot beyond the other, making no sound at all. Bending low he tied one end of the rawhide rope to a sturdy sapling. Using the long stick he draped the snare's loop directly in front of the opening below him. The branch held the noose at what he hoped would be the right height for the adult wolf's head and neck. He crawled back until he was far enough away to stand up and walk. Now he must return to the knoll and wait until something happened.

Otah once again lay curled under the sleeping robe, only his head visible over the hilltop. The good spear was stationed close to his right hand. By making tiny movements and flexing his muscles he hoped to avoid any cramps or muscle spasms. He must be ready to dash out and fight the wolf the moment she appeared! There was no guarantee that all of his planning and preparations would even work. The wolf's uncanny sense of smell would certainly alert her to the strange piece of rawhide dangling before the entrance. Otah's attempts to disguise its smell would probably amount to nothing. Still, he had done all he could. He had exercised patience and had planned carefully. He was *ready!*

There was movement! Otah could feel the hair prickling at the back of his head. A short black snout appeared, then the muzzle and pointed ears. It was a *pup!*

"Oh *no!*" he thought. The young female would ruin everything! He was almost ready to give up the entire affair when the pup raised her head and sniffed at the snare. She nibbled at the rawhide for a moment then took it in her teeth and tugged. The branch that held the noose wiggled and dropped a dollop of snow on her head. She shook it off and without another look re-entered the den. "They have been gorging themselves on the mother's kill," Otah thought. "Were it not so the little one would certainly have tried to chew the rawhide."

Then she was there! The big wolf's head and shoulders appeared. She took one step forward. Her head was inside the loop! Startled, she leaped backward with a snarl. This was the wrong thing to do. The bottom of the loop caught in the rough fur below her neck. The circle slipped tighter. She panicked. Snarling and thrashing, she tried to bite the thing which was holding her. As the snare tightened it buried itself deeper and deeper under her fur. Furiously she fought the noose. Rearing up on hind legs was a mistake, for as she came back to all fours the slippery band was beginning to choke off her breathing. The rawhide held!

Otah leaped up. Slipping and sliding in the snow, he rushed down the knoll toward the den. The wolf's first struggling was as nothing compared to that which began when she saw the approaching human! He stopped well beyond the length of the rawhide snare and watched.

The wolf was strangling, but surprisingly Otah took little pleasure in his revenge. Her eyes were bulging. A red tongue slipped in and out as she tried to breathe. It would take some time for death to claim her.

He had seen enough. It was not right for the animal to suffer so, killer though she was. The wolf lunged at him so suddenly that he was barely able to leap clear. Gripping the spear with both hands he taunted her into attempting to attack again. In the instant the rawhide rope checked her charge, Otah struck. His father's thin stabbing spear drove deeply into the chest just under the wolf's jaw. She staggered back, still fighting the snare, but she was rapidly weakening. In but a few minutes she fell heavily and died. Trembling, he worked the loop from her neck and threw it aside.

Breathing hard, Otah shouted out a roar of triumph. So elated was he that he made a serious mistake, one which would nearly cost him his life! He had not thought to retrieve the spear! The wolf was obviously dead, so he had felt no need for further protection.

Suddenly a snarling, bristling force came hurtling from the tunnel. *Sand!* The male pup, now nearly as large as its mother, launched itself directly at its enemy. In two tremendous bounds it crashed into Otah's chest. Knocked from his feet, the hunter scrabbled desperately for the other spear which was still held loosely over his shoulder. The raging wolf bit savagely at Otah's face. With great presence of mind he flung his left arm upward to protect his head and neck. He felt teeth meet bone as the jaws sank deep into his forearm. Otah's other fist came up fast. With all his strength he struck the pup behind the ear. Stunned, it released its jaws and Otah's hand closed over the wolf's open lower jaw. Fear and pain helped him twist the head over until the animal finally lost its footing. The hunter fell on the thrashing body. With one knee he pinned the animal down in the bloody snow. Hardly knowing why he did so, he yanked the snare over the wolf's muzzle. Whipping his bloody left hand free he cinched the noose tight.

"Sand!" Otah gasped, "I knew you would be a fighter! But let's see you try to bite me again with your mouth tied shut!" He quickly looped several more strands around Sand's snout. The cub continued to struggle, but Otah used his body weight to keep it pinned to the ground. After a while Sand was tiring, but his rage and hatred appeared as strong as ever.

Still holding the struggling animal in the snow Otah was able to loosen one of the strips of rawhide which helped hold his coat together. He looped this around the forelegs and tied it off. Carefully he eased himself from the wolf's body.

Sand made a valiant effort, but was unable to gain his feet.

"Well what am I going to do with you? I'm through with killing!"

Until that moment he had paid little attention to the wound in his arm. The pain struck then! His legs felt suddenly weak. He sank to his knees and tried to get his breath.

Blood was trickling down his arm. Of more concern was a strange numbness in his first two fingers. The fangs had injured a nerve! Otah scooped a handful of snow and packed it over the wound. Next he used his knife to cut a strip of deerskin from his coat. "That will have to do for now," he said aloud. There was work to do!

Otah prepared to take the mother wolf's pelt. Sand watched with hatred, his growling garbled due to his bound snout. Suddenly the cub scrabbled away, digging desperately with his hind feet. It was necessary then to circle his body with the rest of the rawhide snare, one end of which was still tied to the tree. The wolf still tried to escape, but after a few unsuccessful lunges it gave up and lay panting in the snow.

"I should kill the pup now," Otah told himself as he finished the skinning work. "I could turn him loose, but it's doubtful he and his sister could survive the winter. Why am I waiting?" He was thankful that only one female remained. Anything could have happened to the other sister. Accident? Taken by a mountain lion? Disease? Who could tell? He was only thankful that it was gone!

The remaining female pup! Otah was struck with the thought. "Well it will have to take care of itself," he said, knowing full well that that would not be possible. She was too young and inexperienced to hunt successfully. He checked the tether which held Sand. The pup had stretched the rawhide as far as it would reach but did not struggle. The hunter faced what he must do. The area around the tunnel was trampled and bloody from the fight. Otah knew that the longer he waited the harder it would be. He cleaned his knife and spear in the snow and dropped to hands and knees.

He slipped head and shoulders into the entrance and waited for his eyes to adjust to the gloom. Wolf scent was strong. Hair and scraps of bone littered the floor. Slowly he was able to make out the larger space that had been dug out to accommodate the wolf family. The pup was backed against the far dirt wall. She was whimpering in fear. Otah extended the spear until it gently prodded the animal. She yelped and suddenly charged! He was just able to fling an arm over his face when she burst past him and bolted from the entrance. By the time Otah had scrambled back out she was gone.

Sand lay very still in the snow. The rawhide loop was cutting into his flanks but he seemed indifferent to the pain. Otah rolled the wolf pelt and tied it with sinew. It would make a fine coat, which he badly needed. He untied the rawhide from the tree and held it. He spent a long minute eyeing the cub. It looked back in cold fury but made no move to escape. Otah gave a yank on the rope. By making a great effort Sand gained his feet despite his bound forelegs. His fur stood up along his back as he faced his captor.

"You are a brave one! What will I do with you? Shall I use the spear right now?" The hunter could not understand why he hesitated, but in the back of his mind a thought was forming. It was a thought so ridiculous as to be unworthy of consideration. Finally he gave a long sigh and allowed himself to explore the idea that lingered in his mind.

"I will tame this vicious creature! Then I will train him to help me hunt game. He will be a companion for me."

Taking a better grip on the end of the rawhide, Otah gave it a tentative jerk. Sand was yanked off his feet and floundered in the snow. "You'll need to walk, little one," Otah told the wolf. "I am going to untie your legs now. You cannot bite me with your mouth tied shut, so don't try." Hand over hand he dragged the wolf closer and closer. It gathered itself and despite the hobbled front legs, managed to spring at the hunter. Otah fell on its thrashing body and pressed it into the snow. The flint knife flashed twice and the leg bonds were cut free. Otah was afraid now. If the wolf was allowed to get up it could certainly attack, even with its jaws secured. A grim smile creased Otah's face as a plan formed. Still lying prone on the wolf he gathered a handful of soft snow and packed it over the animal's eyes. It would have to serve for at least a few minutes, which might be enough to let Otah control the pup.

He retied the thong to a bush until he could gather up his equipment and robe. Holding the leash with his good arm he started toward home, dragging the snarling pup behind him.

*   *   *

Otah found himself talking to the young wolf as he went about his activities. "So you won't eat? Well then I guess you'll just have to starve!" He threw another bit of venison to the pup. Although the wolf could eat solid meat, Otah had chewed the morsel until it was soft and moist, much as its mother would have done. He hoped this might entice it to eat. *"Sand!"* he shouted, "Eat that meat or *be eaten!"* With a shock Otah suddenly realized what he had just said. Could he really do it? Suppose his supply of dried meat and pemmican was gone and he was unable to get more? He eyed the wolf with new interest. He was thinking terrible thoughts!

As if it knew the man's mind, Sand took that moment to snap up the scrap of meat and whined for more.

Otah was well aware that although Sand was still a pup of less than a year the animal was growing fast. "If I expect to keep this wild thing he must be trained and trained well. Otherwise he will certainly attack me at the first opportunity." But Otah had no way of knowing how to go about the task. The pup was eating now. In fact it was alarming how much meat was disappearing down the wolf's gullet! It took little water, but even keeping the wooden bowl full was becoming a chore.

Patience . . . patience. . . plan . . .

Sand's eyes never left the man. Whenever Otah moved or worked on the hides the wolf kept watch. The small fire, which kept the hut almost too warm, was reflected in the animal's eyes.

Otah had fashioned a heavy collar of leather which had been smoked over the fire. He had been bitten twice before he could secure it on the animal's neck. Attached to it was a short length of braided rawhide rope. This, in turn was tied to a heavy section of log wedged against the hut's far wall. Only when this was completed did he feel safe while he slept.

"Sand will kill me if he can," Otah murmured aloud. "And who can blame him? I killed his mother just as his mother killed mine. Am I alone to have the privilege of revenge?" As he sat eyeing the wolf in the firelight, not knowing how to proceed, a sudden thought leaped out from the past. *"Crow Swims!"* he shouted. Sand's ears came forward and he half rose. A low growl rumbled from deep in his chest.

*   *   *

"Crow Swims!" Otah was laughing now, for a plan was forming. As if it were yesterday he remembered a funny scene from many years before. His sister, Leaf, had been playing along the river on an early summer day. He had caught four large fish and was cleaning them on a rock.

"*Look! Oh Look!*" Leaf had cried, pointing up at the lower branches of a large sycamore tree. "See it? See it?" she cried. A half-grown crow was dangling precariously, one foot holding to a swaying branch. Far above could be seen the nest from which it had fallen. The bird struggled with the other foot but could not get a grip. "It's going to *fall!*" Leaf cried. "It's going to fall into the *river!* Do something Otah. Please do something for the little birdie!"

Otah had laughed at her concern. There was nothing he could do anyway. Death came in many ways in the Black Swamp, be it for bird or person.

"It's falling! See? See?" she moaned. But then an amazing thing happened. The crow did indeed fall into the river but it did not drown at all. As brother and sister watched, the shiny creature began *swimming!* It stepped onto the sandy bank almost at Leaf's feet. Without a thought she dove on it and held the dripping thing in her arms.

Leaf named the bird "Crow Swims", and even though her mother tried to dissuade her, she raised it as her pet. Hour after hour the little girl could be seen scratching in the earth or turning over logs. Keeping the hungry crow fed was a big job for a little girl but she did not complain. Crow Swims was never tied or put in a willow cage. Instinctively Leaf had known that kindness and care would keep the bird true to her better than any restraint. Even after it learned to fly it was never far from the hut. With first light every morning its raucous call would wake the camp.

Leaf used the grubs and worms she found to train the crow. When she fed it, she would make a squealing sound with her lips against the back of her hand, so Crow Swims would come flying down whenever it heard the sound. Sometimes it would land on her shoulder or even on her head! Mother would not allow the bird inside, even though Leaf had begged for it.

"Too messy!" Mother had decreed.

*   *   *

Otah observed the wolf as it lay sleeping. Having gulped down a good-sized chunk of venison, it was content. It was now taking unchewed food and plenty of it! The man approached cautiously. Sand's eyes opened but he did not raise his head at Otah's approach. "I know what you're up to. You'll pretend to sleep, then bite me when I get closer! Well not this time!" Two more careful steps and the wolf attacked. Only the rawhide stopped him. He snarled at the man as saliva dripped from his open jaws. Gleaming teeth were very apparent.

"You were very clever, Leaf. You tamed Crow Swims with food and kindness. I am not, however, dealing here with a small black bird!" Otah's voice, kept low and soft, did seem to soothe the cub. Its ears flipped forward whenever it heard the human voice. Otah was aware of this of course, and continued to do it often during the day. "You are not a crow," he told the pup. "Therefore you will not be tamed like one. If I had captured you when you were younger, perhaps I would not need to be so rough. But you were *not* younger.

Again Otah approached the animal. He extended one hand and waited. Just as he had expected, Sand charged, growling. Now the man raised his voice to a near shout. "In your world there must be one member of the pack which is in charge. You and I are now a small pack and *I am the leader!* These last words were so unexpectedly loud and menacing that Sand backed off a step, but not for long. The wolf recognized the challenge and welcomed it. His instincts told him that this was expected procedure. He had no intention of allowing this puny human to boss over *him!* He lunged.

Crack! Otah's open hand struck the wolf across the muzzle, knocking it backward. Sand charged again, almost strangling from the tightened collar. *"No!"* Otah shouted, and again his hand flashed forward. The blow took the wolf across the ears this time. It cowered back, whimpering and watchful. "So you are a little afraid of me now?" Otah growled. "That is good. Fear of me may keep you alive. I am your *master!"* These words also were loud and menacing. Sand backed up against the log which held him. After a few moments his hackles rose again. The man noted these indications and kept his eyes locked with those of the wolf.

Clearly unsure, Sand finally lay down and rested his muzzle on his front paws. His training had begun.

During the following days, as the wind-driven snow packed itself around the hut, Otah patiently continued the training. He alternated rough treatment, even sometimes using a short stick, with soft words and bits of food. A great day came when Sand delicately took a piece of meat directly from Otah's hand without any attempt to bite.

After this the growing pup learned rapidly. At times Otah even felt the wolf was enjoying the sessions. As his tether was lengthened a little more each day, Sand made no move to attack or even snap at the man. Otah cautiously attempted leading the wolf a few steps inside the hut. It hung back at first but Otah was thankful that it did not even growl!

The final test came in mid-winter. Shortening the leash even more, Otah dragged the wolf out into the snow. He walked fast and was delighted when Sand stayed close, not pulling on the rope at all. For many days he kept the lessons coming. With the world held in winter's frozen grip there was no point in hunting. Also Otah had finished working the skins he had accumulated, even making himself a simple hooded coat of wolf hide. The time was well spent in completing Sand's education. That the wolf was highly intelligent was very evident. It quickly learned a few simple commands, such as "stop" or "go". Otah kept a supply of meat scraps at hand to reward the wolf every time it obeyed. He no longer needed to strike the animal.

The day came when the effectiveness of Sand's training was put to the final test. Far from the hut, Otah untied the rawhide rope from Sand's collar. The man held his breath as the wolf shook itself vigorously then trotted off. It rolled in the snow and leaped about, free at last from the hated tether. His heart pounding, Otah watched his companion [for this was now how he thought of it] range about, thrusting his muzzle into every track and rabbit hole in the snow. Eyes closed, Otah called out loudly, "Sand, *come!*" He made the squealing sound on his hand the way Leaf had called her crow those years ago. The wolf's head perked up and he bounded over the drifts directly to his master's side!

Otah gave the wolf the largest piece of venison he had with him!

Several days later it seemed that something was wrong. Otah had no energy, nor the desire to leave the hut. In the night he would find himself too hot, even when the fire had long since gone out. An ugly blue-black bulge seemed to be growing larger on his left forearm. "You did this to me!" he growled, glaring at Sand. The wolf perked up his ears, but did not stop gnawing on a bone it had dug up from some frozen carcass. Opening and closing his left hand was agony. Two fingers continued to be numb and almost worthless. Once again he examined the lump on the side of his arm. He pressed it gingerly and found it hard and hot to the touch.

"Well Sand, my friend, the time has come. I know what father would do, but he has long since gone to the Other Place. Mother no longer with me either, and Leaf . . .little Leaf! Who knows if she still walks the land? If Fox, or Kardo as he likes to be called, did take her, where are they now? Does he beat her? Must she gather wood and carry water? Does she have enough to eat?"

He suddenly realized that his thoughts were wandering everywhere. "I must do it! I must do it *now* Sand!" The wolf, hearing a strange new note in its master's voice, gave a soft lingering whine and stood up uncertainly. Even Sand knew that something was wrong with the man.

Otah dragged two thick chunks of wood onto the small fire. Forcing himself to move, he left the hut with his gathering bag. This he packed full of clean snow. The small sack now seemed almost too heavy to lift, but he managed to slide it inside. Sand's wooden bowl was filled with snow and placed near the fire. "There, you brute," he whispered. "That is water for you. If I go to the Other Place you must leave the hut and find a pack to join." Very little dried venison was still hanging from the roof. Otah's knife freed a large segment, which was allowed to fall to the floor of the hut. Sand started toward it but Otah's "NO!" stopped him before he could devour it. "It may be that soon you will no longer have orders from me. If that time comes you should finish the dried venison then hunt for fresh meat." Sand's yellow eyes never left the man's face. It seemed to Otah that the wolf actually understood his words, but there was no way to be sure, since he knew he was hallucinating again.

"It is *time!*" he told the watching animal.

Otah plunged his bad arm into the snow-packed bag. While he waited for the cold to numb the ache, he prepared his tools. Sliding his fingers along the edge of his knife confirmed what he had half expected. It was dull. Too dull! "I should have been caring for my weapons during these short winter days," he thought. "But what have I been doing? Attempting to train this wild creature, and for what purpose? Already he eats more than I. Also, can I really trust this beast? If our food gives out during the hunger moon will he start to see *me* as food? Would I do the same for him?" This time Otah was aware of his feverish babbling.

He withdrew his aching arm and wiped it dry. His father's spear would have to do the work. He arranged himself as comfortably as he could, next to the now blazing fire. Standing the spear upright, he carefully placed the point against the largest part of the swelling. He clamped his teeth tight, closed his eyes, and gave a mighty thrust. The thin blade sank deep until it struck bone. Blood and a foul-smelling brownish liquid gushed out. The spear fell free as Otah slid backward in a faint.

Otah had no idea how long he had been unconscious. He felt sick and his arm seemed on fire. As he came fully awake he was startled to see Sand standing over him. The wolf had been *licking the wound!* Otah would never know that for the first time, but not the last, Sand had saved his life!

       *   *   *

The food was gone. The Black Swamp was a frozen glare of silent white. Two rabbits, taken in his snares, had hardly dulled Otah's hunger. Sand had caught a rabbit too, but his snarls and raised fur warned Otah that the wolf meant to keep it for himself. Sand had carried it home in his jaws and crouching down, ate it noisily outside the hut.

"Sand, old fellow, I know it is very cold but we must hunt. It would be too much to hope for a deer or an elk, but a beaver or even a muskrat would help fill our bellies. Also," he told his companion, "we must dig beneath the snow for anything still green. Mother always said, 'too much eating only meat makes the stomach cry!'" When his parents were still with him they had always had plenty of pemmican. Not only pounded meat, but lots of ground up berries were always packed into the casings. So far as he could remember in those days Otah had never felt his stomach cry!

Anything *green* in this frozen land? Hardly! Bundled in his rumpled robes and wearing his wolf skin coat he left the hut. Sand forged ahead, his big feet breaking trail for the man who followed. Otah watched the wolf as it suddenly slowed to a careful walk, its muzzle punching here and there into the snow. The animal continued this curious behavior for some time, ranging back and forth among the snow-covered bushes. Then stopped, dropped to his haunches, and began to gnaw at something on the ground. "So you've found a frozen rabbit, have you?" Otah said as he approached the wolf. Three paces nearer, a low growl warned him to come no closer. He was surprised to see that Sand was gnawing on the knobby frozen roots of the fiddlehead fern. There were many of these ice-covered roots emerging from the sandy soil above the river's flood plain. "So you know what your stomach needs do you? When you finish there I'll gather some for myself. If you can eat them I can too, but I intend to boil mine!" It took half a day's tedious work with the axe to chop even a small bag of roots from the frozen turf. Although the axe handle had been chewed nearly through, a rawhide wrap had fixed it. "These may keep my stomach from 'crying'," he told the wolf "but we need much real food. If we don't make a kill soon it will be the end for us." "Well," he went on, "maybe not for *you*, but certainly for *me!*"

They trudged on, tired and hungry. Game trails when they appeared at all were old and unused. Otah's lack of food made the cold harder to bear. He tired easily, and longed to just sit down in the snow and rest. Sand would have none of this. He turned and regarded his master every time their progress slowed. "We must face what is," Otah said aloud. The wolf eyed him with what looked very much like disgust. The man finally sank down on his haunches, pulled the skins over his head and let his face fall on his knees. Sand turned back and whined uncertainly. He took a few steps back toward the man, hesitated a moment then left at a lope. Otah was too tired and too cold to care much, but he feared his companion was gone for good. "Go on, go *on*", he murmured. "If you can save yourself do it!"

Otah had given up.

The cold was invading his starving body. He must have slept for a short time when he was suddenly awakened. A wild commotion was going on a short distance down the river. Otah could hear Sand's growls. The man found a reserve of energy he did not know he had. He ran toward the noise, floundering through the knee-deep snow. An amazing sight greeted him. Sand was out on a wind-swept section of the frozen river, the ice at this point completely clear of snow. Two deer, a doe and her yearling fawn had been driven from the trees and were trying to escape from the creature that meant to kill them. Their small, sharp hooves, so effective in the forest, could find no purchase on the glare of smooth ice. Sand's huge pads, on the other hand, served him well. He faced the animals, snarling and threatening, while the doe, with the courage of motherhood, continued to turn and face the wolf's charges. Sand circled fast, wanting to get a grip on her flank. She circled as well, slipped and fell spraddle-legged on the ice. Sand charged. His fangs sank deep, high on one hind leg. The deer struggled violently but the smooth ice was her undoing. She could not get up. The yearling did not know what to do. Foolishly it stayed near its stricken mother. Otah leaped out onto the ice, slipped and fell heavily. He regained his feet but moved more carefully now. The smaller deer was so terrified by what was happening to its mother that it did not at first see the man approaching. When it did it made its second and final mistake. Trying to run in terror it went down a few paces from the doe. Otah did not hesitate. The axe rose and fell, killing the yearling instantly.

The man approached the struggling pair warily. The doe's sharp hooves could do great harm if they found their target. Sand's hold on the hind leg did not waver. Both animals were tiring, but there was still much fight left in them. Otah watched until Sand had pulled the deer backward a few paces. He saw his chance. The spear slipped through hide and muscle low down behind the shoulder. The finely chipped point found a lung. Otah ripped the weapon free and struck again, this time in the neck. Death came quickly then.

Sensing the deer's demise, Sand ripped a large chunk of meat from the throat and devoured it hungrily.

"Good boy, Sand!" Otah shouted. He dragged the yearling's body onto the shore and wasted no time twirling the fire stick. He did not begin the skinning until he had eaten well of a hefty piece of half-cooked venison. Sand too was filling his belly.

When the wolf had eaten all it could, Otah approached the kill site. The wolf surged to its feet, bloody jaws and teeth gaping. Its snarls left no question for the man. Sand had made this kill and he planned to claim it as his own. This would never do! "Sand, *no!*" Otah commanded. The wolf only growled the louder. He stood over the carcass, fur on his back and neck raised in warning. The man backed off, keeping his eyes on the wolf in case it decided to attack him. "Go ahead. Eat some more, then we'll see. After all it is your kill."

Otah skinned the yearling and quartered the meat. For once he was thankful for the cold. He talked to himself as he worked, stopping often to warm his freezing, blood-coated fingers at the fire. "Sand, my friend, we'll do well for quite a while now! I'll hang this meat in that big oak behind the hut and let it freeze out. That is we will if I can get what's left of that doe away from you long enough. We'll not have to fear the bears robbing our meat, since they are all fast asleep in their dens until spring. Wouldn't it be great if we could do that? But before I eat any more of this I'll have to boil up a mess of fern stew. It may taste awful but if it works for wolves it will probably work for me too."

Sand had dragged his prize off the clear ice and was lying next to the body, fast asleep.

*   *   *

The small clay pot bubbled in the edge of the fire. As melted snow quickly disappeared Otah kept adding more until the vessel was half full of hot water. Fern roots had long since thawed in their bag hanging on the wall of the hut. Sand lay head on paws watching his master. The man chuckled as he remembered the battle it had taken to take the doe from the now full grown wolf. "You would have done for me wouldn't you boy? Maybe the deal I made with you wasn't exactly fair but now we both have food to spare." While Sand had held a hind leg and continued to growl Otah had quickly used the knife and axe to cut the leg free. Sand had been content with that. Otah had hauled the rest back to the hut for skinning and butchering and it was now hanging from a high branch in the oak.

Otah dropped the ugly yellowish roots into the pot one by one. After a time the concoction came to a boil again and the man slept. When he awoke the fire was down but the mess was still steaming in the cold hut. Using a pointed bone he kept for the purpose,

Otah stabbed one of the sodden globs floating in the bowl. He smelled it [terrible!] then gingerly took a bite [worse!].

The roots' outsides were thick and slimy but inside they were so tough he could hardly chew them. "It has to be done!" he told himself. By holding his nose and chewing as fast as he could Otah managed to choke down three of the awful things. He tossed one to the wolf. Sand sniffed at it briefly then backed away. "I guess you prefer them frozen. Can't say I blame you!" There were still four of the boiled roots in the cooling water, but Otah could not stand another. He promised himself he would eat one every day until they were all gone. There is no doubt that the fern tonic had kept him well during most of the winter.

The clumsy, dull spear he had made must be discarded. If he were to depend upon such a poor weapon harm would certainly follow. He shuddered to think of what his life would have been had he not had the one good spear made by his father. But it too needed some care.

Sand lay in his usual place against the back wall, the slanted golden eyes never leaving the man at his work. The wolf, now an adult knew several simple commands and generally obeyed, but he did not fear the man.

Otah unrolled the bag of tools and spread them out on the sleeping robe. A moment of sadness touched him as he picked up a short section of elk antler. It was polished smooth and shiny by many hours in the hands of his father. Taking it in a firm grip with his good right hand, he placed the pointed tip against the very edge of the flint knife. It too had become dull with use. Before much more could be accomplished the knife must be sharpened. Trying to hold it firmly in his left hand was very difficult. The two first fingers remained stiff and sore even thought the wound in his forearm had healed well enough. A jagged reddish scar was sufficient reminder of the battle with Sand and its mother. Taking another hold on the flint blade he brought the pointed tool against its edge and pressed hard. A tiny flake of stone popped loose. Otah was elated! This was not as difficult as he had imagined. He began to chip the stone faster.

Patience . . . patience. . . .plan . .

Otah smiled and proceeded more carefully. Sharpening the existing knife was one thing, but if by carelessness he broke it, that would mean the whole process would have to be attempted. A flint core-stone would be needed from which flakes could be driven off. This was a process that even Otah's father had difficulty with. Furthermore there was no flint supply left.

The sun had climbed high by the time the job was done, but Otah was proud of the new edge he had given to the knife. He held it up and slowly turned it over and over. "What do you think Sand? Not a bad job, eh?" The wolf pricked up his ears at the sound of his name but did not rise. Such activities held no interest for him.

The following day Otah decided to see what could be done with his poorly made spear. The shaft was crooked and full of knots. New binding on the blade was ragged and beginning to unravel. In short, the entire weapon needed to be rebuilt. The first step must be a new shaft. It would not be easy to get one, since snow had built and now lay knee deep across the swamp. But he was tired of staying inside the smoky hut.

"Come Sand!" The wolf rose eagerly, and pressed its nose against the double buffalo hide door flap. He got in the way as Otah undid the ties that held it in place. Sand was tired of the hut too! Otah no longer used the rawhide leash. He was satisfied that his companion would come when called, but also aware that the animal might at any time run off for good. If that happened the man would be lonely indeed, so he did what he could to satisfy the wolf's hunger. He also petted the animal at times, but this was dangerous. Sand did not like to be touched. He was still a wolf!

The glare was dazzling after the darkened hut. Man and animal headed west, finding travel difficult in the snow. Before long the sun had disappeared behind a bank of blue-gray clouds, and the glare was gone. Otah was heading for a grove of hickory trees where his family had gone nutting every fall. Hickory was good for axe handles so the man thought it might serve for a spear shaft as well. Osage orange would have been better but Otah did not know where such a tree could be found.

The shagbark hickory trees stood together on the little knoll he remembered well from happier days. Leafless and bare, they were silent as skeletons against the winter sky. Sand had ranged out of sight looking for rabbit sign as Otah circled each tree. He was looking for a straight branch as thick as two fingers and as long as he was tall.

The wind was getting stronger. As the limbs and branches began to whip back and forth it became more difficult to see what he was searching for. Finally he spied a limb which he thought might do, and luckily it was low enough that there was no need to climb. Using the newly sharpened knife as a sort of saw he set to work cutting it loose.

Twice he stopped briefly to peer up at the darkening sky. Snow was starting to fall but he was not worried. A little snow was not a problem since he was but half a day's journey from the hut.

More than a little snow was coming. Much more!

The limb was nearly cut through. He whipped it back and forth until it finally snapped free. He was relieved. The wind was coming at him from the southwest and its voice could be heard in the top branches of the hickory trees. Holding his wolf-hide hood with this good hand, Otah tucked the new spear shaft under his arm and gave the call for Sand to come. The wolf did not appear.

For the first time the man became concerned. The snowflakes had started large and feathery, but as he watched and called to his companion they were quickly turning to small hard-driving missiles. Otah tried to tighten the poorly made clothes around his body but the wind and snow found every gap and seam. "Sand will find his own way," Otah said aloud. He turned his back to the growing storm and began floundering his way east toward his hut. He continued to call, but knew that the high-pitched squeals would immediately be carried away on the howling wind.

Patience. . . patience. . . plan. . .

He realized that once again he had failed to heed the cautions his father had tried so hard to hammer into his son. With no pack he had started the trip in bright sunshine. No pack meant no emergency food, no heavy robe, and worst of all, *no fire kit!* As these facts crowded in upon him he made a very serious mistake. The hut was his home. There he had food and a warm robe he could crawl under. There was safety. There was *life!* He began to run, floundering heavily in the deepening snow. "East! I must keep going east!" he repeated as he attempted to hurry. "I will soon find my own back trail. I need only follow it and I will be able to reach my home before full dark."

There was no back trail. It had long since been obliterated by the wind-driven snow. Otah was still not overly concerned about this. "I will have no trouble traveling east," he assured himself. "I'll just keep the wind on my back." While he was correct in this he could not know that the furious west wind had gradually veered more to the south. His laboring footsteps were leading him northward, away from his home, and more seriously, away from the river and ever deeper into the frozen Black Swamp.

Otah's makeshift clothing did little to keep out the wind and snow. Only the wolf skin was effective at all. Even with his hood fastened as tightly as possible, still the snow was soon matting his hair and eyelashes. It was hard to see.

He plunged on, sometimes tripping over obstacles hidden under the deepening snow. "I am not afraid!" he shouted, shaking his fist at the storm. The spear shaft he had cut from the hickory tree served him well. He was now using it as a walking staff. At times it even helped to push him forward.

"I must find the river and soon," he mumbled. He changed his course enough to feel the wind on his right cheek. "All I need is the river to guide me," he thought. He tried to hurry but this only caused more stumbling and falling into the drifts. He could not know that the river he sought was now far to the south. Hunger was becoming noticeable. He had packed nothing for this emergency, a fact that was becoming steadily clearer as the storm raged around him.

For the fourth time he fell headlong. His left knee punched through the snow and struck something hard. A rock? A log? He didn't know but what he did know was that the joint seemed badly hurt. "Not *again!*" he groaned. Using the staff he was able to pull himself erect, but the pain was building. Otah realized that very soon he may no longer be able to fight his way through the drifts. "I must find some kind of shelter soon or I will die!" he thought. Almost at that very moment his way was blocked by the four joined trunks of a large clump birch. The wind had cleared a sort of hollow on the lee side of the trees. He collapsed into this tiny refuge and attempted to cover himself with his deerskin clothing. He pulled the wolf pelt completely over his head and face, leaving only a crack for breathing. Curling up with his aching knee against his chest he prepared himself.

"Prepared for what?" he wondered. "Prepared to die, of course!" he answered himself.

The wind continued to cry through the bare branches of the birches above him. "I didn't plan did I?" he asked the wind. "No robe, no food, not even the fire drill! I deserve to end my life here in this frozen place!"

He was still fairly warm from the recent difficult travel. The snow piled over the small mound that was the man, Otah. This helped capture the pitifully small amount of heat from his body. He was feeling sleepy, but instinctively knew that to sleep now meant death. He tried everything to keep awake. Leaf's small figure seemed to appear before him. He talked to her but she did not answer. Then his father's face wavered in and out of Otah's mind. It seemed that the man was frowning. "As well he might!" Otah thought. "He taught me well but I have been a fool."

The cold was not to be denied as it crept in under his clothing. The clumsy boots did little to warm his feet, even though he *had* thought to stuff them with cattail fluff before leaving on his trip. The cold helped in one way however. The twisted knee no longer ached as it had at first. In fact he could hardly feel it at all! This was not a good sign.

"I will sleep now."

Otah did not die. Some time during the long night he awoke. He was almost *warm*, and was not alone. "Have I gone away to the Other Place?" he wondered. He felt movement.

"Sand!" he cried. "You have come to me. Your rough furry body has kept me alive!" He carefully put one arm across the wolf's back in a gesture of affection. Sand growled at the touch. The big animal's teeth were bared as a furious snarl echoed from deep in his chest. The dim half-light of the snow cave showed the fur across his neck and back standing high and menacing. Sand was about to attack!

Almost without thinking Otah balled his right fist and smashed it deep into the wolf's belly. Sand gave a yip of surprise and pain and shrank back against the frozen snow. The batting eyes and flattened ears showed the man that his companion had received the message! Otah immediately followed the blow with a growl of his own. His angry voice was magnified within their ice-bound shelter. Sand cowered in fear, then wriggled until his head and throat were vulnerable. Otah kept his voice low and menacing.

"You thought your master was too weak to rule over you did you? I am tired, hungry and cold. My knee is aching and my left arm throbs where you bit me. But [and here he raised his voice to a shout] I am *leader* of this pack!" Otah knew of course that the big wolf understood not a word, but the animal understood the actions perfectly!

The man knew that it was the animal's nature to challenge any leader. This was especially true as a male neared full growth. There would be other challenges as the wolf matured, so he must always be on guard, but for now Sand had submitted to the man's leadership. Together they could make a formidable team. Apart, probably neither would long survive.

Only the wolf's remarkable sense of smell had enabled it to find and follow its master's trail through the snow. Sand had saved Otah's life *again!*

Man and wolf slept until dawn.

*   *   *

As he worked on the new spear shaft Otah could not help recalling the horror of that full day's journey back to his hut. Hopelessly lost in a blinding wilderness of white, he had simply let Sand lead the way. With the wolf in the lead breaking trail and the hickory shaft to lean on he had dragged himself back to safety. Back to life!

The man vowed never to be caught in such danger again. Sand had watched as his master carefully packed a small parfleche with survival gear. A few fragments of smooth, sharp flint, a hunk of dried venison, and most of all, the fire-making kit. "I owe you my life, good friend," he murmured as he tossed the wolf still another strip of frozen meat. Sand's ears came forward as he gobbled the meat. It seemed that his eyes told Otah that his master had certainly been a careless fool! *Humans!*

The hickory limb was fairly straight but had a decided bow near the thicker end. Otah was attempting to remedy this by the method he had seen his father use. First he wet down the crooked area with snow water, soaking it again and again until he judged the wood to be wet nearly through. The fire was low, just right for heating the wet limb. With the shaft propped under his left instep he leaned his weight along the length of the wood. Gently he pressed and released until the wood was dry again. Otah kept this process going for half the day, keeping the fire low and smoky.

The snow had stopped but the wind remained strong out of the west. Occasional gusts came down from the smoke hole in the roof, and Otah's eyes were streaming from the smoke. Sand sneezed twice, stood up and shook himself mightily. Again his eyes seemed to suggest that all humans were fools! He wormed his way out of the door flap and curled up nose to tail in the snow.

Otah continued the straightening process, and between the heating sessions he was busy scraping down the shaft. He was using the same flint fragment shaped like the crescent moon that had served him before. By pulling it back and forth across the rounded wood he very gradually shaved away every knot and high place. He was proud of the result. All that remained was to saw a thin slit in the end and bind in a flint blade with sinew. The problem was that he *had* no blade and no flint to make one!

It would be necessary to try to make a trip to the flint quarry, but there was no point in going there until the snow was gone for good.

Otah had not eaten much during these frozen winter days. Staying mostly in the hut had hardly fueled his appetite. Sand had consumed less also, spending much of each day curled up in his favorite spot against the hut wall. Otah noticed however that the animal became restless at night. He often squirmed out of the hut and would be gone for most of the following day.

"He is free to do as he pleases," Otah reminded himself with a smile. "I only hope and trust that he will come back to me after each of his wanderings. Life now would be very sad without him!"

It was not long after this that what he feared did happen. Sand had left the hut shortly after dark. Another snowstorm was coming in, this time from the north. Otah was not concerned when his companion did not appear all that day or the next. However, when the third day dawned with the wolf still gone Otah knew he must act.

Patience . . . patience. . . . plan. . .

He would not be caught unprepared this time! Telling himself that his companion would surely show up before long anyway, still he prepared carefully, in case he must spend some time in the weather. Leggings, hood, and coat were inspected and repairs made where necessary. All was ready, but he decided to wait one more day to make sure that the latest storm had blown itself out. Also he still maintained a slight hope that the wolf would indeed return.

A weak sun had risen over the trees to the east when he left the hut. The cold seemed a living thing which meant to kill him! He wrapped a tanned snowshoe rabbit skin over his nose and mouth, chuckling aloud as he remembered the fight it had taken to tear it away from the wolf. Sand had caught the rabbit in a patch of swale that had been blown free of snow. The small animal's huge feet had served it well as it bounded over the drifts, but Sand had managed to drive it onto the bare ground where he had quickly run it down. The wolf carried the dead rabbit back to the hut and prepared to devour it. Otah had heard the sound of bones crunching just outside the hut. Rushing out he risked being bitten by yanking the rabbit from the wolf's jaws. He had quickly skinned it and thrown the meat back to the wolf. This warm pelt was exactly what he needed to avoid a frozen nose or frostbitten ears.

He circled the hut several times, each trip in a widening path. On the third pass he saw what he was searching for. In an area somewhat sheltered from the wind a faint set of tracks led away to the east: "He will follow the river," Otah thought. He drew a sight on a dead tree which stood far off in the direction of the spoor. He did not hurry, not *this time!*

Approaching the river bank, the man saw where the wolf had started across on the ice. Otah sighed with disgust at how easy it was to gain the far side now! He would never forget those freezing plunges he'd had to make across this same stream the past fall! Sand's tracks disappeared and reappeared on the ice, but Otah found them often enough to keep heading in the right direction. At last he came upon a gouged out drift where the animal had bucked its way off the ice. Stands of willows had held back the snow somewhat, so here the trail was clear.

The wolf had ranged far during the three days it had been gone. Although its direction was generally east, Sand had crossed and recrossed the river several times. Otah made steady progress, taking his time to relocate the wolf's tracks whenever they disappeared.

Sand's tracks were quite clear now, having been made after the last snowfall. Confident that he would soon encounter his traveling friend, Otah cleared a place to sit down and rest. As he chewed at some of his supply of dried venison he puzzled at the changes in the wolf's trail. For over half a day the tracks had been haphazard. They had curled around thickets, backtracked for long distances, and generally showed no intense purpose. Now however they led straight away. Something had happened here!

Food forgotten Otah rose to his feet. He moved much faster now, a strange sense of urgency pushing him forward. Near a thick clump of bushes Sand's trail changed dramatically. Plainly the wolf had crouched down in the snow long enough to leave the distinct print of its body. From that hollow place in the snow Sand's tracks had indicated a series of great, long bounds into an alder thicket.

Otah was not surprised when he came upon the story written in the trampled snow. It was plainly evident that Sand had made a kill. From the tracks Otah could read what had happened. A small herd of whitetails had yarded up in the alders. By staying close together they were able to trample down the snow to expose enough grass and low-growing shrubs for grazing. Sand had watched them, lying half-hidden in the snow. Evidently one or more of the deer had wandered too close to the waiting wolf.

There had been a battle it was clear. Sticks and brush were scattered all around. The snow was disrupted in a great circle peppered with hair and spots of dark blood.

"I hope you didn't eat it all!" Otah said into the wind. "When I find you I intend to take most of the meat away from you. That shouldn't be hard to do since by now you have probably eaten so much you will only want to *sleep!* Now, what have you done with your kill?"

Otah stood at the edge of the kill site and considered the question. Why was the carcass missing? Sand could, he knew, eat great amounts of meat at one time, but it was not possible that the animal could have devoured a whole deer in a day or two. He started off to make a wide circle around the area. He had gone less than a hundred paces when he stopped in shock. The deer's body, what was left of it, lay there before him, but something was not right. It was almost covered with snow, sticks and dry leaves which had been scraped from the ground nearby. Something had attempted to hide the body, something a wolf would never do. Otah gingerly kicked away some of the debris in order to see what else he could learn. Large portions of flesh had been torn from the flanks. This would have been Sand's feeding and was to be expected. What caused Otah to draw a quick breath of fear however, was the sight of the ripped open stomach.

Now he knew!

Otah slipped the good spear from its sling over his left shoulder. He loosened the axe riding in his belt, thankful for the rawhide repair on the heavy tool. Cautiously he made one step back, away from the deer, his eyes raking the nearby bushes and low-lying limbs. Another careful backward step was all it took.

The yellow-brown body came crashing out of the brush, teeth bared, ears laid back, and snarling. It crouched over the kill, long tail thrashing. Otah was terrified but he kept his wits about him. The cat was guarding its food. Otah took another cautious step backward, keeping the spear pointed at the animal's head. It made a false charge of only a few paces. Otah nearly dropped the spear in terror, but he did not run. *He must not run, he knew!* Step by careful trembling step he retreated, never taking his eyes from the crouching panther. It made another half-hearted charge but chose to remain guarding the carcass.

Finally far out of the danger area Otah sank to his knees in the snow. His wolf skin hood was wet with sweat. He made a small fire and crouched almost on top of it to warm himself. He had no doubt that this had nearly been the end of him. The experience left him weak and very afraid. Still he meant to find his companion if that was possible. Otah did not try to fool himself. Sand was probably dead, his body by now nearly consumed by coyotes and other scavengers hungry after the blizzard. But, he had to *know*.

Afraid to go anywhere near the area now claimed by the panther he simply walked a zigzag path westward, keeping the river in view on his right. Chances of cutting Sand's trail were slim he knew but he kept on.

The short winter day was nearly gone. Long shadows rippled across the snow-covered landscape. Sand's trail had not been found. "Perhaps," he thought, "there *is* no trail. Somewhere there may be another debris-covered body waiting to make another meal for the big cat. I'm tired now and hungry," Otah told himself. He must make camp for the night. "Tomorrow I begin again. I will not give up!"

Feeling slightly proud of himself, Otah quickly made a serviceable camp. Curled up on a section of hide and with the sleeping robe covering him he was warm. No fire was needed but the fire drill was safely at hand to make a warming blaze in the morning.

He slept.

The sun was well up by the time the man had wakened, made a fire, and eaten some pemmican. The sky was clear except for a roll of low-lying clouds to the south. He knew about that sort of cloud formation. Wind and snow would be coning again soon. He hardly knew why he was continuing on this useless quest. If the snow was heavy at all, every track and trail would be buried.

Hope continues so long as there is breath!

Otah shook out his robes and repacked them with care. The sky was heavy but the snow had not yet started to fall. Wandering slowly along, several hundred paces north of the river, he began to experience a strange feeling. What was it? Having kept his eyes on the ground as he searched for tracks, Otah had paid little attention to his surroundings. "Why . . why .. ." he stuttered, "I think I'm beginning to *recognize* this place. There, that twisted tree . . those barren ridges . . that . . that. . .*I know! I know!*"

He was sure not only of his position, but where he would find the wolf! He was tempted to begin running, but he fought down the impulse. It was no longer necessary to watch for glimpses of half-buried tracks. He kept his eyes far ahead, hoping . . hoping. . .!

Otah was almost upon them when they appeared in his path. The *"family trees"*! He was nearing the wolves' old den site! The faint trail of tracks appeared then as he knew they would. They led north, the direction of the den, but that was of no concern. He stopped long enough to examine the tracks more closely. There was a little blood in the snow and the trail clearly showed that one foot was dragging.

Sand was hurt!

He approached the den cautiously. How different it appeared covered with winter snow. Stopping well away from the entrance, he was not encouraged by the faint trail. Brownish stains of dried blood were apparent every few paces. Snow had drifted across half the opening to the den, and tracks here were but faintly visible under the new skift of white.

"Sand! Oh *Sand!* I know you are in there for there are no tracks leading out. But are you alive? Did you crawl back into your old home to die?" Otah hesitated. He couldn't crawl right in as he had done last fall. He relived the sight of the small female bursting past him and away. "I wonder what became of her?" he mused. Otah well knew that he must act, but what would be his best option? Whatever he did it must be done soon. Crawling into the den to confront a terrified half-grown female cub had been one thing. Doing the same with a mature wolf was quite something else again, especially one that was undoubtedly injured and in pain.

Otah approached the opening on all fours. He spent long moments listening, but not a sound was heard. Crawling up to the very entrance, he pressed his lips against the back of his hand. He gave the squealing call which Sand had learned meant "come". The man stopped breathing and listened. *There!* Faint but unmistakable, the wolf's familiar low whine of greeting floated from the den. Otah was ready to scramble into the den and greet his companion!

Patience. . .patience. . .plan. . .

Smiling to himself, Otah sat back in the snow and considered. "I know you, my friend." He spoke softly but loud enough for Sand's sharp ears to hear. "Yes, I've learned to know you very well over the past months. You do not like to be touched. In the narrow den I could not defend myself were you to attack. And you *would* attack!" He kept talking in the most soothing tones he could produce, but he was thinking. *Planning!*

"I don't know how badly the panther dealt with you but I can guess it was serious. You are not going to like what I am about to do, but I must. You have saved my life twice. Now it is my turn to try to save yours."

Otah uncoiled a length of sinew from his well-stocked travel pouch. Working quickly lest his bare fingers freeze, he formed a loop secured with a slip knot. The strands, much like a rabbit snare, he draped over a short section of a downed limb dug from beneath the snow. The other end of the sinew rope he tied securely to his belt. He was ready. The entire scene was almost repeating itself. How *strange!*

With exaggerated caution he entered the tunnel. Low, rumbling growls greeted him from far back in the cave. He continued to slither forward but with every foot of progress the growls and snarls increased. He had left the pack bundle outside, but had thought to bring a section of pemmican with him. He threw the food toward the glowing eyes, visible in the darkness, and waited. Sand ignored the food. A bad sign. In other circumstances Sand would have snapped up the treat in two gulps. Otah waited some more, talking softly all the time. His eyes had adjusted enough by now that he could see the animal, but was unable to tell what sort of injury it had suffered.

Sand lifted his head with teeth bared. One ear hung crookedly beside his eye. It was chewed half in two, the pointed tip barely hanging on. Otah could see bloody furrows across the neck, but the rest of the animal was still invisible in the darkened den. The noose dangled close to Sand's snout, and fortunately the sinew held a scent that the wolf found familiar. He dipped his head, eyeing the sinew with distrust. Otah tossed a small piece of venison almost under the animal's nose. Sand had not eaten for two days, so still watching his master he grabbed the meat and quickly swallowed. The man had his chance! The noose encircled the still moving jaws perfectly and Otah jerked it tight. Sand fought the snare but this only tightened it over his muzzle. He would not bite anything now!

Otah carefully slipped one hand under a front paw, still keeping his end of the sinew rope taut. The wolf's hackles rose but he didn't struggle. The man could feel no wounds along the front legs and across the chest, which confirmed what the snow trail had told him. The injury, at least one of them, was in the right hind leg. Otah began gently but firmly pulling the heavy animal forward. Sand's attempts at snarls would have seemed funny in other circumstances. They came out in sniffs and squeaks, and Otah ignored them. His attention was centered on the loop of sinew that held the wolf's mouth tightly closed. Finally Sand began to crawl forward.

The sunlight was dazzling as Otah backed out of the tunnel. He urged Sand out of the den. The wolf did not struggle, for which Otah was thankful. The wounds were evident. The deep claw marks across the neck were swollen, with dried blood hanging in the rough fur beside each of the nasty gouges. With his first good look at his companion Otah noted the right hind leg lying crooked and swollen. Deep bite marks left no doubt of how the panther had crippled the wolf. "You might learn to walk on three legs," Otah said soothingly, "but you may find it hard to make a kill with that bad leg. No, you might

not make a kill, but you would certainly *be killed!* You must let me try to fix the break.

Even if I am successful in that, it will be a miracle if your wounds do not become

infected."

Patience . . .patience. . . plan. . .

"No my friend, we cannot attempt the trip back to the hut. Not yet. I will build us

a shelter and here we will stay until either you are well enough to travel or you have gone

to the Other Place. I will not leave until one or the other happens."

Otah had already begun gathering some long branches for the shelter when the

thought hit him. "Sand my friend, you are smarter than I! There is no need to build a

shelter when one much better stares us in the face! I will try to clean your wounds with

new snow. Then we will see if you will tolerate a sturdy stick bound to your broken leg.

Then. . . *then* . . . we shall both re-enter your den!"

Sand made it clear that he did not intend sharing the den with his master.

Whenever Otah crawled into the tunnel the wolf refused to be enticed to enter. "Very

well then," Otah snapped, "you stay out in the snow. I will sleep warm in the den." This

was what the animal preferred, his thick coat adequate insulation against the late winter

cold. Curled into a rounded hump, he simply let the snow cover him completely.

Otah was becoming concerned about food for the wolf and himself. "When you

can walk well enough we must travel back to the hut," he said. Talking softly and with

many soothing sounds and gestures he gentled the injured animal until Sand finally

allowed the man to touch him. Even a careful examination of the injured leg brought only a few half-hearted growls. "We still have a haunch of venison hanging behind our hut. That is, if the raccoons and squirrels have left any of it! Yes, we must get home soon."

Both man and wolf were becoming sick of rabbit flesh. Otah's snares had been successful but he was forced to cross the river to set them. The she-wolf and her pups, including Sand, had long ago depleted the rabbit population north of the river where the den was located.

A big kill was needed soon. Sand had eaten little as his wounds were healing but Otah could see the wolf's need for meat rapidly returning. It was a good sign but did not solve their problem. Not only did he have little hope of finding and taking an animal, but he was concerned about leaving his wounded companion while he was off on an extended hunt.

Patience . . .patience. . . plan. . .

Otah felt confident that the wolf would be safe only if it remained in the den. Outside, handicapped as it was, even a pack of roving coyotes could easily surround and kill it.

Otah considered several options while he busied himself preparing a splint for Sand's leg. He had cut and smoothed a section of green willow as thick as two fingers and long as his forearm. He had allowed the wolf to sniff at it often, and he kept the stick in his hand as he stroked the animal's head and back. Sand growled at his master's touch, but for once tolerated it. When Otah finally felt it might be time to try the splint he spent longer than usual talking to the animal. Then with quick but gentle hands he laid the wood along the broken limb and secured it with several strips of green rabbit hide. The leg was slightly crooked, but Otah knew it would be worth a vicious bite if he tried to manipulate the broken bone in any way. He was elated, as Sand had allowed the splint to be secured without fighting it!

Sand stretched his nose to the bandages, sniffed at them, calmly chewed them off and ate them!

While all of this was going on, Otah was developing a plan. He fished the last strip of dried venison from his pack. He waved it enticingly before the hungry wolf's nose, then tossed it as far into the den as he could. Sand crawled in after it, just as Otah had hoped. "Now stay in there until I come back!" He commanded, well aware that the wolf understood none of this, and would not have obeyed even if it had! "I tried to help your broken leg but you would not cooperate. I know of nothing more I can do, so hopefully the leg will heal itself."

It was fortunate that Otah's attempt had been unsuccessful, for with such a splint in place Sand would have been unable to lick the torn flesh from the cat's bites. The bones would knit together eventually, but without his tongue patiently cleansing the wounds, Sand would have soon died from infection.

*   *   *

Once again Otah prepared as best he could before the hunt. Sand had remained in the den for the present but the man could not tell if it would stay there. That morning he had made a hurried trip beyond the river to check his snares, hoping to find a rabbit or two. He was disappointed to find none. "If I had a rabbit to throw into the den Sand would probably stay in there long enough to eat it." Checking his pack one more time he left the wolf and headed east.

A thaw was coming, indicated by a gentle, restless breeze which came sliding across the frozen swamp. While the warmer weather was a relief, it made traveling difficult, since the wet snow clung to his clumsy boots. It was slippery as well, causing Otah to take each step with caution. Forced to travel slowly he began to feel depressed.

"What am I trying to do anyway?" he asked himself sadly. "I have father's spear of course, my flint blade is safe, and the big axe rides against my hip. But what good are these? Alone and without an atlatl my chances of successfully taking anything larger than a rabbit or a porcupine are futile. Were it not for Sand, my companion, I would head back to the hut. There is meat there [or there *was*] and I would be safe. But as long as he lives I must do all I can to save his life, just as he has saved mine!"

Otah's steps continued but came slower and slower. He wandered aimlessly, paying no attention to the tracks of deer and elk which were plentiful here on the ridge which in summer held back the swamp. He decided to give up and turn back.

Patience. . . patience. . . .plan. . . .

With a grim smile Otah once again remembered these words of his father. Still with little hope he spoke into the breeze, "Very well. One more half day, but then I am finished!" A half day was not needed! Wearily topping yet another snowy ridge he saw not far in the distance a feeder creek. It was still frozen over of course, but what excited the man was the long, curving dam that held back the water. This created a small pond, near the center of which was a large dome-shaped structure of sticks and mud.

"A beaver lodge!" Otah whispered, his fatigue instantly forgotten. He slipped and slid down the ridge to the edge of the small stream. Beaver sign was everywhere. Saplings and even fairly large trees had been felled by the animals' long orange teeth. The stumps were evidence that a family of the creatures had been hard at work around the pond.

By this time Otah needed no reminder. Taking one of these large animals could mean the difference between life and death for the wolf, if not for both of them. He seated himself behind a screen of bushes on high ground above the pond where he could wait and watch. It wasn't long until he spotted movement under the clear ice near the stream's edge. A large brown shape glided gracefully toward the shore. Its webbed hind feet, plainly visible from his vantage point above, propelled the animal effortlessly. Otah watched, unmoving. The beaver was heading for the bank, almost directly under Otah's hiding place. Its destination was clear. A branch, cut down from a paper birch tree, lay half in the water. The ice was thin at that point due to the current eddying around the thicker end of the branch. Hardly breathing, Otah watched the beaver trying to work the limb under the ice, but it was stuck. A fork had caught in the bushes on shore. No matter how hard the animal tugged, its food supply did not budge, and the beaver finally gave up. Then Otah noticed a most peculiar thing. Rather than turn around to swim back to its lodge in the center of the pond it wriggled awkwardly backward. It was trying to back up! In a flash Otah saw the reason. The heavy-bodied animal was following a sort of half tunnel which allowed it to move along in the shallows under the ice.

Otah waited some more. The inactivity had allowed the cold to creep under his clothing. He shivered constantly, but did not allow himself to move. There would only be *one chance!*

Rising carefully at last, he slipped away, out of sight. When his legs had stopped shaking, he peeked into the pond again to make sure the animal was gone. He must hurry now! The thin ice crackled alarmingly as he stepped out upon it. The little channel the beaver had used was plain to see. Kneeling on one knee he brought the axe down on the ice again and again. When he had chopped a hole as big as his palm he rose and skated his way to the bank. Then he ran!

Finding a limb of a size to fit in the hole he had made, he used the axe and his knife to sharpen one end of it. Moving as quietly as possible he returned to the same vantage point as before, the stake ready in his hand. Time passed slowly as he watched for the beaver's return.

There! The big animal came slipping along, its back rubbing on the ice above it. The webbed hind feet stirred up mushrooms of muddy water as it came. As before, the beaver began gnawing and worrying at the sunken end of the branch. Otah did not hesitate, but burst through the bushes and leaped. Luckily he landed with both feet on the ice. The beaver panicked. It was trying frantically to back up when Otah jammed the stake through the hole and deep into the muck on the bottom. With its escape cut off the big animal charged forward, making for the shore. As Otah leaped after it, the thin ice broke under him. Freed from the ice the animal scrambled ashore and started up the bank through the snow. A thing of beauty and grace in the water, the beaver was hardly that on land. It waddled along as fast as it could but it was not fast enough. Wet to the knees, Otah thrashed through the broken ice and gave pursuit. Bravely the beaver, knowing he could not outrun the creature that chased him, turned to fight. With its broad scaly tail propping it up he rose on his hind legs, gnawing teeth bared.

Otah killed it with a single slashing blow of the axe.

"Sand, we will eat *now!*" he rejoiced as he dragged the heavy body to higher ground. Its weight appeared to be more than half of Otah's own. Furthermore it was heavy with the fat that their diet of rabbit and dried venison needed. "Now to head back west to the den!"

Patience. . . patience. . . plan. . .

It was late in the day with wet snow falling again. Otah's soaking legs and feet were becoming numb. He shook his head at his own folly. Sand would have to wait another day. What must be done now was the building of a strong fire. Frozen feet would mean two deaths, and very soon.

Working rapidly as close to the fire as he could get, he hoisted the beaver to the low branch of a tree. He tied it upside down by the tail and did a quick but very creditable job of skinning. He gathered the largest logs he could carry and placed them in a circle around the fire. Once again he would sit up all night and keep the fire blazing. The precaution had worked before and he was getting good at it! The scent of the hanging carcass could bring predators, but even the panther; were it still about, would not brave the fire.

He dined on a good sized portion of beaver meat, the best food he had ever eaten!

Although he had fallen asleep several times during the night there were no predators. The fire had warmed him all the way through. His clothes and boots were fairly dry, and the snow had stopped before dawn. "We're coming Sand!" he shouted, packing his gear. Every bit of the meat must be saved, even the entrails, but Otah was not concerned. He split the beaver pelt down the middle and fastened a sinew rope to one end. Spreading the raw pelt flesh side up, he packed the meat on the makeshift sled, just as he had done with the deer. The oil-treated fur slid effortlessly over the snow. He could travel fast and he did. He was going *home!*

*   *   *

Sand tore off large chunks of half-frozen beaver. Growling possessively the wolf gulped them down until he was finally full. Still he lay with one paw over the meat and kept his eyes on the man. "So I see you are much better now. Do not forget who is chief here or you may believe that I will use the club again!" Sand was unimpressed.

The animal could walk now but with a decided limp. The deep scratches across his neck and shoulders were healing, but would leave scars. His broken hind leg remained crooked and appeared to be slightly shorter than the other, but all things considered, Otah was very pleased. He still had his companion, although it remained to be seen if the wolf would be able to hunt. "Soon," he told the wolf, "we will make a long journey. I intend to find my sister if she is alive, and bring her back to us."

Patience. . . patience. . . plan. . .

Otah could not believe how much meat the wolf was able to eat. Had he allowed it Sand would have gorged himself until there was nothing left. "We must take another deer

Sand, my friend," he said, eyeing the sleeping wolf. "You are probably as well now as you will ever be. The days are getting longer and soon the ice will be gone from the river. I'm not about to brave that cold water ever again. Yes, we must prepare soon while we can still cross on the ice. The deer herd will probably leave when the Black Swamp thaws. They will seek other pastures on higher ground, just as we would."

Sand watched as his master spoke his thoughts aloud. The words were soothing to the animal and Otah was well aware of this. More and more he spoke audibly of his concerns and ideas while the wolf was present. Sand was not a pet. He remained a wild animal that, for the present at least, was willing to accept this two-legged creature as his pack leader. Were Otah to relax his control at any time the wolf would probably challenge him, even to the point of a serious attack. This was the way of things at that prehistoric time.

Luck had certainly been with them as they had sought food in the past. Luck, however could not be depended upon. Otah intended to be better prepared before their next hunt. This was especially necessary since it was highly uncertain if the limping wolf would be able to do its part.

Otah sat against the hut wall, knees drawn up and arms folded while Sand slept as usual in his spot on the opposite side. The small fire was adequate to warm their small house, as snow still covered it almost to the smoke hole. Otah was planning to build an atlatl. Angrily he recalled the way he had carelessly lost the beautiful one made by his father. He had been much younger then but old enough to have followed his father's instructions. Excited by his first real deer hunt the young Otah had dashed through the forest in pursuit of the deer he had wounded. Somewhere in the thickets he had dropped the atlatl, losing it for good.

Otah sat brooding, angry at his former foolishness. He could almost feel the smooth, slightly curved wood which so cunningly held the spear. He had been too young to remember how his father had crafted the device but he felt that he might be able to make one that would work. "The atlatl will keep us alive," he told the wolf. "Also it may well be needed when we confront my sister's captors. All this *if* I can make one, and you are well enough to be of some help in hunting or fighting." Sand rose and stretched, paying little attention to his master's musings. He was too warm. The coarse outer hair above the thick body fur served him well even in the coldest weather. He disliked the smoky heat of the dwelling, so nosed his way out of the door flap and disappeared.

Otah, dressed for the cold, left the hut. He needed to find several items if he were to be successful in building the spear-thrower. First must be a section of seasoned wood as long as his arm and nearly as thick. Green wood from a living tree would not work he knew, for he had seen the difficulty working with such material when working on the spear shaft.

The search was made more difficult with everything covered with snow but he kept looking. Finally he saw what he felt might be usable. A wind-blown poplar tree had been uprooted near the northern edge of the swamp. It appeared to have been there, roots exposed, for some time. One root jutting upward from the snow looked about right. Otah brushed it off and examined it from every angle. It was not quite long enough but it was the best he had seen, so it would have to do. Using the tiny flint saw from his kit he began to cut it free. The wood was just right, not too green nor too dry. Otah was elated! When it finally came loose he followed his wandering back trail to the hut.

Sand was gone but Otah was not concerned, as the wolf came and went as it pleased just as Otah did. "I hope he can get a rabbit or something. Our food supply is dwindling," Otah thought. Food! Always there was the problem of food! The man sometimes considered how much easier it would be if the wolf were not with him. On the other hand, Sand had been a real help in obtaining food. Of course the most important reason was that the wolf was very much a companion now. The animal had done a lot to take away the loneliness.

He started a fire in the pit at the center of the lodge, and warmth came quickly in the small space. He would not need much heat. He examined the poplar root carefully, turning it over and over and sighting down its length. There were no cracks he could see, and since it was a root it was free of knots.

Otah settled himself as comfortably as possible and began the tedious job. Using a "thumb scraper" no larger than the first joint of a finger, he began scraping away, removing all the bark. Finishing that he selected the same crescent-shaped tool that had served him so well on the new spear shaft.

The work went on until it was becoming too dark to see. He ate some of the remaining pemmican, put a thick branch on the fire and prepared to sleep. Sand had not returned.

Shortly after dawn of the following day, Otah was awakened by some suspicious sounds outside. Half growls and part whine, the noise sounded somewhat like Sand, but then again it did not. He grabbed the good spear and carefully pulled back a thin slit in the door skin. With one eye pressed to the opening he scanned as much of the area as possible. It *was Sand*! But why had the wolf not come scratching at the door flap as usual? The animal limped nervously about, casting glances at the hut, but did not venture closer. Otah opened the flap wider, stuck his head out and checked the entire area. Sand made the same sounds, keeping his eyes on his master. "Sand, *come!*" Otah called, then made the squealing sound on the back of his hand. Sand paced hesitantly back and forth but did not approach.

Otah held a strip of jerky toward the wolf and continued to call. Sand suddenly crouched down in the snow and began scratching at his snout with both front paws. Otah stepped out and moved carefully closer. Then he saw the trouble. "You are a *stupid* wolf!" he said, shaking his head. "I hope you had a meal for all that trouble!" Sand's lips and chin were bristling with porcupine quills! This was no laughing matter. Left alone the barbed, needle-like spikes would keep working their way in, and infection would probably follow. It looked as if there might be as many as ten quills. They must be removed, but how?

By commands and squealing sounds Otah finally coaxed the animal inside. Sand eyed him suspiciously, a low growl giving warning. The wolf had no intention of allowing the man to even touch the stinging, painful quills that protruded from his lips. "Now my friend, we shall see just how much you trust your pack leader. If you bite me I must leave you to suffer. You will not be able to eat and the pain will get worse."

Otah stayed clear of the wolf, circling to get a better look at the position of the quills. He picked up the fist-sized stone his mother and sister had used to grind seeds and dried berries. The rock felt good in his left hand. He knelt at arm's length from the wolf and very slowly extended his right hand, intending to pull out one of the quills. Sand lunged forward, his lips curled in a snarl. Mouth agape, it was clear that he meant to bite that hand if it came any closer! The animal was in pain and was not about to let the man touch his wounded mouth.

Otah did not hesitate. The rock smashed into Sand's head just above the eye. The wolf batted his eyes and fell back, whining. Blood trickled from a cut made by the blow.

"Sand! *Down!*" he roared, again using his "leader of the pack" voice. Surprisingly Sand obeyed, exposing his throat and stomach just as he would have if the number one wolf of a pack had demanded the action. Quickly Otah knelt, pushing his good knee hard against the back of the animal's neck, just behind the head. Sand growled and whimpered but made no move to bite. The man kept him pinned to the floor of the hut and wasted no time. He was not gentle! There was only one way to do this job; it must be quick and painful. Sand yelped each time Otah gave a sudden tug on a quill, but instinctively he seemed to sense that his master was helping him. It did not take long. All eleven of the brown and white tines were extracted before Otah allowed the wolf to rise. It stood up, shook itself mightily and backed off to try to lick the sore places below its nose.

Otah was elated that the painful problem was so easily solved. But was it? Four days later he noticed the wolf worrying a front paw with his teeth. The man paid little attention, but after two more days Sand was still at it! "Sand, *down!*" he ordered. This time the order was quickly obeyed. It was almost comical the way the huge, dangerous animal submitted to its "pack leader". Otah pinned the animal with his knee as before and lifted the paw. He had an idea of what he might find, and sure enough there between two calloused pads on the huge foot the very end of a quill protruded. There was not enough showing to get a grip on the thin, tapered quill, so there was no other way! Otah spread the pads with his fingers, bent down, held his breath, and withdrew the quill with his teeth!

Sand did not try to bite. He didn't even growl! The wolf would never attack a porcupine again, no matter how hungry he might become!

*   *   *

The finished atlatl was far from a thing of beauty but Otah was proud of his work anyway. Lacking the skill to make the thin, feathered foreshafts for it, he would be forced to use his father's spear as a substitute until he could craft some of them. With longing he remembered the graceful beauty of the Mastodon Hunters' weapons. "It may be," he thought, "that when I find the Clan I can learn the skills I need. But would they be willing to teach me? Will I be welcome at their camp? Can I even *find* them?" These and many other questions plagued him as he oiled the atlatl with a little remaining fat from a pemmican casing. They were difficult questions but not the most important one. "Sand," he said one morning, "we can wait no longer. Your leg has probably healed as well as it ever will. Our food is nearly gone, and there are several moons left of the winter. Once again we must hunt or die! That is how life is when we are alone."

The rains of spring had begun but there could be no excuses because of weather.

Otah had prepared as best he was able, packing the last bits of venison and pemmican.

The pouch with his precious tools and fire drill had been reinforced by sewing with sinew

but it was a poor job. "Women's work!" he had repeated often. There had been little time

to practice using the atlatl to cast the spear. Although a work of art in itself, his father's

spear was never meant as a missile. It was stabbing lance to be used for defense or to

finish off a wounded animal. Without the necessary fletching of turkey feathers it would

never follow a true flight, no matter how hard the atlatl propelled it. "Making a kill with

this concoction will be a miracle indeed," he said aloud. Sand seemed to agree. "But what

choice have we, my friend? We will do all in our power to get food, as if our lives

depended upon it. Because it *does!"*

The wolf had lost weight during the winter months as had his master. Sand had

managed to kill several rabbits, but devoured them on the spot. Returning to the hut he

would slink inside, looking guilty as he licked the blood and rabbit fur off his muzzle.

"Cheater!" Otah would cry, but he was glad that at least his friend had found some food.

The rain had stopped as they set out but the melting snow made mushy traveling.

As leader of the pack Otah was expected to make plans and lead the way. Sand accepted

this, and limped along behind, using the trail made by his master.

The hunters would cross the river and head west on the other bank, hoping that the deer

herd was still yarded up on high ground above the swamp.

The river looked somehow sullen and menacing, with wet snow lying knee deep

on the ice. Not a single track marred the surface. With the atlatl and spear strapped across his shoulders Otah used his own spear for a probe as he eased himself out on the frozen

surface. He took a few careful steps, tapping on the ice with the butt of the spear, to see if

it was safe. So far it appeared to hold his weight but he did not like a sort of groaning

sound which seemed to come from further out. He took a few more tentative steps before

he looked back at the wolf. Sand remained, pacing back and forth on the bank and

whining. Otah pulled off one beaver skin mitten and sucked at the back of his hand. The

wolf pricked up its ears but refused to venture out on the ice. "Very well then. You can

come or not, but we must cross if the deer are to be found at all."

Almost to the far shore the ice gave way! Otah fell through, the icy water chilling

him instantly. Fortunately his feet touched bottom but he was up to his shoulders in water

and chunks of ice.

The precious pouch of tools and fire-making equipment was carried away under

the ice. All but the atlatl, two spears, and his backpack were gone. Otah felt death very

near! He thrashed through the shallow water, pushing chunks of ice out of the way, and

scrambled, dripping and freezing out of the water.

Sand was nowhere in sight.

He stood in the soft snow, water dripping from his clothing. Only the hood of his

wolf skin coat was still dry. Almost in shock he peered around looking for any kind of

shelter. There was none. With nearly numb feet he tried to kick the snow away from a

clump of weeds behind a small hill. He began to shiver so hard he could hardly stand. His

teeth clicked together. *Fire!* He must have fire, and soon. He spent no time thinking of

the loss of almost everything of value that he owned. Clumsily he pulled off one dripping mitten and felt for the axe and his knife. He breathed a little easier when he found them still safe in his belt. There was no time to lose! Before long he would no longer be able to twirl a makeshift fire wand, even if he could devise one.

A dead and dry alder sapling caught his eye, and the axe knocked it over quickly. Using the knife, he rounded the thicker end and began trying to remove the dry bark, which might work for tinder. From a rotten stump poking up from the snow he tore a slab of wood. It proved to be still wet from the rains, but a fragment beneath it was dry and punky.

Unmindful of the wet snow, he knelt and pressed the rounded end of the dead stick against the crumbling wood. Starting high and using both hands, he sent the stick twirling. It wasn't working. Otah was ready to give up. His possessions washed away down the river, clothes wet and freezing on his body, and little hope that his clumsy atlatl would work at all. Still he kept on drilling away, although tiring rapidly.

A whine and a short "whuff" raised his spirits a little. Sand stood watching from a distance. His coat was dry and bushy. The wolf seemed almost to be making fun of his wet and bedraggled master. "So you are warm and dry are you? How did you manage to keep from falling through the ice? You probably weigh more than I!"

Sand listened to the words with interest, but Otah noticed that the big animal made no move to come any closer. "Sand, *come!*" Otah commanded. The wolf gave a soft whine but only settled down in the snow. "You saved me from the cold once, now you must do so again! *Sand, come!*"

Sand had no intention of approaching the quaking, water-soaked human. There was something in the man's voice the wolf did not like so he kept his distance. It was, after all, the man's fault. He had tried to warn him not to try to cross where the ice was unsafe. The animal's keen hearing had detected the gurgling sound of running water just below the surface. Also, too much snow lay on top, so the ice was rotten. Only a fool, such as this human, would venture out upon it. Wisely, Sand had traveled along the bank until he found a place nearly clear of snow and without the sound of running water. He had crossed without incident.

Disgusted with his companion, Otah began twirling the stick again. Smoke appeared but without powdered buffalo droppings for tinder he could not get a flame. He staggered back to the river's edge and ripped up all the cattails he could carry. The dark brown fluff from the tops of these he quickly crushed up and piled around his makeshift fire wand. Desperately he spun the stick into the soft slab of rotten wood. There! The cattail down began to smolder. He twirled harder and faster, his strength almost gone. A tiny flame appeared on the fire board. Desperately Otah leaned over the flickering flame and blew very gently. Now the bark he had first shaved off caught fire. Shaking all over, the man carefully added small twigs. Bigger sticks came next. When the flames were bright and steady he dragged a large rotten log to the edge of the blaze. It caught quickly but Otah took no chances. More and larger logs, once they had dried somewhat, soon had sparks and flames shooting upward.

Sand backed away from the growing heat, as he did not like fire! Otah, on the other hand, was rejoicing. His wet clothes were steaming on his body and for the first time his teeth had stopped chattering. He became almost obsessed with fire making. Piling on additional fuel soon had a truly impressive blaze crackling away. When he finally felt really warm he took off his wet leggings and hung them from sticks propped up near the fire. By this means, although it had taken far too long, he finally put on dry clothes once again. Thankfully his backpack had not been lost, but nearly everything in it was soaked. He took each item out and hung them on sticks to dry.

Although he was now warm and dry the danger was far from over. No food, no tools [except for the axe, his knife, and the spear] there was no real chance of making a kill with the clumsy atlatl he had made. "There is almost no hope for us," he told the watching wolf. He envied the animal, curled up in a nest of snow, the injured leg poking out from under.

"Yes, hope is almost gone," he repeated.

Almost!

Patience . . .. patience . . . plan . . .

The warm wind from the south was rapidly bringing the swamp alive again. Ducks and geese were finding small pools of open water and settling in. Deer, elk, and the occasional forest buffalo were seeking higher ground as the bogs became treacherous under their hooves.

"At least we will be able to find plenty of eggs to eat, Sand, my friend." The wolf pricked up his ears at his master's more hopeful tone. It was still too early for the morsels, but the birds were pairing off to find dry nesting areas. There was no way Otah could survive that long. They needed to hunt. Sand was looking gaunt and Otah even worse. He fastened Sand's collar and attached the length of braided rawhide rope. The wolf's crooked hind leg would make any sort of successful pursuit difficult if not impossible, but there was nothing at all wrong with Sand's incredible sense of smell, or his keen eyesight.

Otah had a plan, devised while his clothes were drying. He reflected upon the changes that had come about over these past months. Earlier he would have wasted time and energy cursing his fate and feeling sorry for himself. Now, he honored the memory of his late father by taking the man's good advice. With Sand tugging at the leash they set out to find the deer herd. Several times Otah had to alter their course in order to avoid the growing areas of muck and open water. They kept to the higher ground, still heading for the area where they had last encountered the deer. He hoped they would still be there, as any sort of longer travel would be impossible. Hunger and lack of sleep were dragging him down. Sand seemed less tired, but he too was hardly enthused with their hunt.

It took most of the day to approach the area they sought, since as always it was impossible to maintain a straight line through the swamp. In late afternoon Otah pulled Sand up short and moved ahead silently. He recognized features in the landscape that told him they were near the area he wanted. Sand also was aware. Twice the wolf dropped to his belly to watch and listen.

The herd was *gone!*

Just as he had feared, Otah realized that the deer had already left their yarded area to seek higher ground. With the snow nearly gone the animals would browse on leaves and the tender twigs of new growth on trees and bushes. Soon grass would appear and their food supply would be assured. Otah stood and moved wearily ahead, stopping only when he was at the very edge of the trampled slush where once twenty or more animals had wintered. Once again he was ready to quit!

Sand suddenly dropped to a crawl. The wolf's ears, half of one gone from the cat's attack, were pointed forward, his nose twitching eagerly. Otah slipped to the ground beside his companion. "What do you see?" he whispered, straining his eyes at the forest beyond. Then he too saw them! Three deer, a doe and her twin yearlings stood looking back over their shoulders toward the bushes where the man and wolf lay concealed. For some reason they had lagged behind when the herd moved on. Otah and the wolf would have one chance. Perhaps not even that!

"If only you could understand my speech," Otah thought as he watched the wolf preparing to attack. "I would tell you to circle around the deer and cause them to panic. If you could drive them toward me I might be able to use the spear." Both man and beast watched the deer. The doe stepped daintily out of the forest and into the slush, the twins following. She dropped her head toward the trampled snow and pretended to graze. Suddenly her head snapped up. Ears batting she peered around her. She knew something was wrong but didn't know what or where the danger lay. Once more she resorted to the trick, pretending to eat then quickly becoming alert. She stamped a front hoof, trying to get the unseen enemy to show itself, the fawns awkwardly trying to copy their mother.

Otah removed the rawhide collar. Sand was trembling violently, but remained hidden. The wolf did not like approaching an animal that was facing him. His instincts told him to attack a running deer from behind. Cautiously the big animal inched his way to the left, taking advantage of every bush and tree. Otah held his breath. If Sand could make his way all the way around the deer without spooking them, it was just possible that they would run directly past the hidden hunter, the wolf in pursuit. Otah almost smiled at the apparent impossibility of the scenario happening in just that way. Still, he clutched the good spear in both hands and carefully rose to his knees.

The deer caught the wolf's scent before it could make its way completely behind them. They leaped into full flight and, miracle of miracles, raced straight at the man hidden in the bushes. Otah leaped to his feet. The doe swerved to avoid him but not quickly enough. With desperation fueled by hunger and fear Otah rammed the spear head deep into her chest. It was a mortal wound but the deer tried to pull away. He yanked the spear back, ready to strike again but was amazed at how easily the weapon was withdrawn. The dying doe, running only on reflexes, bounded away toward the timber, her twins running beside her. Otah was not alarmed, for even with his limp Sand would bring her down before long! He wanted to dance or give a victory yell, but was suddenly thunderstruck as he glanced down at the bloody spear.

His father's beautifully chipped lance head had *snapped off* just beyond the lashing!

There was no time for remorse. Sand was trailing the dying mother as fast as his three good legs could carry him. His nose was up, taking the smell of blood directly from the air. Otah raced after the wolf, splashing awkwardly through the slush until he reached solid ground under the trees. The sound of growls and snarling showed the way. The deer was down, her legs thrashing in agony. Sand's powerful jaws closed on her throat and held on. The doe died quickly. Her twins were gone, heading west to join the herd.

Otah made no attempt to take the deer from the wolf. Sand had again claimed the kill as his own, and any attempt to interfere would mean an attack, as Otah was well aware! He moved off a short distance and began constructing a rough camp. The wolf continued to gorge himself until finally he lay down near the carcass. Otah waited until the animal was nearly asleep before he made an attempt to get near. Sand watched the man and growled but he was too full and too sleepy to make a challenge.

Although a surprisingly large section of flank was missing there was still plenty of meat left for both of them.

"Well Sand, at least I still have my knife and the axe," he said as he went about the welcome task of skinning. A cold wind was building from the north, and the smell of snow wafted around the trees, causing his bloody hands to feel as if they were freezing solid. How he missed the fire-making kit lost under the river ice. Leaving the skinning half finished he set about the task of once again making fire. The job went quicker this time. He dragged the carcass closer to the fire, warmed his bloody hands and finished the job. Only when all this work was done did he slice off three thin slabs of venison. He hung them from sticks leaning near the fire to roast. The aroma of sizzling meat set his mouth watering, and far too quickly he pulled one piece from its stick, burning his fingers. It was still not done, but he ate all three half-raw pieces and like Sand, sank down to sleep.

*　　　　　　　*　　　　　　　*

Man and animal spent two days and nights eating and resting. The snow had come, but gently with no drifting. Otah's spirits had improved immensely, and Sand, with plenty to eat right in camp had not gone off to hunt since the kill. Otah was *patient,* and he was *planning!*

The broken spear point was a disaster. Not only did it leave him with no means of hunting, but also no real protection. What he was seriously considering might mean contact with other men. Who could tell about them? Friendly? Perhaps, perhaps not! And what of Sand? Most people would kill the wolf on sight, but there was really no choice. He must have flint and a good amount of it!

"Are you ready to travel again my friend?" Sand looked up from the bone he was gnawing, alerted by the welcome note of optimism in his master's voice. He was ready!

Otah began preparing for a trip of many days. Somewhere in the hills far to the south of the Black Swamp there lay a deposit of flint. His grandfather had made the trip twice as a young man. Otah remembered many nights in the hut when his father had told the story of *his father's* collecting adventures. Bitterly Otah recalled that he had hardly listened to these often repeated tales. He knew that his father had passed down careful directions to the site, but his young, impatient son had not found such information important. All Otah could recall after these years was that the quarries lay in hilly country far to the south.

The grandfather had told and retold the story on many nights, the family seated around a tiny fire. Both he and Otah's father had carefully described the route, even scratching a rough map on the dirt floor. "Some day," the grandfather had told Otah, "all this flint will be used up. You, yourself will need to go when that time comes." Otah had paid little attention. What was a trip to the far off flint quarries to a happy boy of six? He would rather play along the river!

He spoke to the wolf as he secured the collar and leash. "We are going for flint my friend! I don't know if we will even find the place. I'm only sure that we must travel to the south. We may meet others going the same way for the same reason. They will surely want to kill you and possibly me as well! I have only father's knife and the axe for protection should a fight ensue, and they are not enough. Still, without good flint we will die anyway!" Sand watched the man as if he understood, and for once did not fight the collar and leash. "You must stay with me," Otah told him. "I have food enough for both of us, and there should be no need to use snares, at least at first. The sooner we find the flint source the better it will be for us."

The following morning they left the hut, keeping the rising sun on their left. Well fed and beyond the rough travel of the swamp, they made good progress. On the third day they encountered the first major obstacle. They had crossed several small streams and brooks with little trouble but this was a river. Fortunately it was flowing in a generally southern direction so there was no need to cross, at least not yet. They followed the river but not directly on the bank. Otah knew that if other people were around they would probably travel along the stream as well. Man and wolf stayed several hundred paces away, traveling through thick foliage to keep out of sight, but they saw no other people.

Three more days of travel were uneventful. The river meandered more to the west, so Otah left it in order to maintain a more southeasterly direction. Sand was behaving well, although he often tried to break free when encountering a fresh track of one of the many animals in the forest. They flushed deer nearly every evening, but without even a spear they had no means to try for a kill. Twice they saw buffalo wallows where the huge creatures had taken their mud baths. Otah dragged the wolf away from these. To meet one of the dangerous beasts would surely mean disaster! Smaller game was plentiful. Sand would have loved to track down the raccoons, foxes, and beaver whose trails they saw but the man would not allow it. He could not stop traveling to wait while Sand was off on a long hunting trip.

Two days later Sand suddenly began to show signs of agitation. He often stood very still, his muzzle pointed to the sky. He whined and looked often at his master. Otah knew his companion well enough to pay attention. The wolf was detecting something, something that made him nervous. That evening the mystery was solved. A narrow path, just wide enough for one person, led away to the south. Otah examined it closely, Sand sniffing along as well. *There!* A definite moccasin print showed in an area of soft earth. Sand's low growl was enough to cause Otah to drag him quickly away from the path. "Easy boy," he cautioned. "That path will make our travels much easier but we must use it only in darkness. Who knows how many may be coming and going on that trail?" Would it lead to the area of the flint quarries? Otah only knew it was heading south, the direction they needed to go.

He made a cold camp well away from the path and waited for nightfall. Sand tore into a rabbit carcass they had taken in a snare that morning. Their food was still adequate,

but with most of a day and evening to wait, Otah had made several sets. One had been

successful. The man chewed his usual strips of smoked venison, but garnished it with

fiddlehead ferns and their roots. The taste was bad, but both knew of the danger in a diet

of only meat. That was one of the many things he had learned from his mother and from

watching the wolf.

When it was fully dark they made their way back to the path. Had any other

people been near they could not have helped hearing Otah crashing and stumbling

through the ink-black forest. He would have missed the path completely had not Sand

tugged at his leash to stop him and lead him to it. At first the wolf led the way, his keen

eyes able to stay on the trail. The man however, kept tripping on unseen roots and

downfalls along the edge of the winding narrow path. Moonlight would have helped but

clouds were thick overhead. They made little progress and would have traveled further by

staying in the forest as they had before!

The next two days they kept off the path but stayed close enough to follow its

leading. Finally there was a clear night illuminated by a full moon. Eagerly they resumed

their night marches, rapidly putting the miles behind them, but the path was becoming

noticeably wider. When the moonlight was good they saw more and more human

footprints. Sand had learned to ignore the man scent as he strained ahead, pulling on his

leash.

A few nights later as they padded along, Sand began to whine and emit his low,

challenging growls. Otah grabbed his muzzle to keep him quiet. The wolf would never have permitted this before, but he was learning, as was his master. "What is it Sand?" Otah whispered sliding off the trail into the bushes. The fur on the wolf's back and neck rose high and stiff. Otah could feel the animal's lips curling in a silent snarl. "What *is it?*" Otah asked again. Then he heard it too. *Voices!* Human sounds that neither man nor animal had heard in years. All at once a great yearning filled Otah's heart. He was so *lonesome!* It was hard not to shout a greeting and enter the strangers' camp, for obviously that was what it was. Wood smoke filtered through the trees from the east. The man was almost ready! *Almost!*

He sat in the darkness and considered what he should do. As in the past his father's voice seemed to come to him on the wood smoke. "Never show yourself to other people," he had told Otah and Leaf many times. "They will either kill you or make you a slave. Avoid them! Run! Hide! Do not trust *any* of them!" Father must have forgotten the help of the Mastodon Hunters, Otah thought with a small smile. Was the advice of his father good or not? And what of the way things were with him and the wolf now? Alone, often nearly starving, without even the rudest of tools and weapons, would it not be better to try to join some others? But again, what of Sand? No one would permit a wolf to live, and many would look with extreme suspicion at a man who could live with a wild wolf! They might consider him a witch! The main reason, however was that the animal meant more to him than he cared to admit. Then a final thought gave him the decision. "What of *Leaf*" he asked himself. "I cannot rest until I find if she is alive, and if so, what is her life like now? The wolf and I are on this journey to get flint, flint that will keep us alive to return to our river and find the Mastodon Hunters. For I am sure that when we find *them*, we will find *her!* Sand, we will stay quiet, avoid these strangers, and keep on with our search for the quarries of flint!"

Before dawn they had made a great circle around the noisy camp, leaving the strangers far behind.

*   *   *

Sand had stopped tugging at the leash. He was tired! Eight more days of travel with little food and little rest had taken their toll on the man and the wolf. But finally they were *there!* More and more trails had crossed their path as they neared their destination. It was apparent that people had been coming to this place for many generations. Hardly a day had passed when the two had not encountered larger, well traveled pathways. Always the footprints pointed south and east, making it even clearer that they led to this vital location. Otah kept to the deep forest, no longer needing the trails for direction. Several times they heard voices and once again were forced to circle wide around another noisy campsite.

That evening, still with no warming fire, Sand began to whine and pull restlessly against the leash. The wolf kept looking off to the east and lifting his nose for scent. Otah knew the animal well, but he had not seen this sort of behavior before. "If you could only speak, Sand!" At the sound of his master's voice the animal pulled even harder at his leash. "Very well, it is still some time until dark. Let's go and see what is bothering you." They didn't have far to go, as Otah also began to detect an odor. It was not pleasant!

They came upon the source of the smell in a cleared area beside the stump of an enormous sycamore. The bones were scattered about, picked clean of any flesh by a succession of scavengers, the last of which was a pair of ravens worrying at the few shreds of flesh remaining on a shoulder blade. The bleached and dry skull still held an impressive set of antlers, making it plain that the kill had not been made by men, as any hunter would have saved the horns for knife handles, flint knappers, and a variety of other uses.

The smell of death and decay lay everywhere in the clearing. Otah held his nose and began to leave but Sand would not be led. "Go then!" Otah told him disgustedly, "you'll find nothing left on those bones." Sand had other ideas. Instinct was a powerful force. Reluctantly, Otah untied the leash to see what the wolf would do. Without hesitation the big animal lay down and began to roll on the bones and the trampled mud around them.

"Now I see," Otah growled, "you are masking your scent with this rotten odor. That may be a good idea, but I must lengthen your leash. I want you as far away from *me* as possible!" Sand stank terribly.

The trails always stayed in the valleys between the hills, but Otah chose the high ground. Travel was much harder but there was less chance of encountering people.

Then they finally realized that they had truly arrived! Creeping near the crest of what was nearly a mountain, he looked down on a sight which chilled his heart. Open pits and rubble littered the area. Ancient fire rings of stone were everywhere, proving that there had been camps constructed here over the ages. None of this was reason for his alarm however. It was the *people!* He counted more than he had fingers and toes. Men, women, and even a few children were moving about. They strode in and out of their cleverly built houses. These dwellings were constructed of skins stretched over a ring of poles set in the ground. Otah marveled at the ingenuity of these people. "I will make a house like that when we have collected enough skins," he whispered. Sand paid no attention, his eyes following the movement far below.

Once again Otah was ready to leave their hiding place and attempt a friendly meeting with these strangers. But several things caused him to wait. He could not help noticing that these people were dressed little better than himself. They also appeared to be lazy, working at the flint pits only when they wanted to. The women, unlike his memory of his mother and sister, wore ragged clothing which appeared to be caked with dirt and grease. Both men and women were gaunt and thin, and the children seemed to be even less well fed. "How can they look like this?" he wondered. "They have access to the finest flint known to man, and yet they are nearly starving. Sand, we must not go down there! We have nothing to trade. They would only consider me to be another mouth to feed. And *you!* They would kill you for your pelt, then probably eat you!" But leaving without the precious flint was never an option. "We came all this way for the stone we must have," he whispered to his companion, "and we will have it *or die in the attempt!*"

All he could discern from watching the activity below was discouraging enough, but then he saw something truly horrible. A small man was actually hard at work in one of the pits. Using a heavy wooden pry bar he was attempting to break a shiny flint free from its matrix, but the work was not going well. A large, ugly man was lounging nearby, making no attempt to help in the pit. This seemed most unfair to Otah, who would have helped the smaller man in an instant. Slowly the larger man got to his feet and approached the pit. In his hand was a short club, decorated with shells and feathers. Angrily he raised the club high and struck the worker across the back! Though far from the action, Otah clearly heard the cry of pain. The big man struck twice more then settled himself on the ground as before.

"*Slaves!*" Otah gasped. "It is just as father told us. These people keep slaves to do their work. Well Sand, they will never make a slave of *me,* or a meal of *you!* We have nothing to fight them with, but we have our wits. Now we must rest and make a plan. Yes, Father, I will be patient and plan what might be done."

Patience . . . patience. . . plan . . .

Keeping one hand on Sand's muzzle he slid backward even deeper into the thicket which concealed them. Many possibilities presented themselves, but were quickly rejected.

As he had watched them at their various activities Otah had noticed a curious sort of behavior. Each time a slab of new flint was handed out of the pit a very old man, dressed in what they must have considered impressive clothing, would stumble forward to wave some sort of rattle over the stone. Next this apparition would croak a sing-song chant while pointing a feathered stick toward the sky and in each of the four directions. It was obvious that these people were filled with fear and superstition. It appeared that they were trying to appease the spirits of the stone so the *stone ghosts* would not be angry!

As a boy during his short stay with them, Otah had seen something like this done by the Mastodon Hunters. Whenever a kill was made their shaman would apologize to the dead creature while making motions much like the ones Otah was seeing now. By doing this they felt assured that the dead animal's spirit would not warn the living animals, and make hunting them more difficult.

It was another cold camp. Otah tried to wriggle into the brush and cover himself with dry leaves. The hide from the deer he and Sand had taken back at the river had never been properly scraped and brained. It was stiff and smelly, but did help keep off the rain that was beginning to fall. Now more than ever he was afraid to release Sand's tether. The wolf would undoubtedly head for the smell of cooking meat near the flint pits. Having lost some of his natural fear of man, the wolf would be easily captured and killed. Otah pulled on the rawhide to drag the animal closer in case it should make noise and betray their hiding place.

The smell was horrible! A wet wolf that had recently rolled in decaying deer remains had an odor that was almost more than Otah could bear! What was it about those deer bones?

Then he had it! The plan seemed to form itself full blown.

He slept then but was often awakened by icy rainwater sliding down his neck or across his shoulders. He did not mind this however, for every time he woke he was able to patiently add details to the action he was soon to take. At first light he was up and slinking back the way they had come. His plan involved the deer remains that Sand had so enjoyed. Otah no longer knew exactly where the bones lay but he was not worried, as the wolf would drag him to the spot the moment its nose detected it. As they came closer the man did not need the wolf's leading! The putrid odor seemed even stronger than before!

When they arrived, Otah tied Sand to a tree several paces away from the bones. He certainly did not need the animal anointing itself a second time! Working quickly while trying to hold his breath he separated the skull and antlers from a still attached section of backbone. Off in the forest he began to prepare the first part of his plan. A long pole was thrust up into the deer skull and secured by stuffing it with broken twigs and leaves. When it was solid he draped the uncured skin around the pole, just below the skull's lower jaw. More leaves and sticks filled the draped skin to give it substance and form. With the knife he cut a narrow slit at just the right height for his eyes. With some doubt he put on his costume. After a few adjustments and careful use of sinew he was satisfied. Rib bones and leg bones, thankfully picked clean by the scavengers, he tied here and there on the disguise. These made a most convincing rattle as he moved around. His final task was to smear his legs and arms with mud. He was ready, but must now return to the hill and wait for evening. Sand did not like his master's creation but tolerated it as long as the man did not yet have it on his body.

Back in the same thicket, Otah arranged his disguise carefully beside them and slept until nearly twilight. Fires twinkled in the clearing below as the people prepared for sleep. The rain had stopped and a full moon was peeping over the surrounding trees, so conditions for Otah's plan could not have been better. He crept forward until he and Sand were at the very edge of the hill. Clutching the pole against his chest, Otah let the contraption down until his own head was almost inside the skull. Carefully he adjusted

the costume to position the eye slits just right. When he stood erect the antlers brushed

the lower branches of a cedar tree, making him appear to be nearly twice as tall. He filled

his lungs and screamed with all his might!

AAIIIIEEEE OOOOHOOOO OOOO!

People below added their own screams of terror while running about in a frenzy,

in and out of their houses. Mothers grabbed up their children and hid themselves in their

wickiups. There was *pandemonium* in the camp!

Otah did it again, rattling the bones and dancing about in the moonlight.

AAAIII EEEEOOOOO EEEEEE OOOOOO!

By this time most of the men still outside had seen the fearful creature outlined

against the sky far above them. They gathered in little groups, obviously terrified. Then

they had reason to be even more frightened! An excited Sand pointed his muzzle toward

the moon and put forth such a tremendous howl that even his master was frightened!

Otah moved backward, step by dignified step. When he was completely hidden

among the trees he quickly stripped off the costume and threw it down. Dragging Sand

behind him he crept once more to his observation point and lay there concealed by the

bushes and watched the scene below. At first it was unclear just what was happening in

the camp. Night had almost fallen, but much frenzied activity was going on. The main

fire was being built up until the whole central area was illuminated. Otah was amazed

when the old shaman, still dressed in his finery, came haltingly into the firelight. Raising

his arms toward where he had seen what he considered an angry spirit, he began a long harangue of words and gestures. The old man was trying to honor and appease the "ghost".

Otah was surprised by what happened next. One by one each man came forward, every one with something in his hand or in a skin bag. These they reverently placed in a circle near the roaring blaze. The shaman shook his turtle shell rattle at each offering, never stopping his eerie chants. Piece by piece the pile of items grew. As soon as each man's gift was presented he ran back to his lodge and began tearing the dwelling down. The women and children helped with the dismantling, casting frightened glances at the hilltop above them

The tents were disappearing! As each one collapsed from its ring of poles it was dragged away into the night. By this time the clearing was nearly deserted. Only the medicine man remained, still bravely shaking the rattle. He had stopped chanting.

Otah, watching from the hilltop, now observed a most curious thing. A little girl, ragged and shrunken with hunger, was being dragged toward the fire by a frightened-looking young man. The child was clutching something in one arm while the man yanked her along by the other. She appeared to be crying, but the man tore the object from her hand, threw it on the pile of offerings, and dragged her away in the darkness. Finally the old shaman also left the clearing.

The area was completely empty!

Otah was elated that so far his plan was succeeding far beyond what he could have hoped. He remained cautious however. Where had all the people gone? Had they seen through his charade and placed gifts near the fire as *bait* to lure him out of hiding? Were they right at this moment watching from the edge of the forest?

Patience. . . .patience. . . .plan. . . .

Leaving the spot they had been using, Otah skirted the hill and worked his way east. If the people attempted to capture him he needed to be far away from the place where he had shown himself. Sand followed obediently this time, which made their movements easier. The full moon helped them, for without its light they could hardly have moved through the forest at all. Even so, the man fell twice, further bruising his bad knee both times. Sands's leash seemed to catch on everything, and it required patience to keep the rawhide free. They kept going but Otah was tiring rapidly. His knee aching, he limped along, trying his best to avoid the bushes and brambles. "Well Sand, now we're both limping. As soon as we find a spot where we can watch the clearing we must stop and sleep." The wolf seemed to agree.

A fire was out of the question, so it meant another cold camp!

When he awoke Otah was terrified. The sun was well above the trees, proving he had slept far too long. Sand, curled up in some high grass, was *still* sleeping! He crept closer to the wolf and grasped its muzzle, as there must be no sound in case the people might be searching for him. Man and animal looked almost alike as they moved silently forward, Otah crawling on hands and knees, and gently parting bushes before slipping through. He had released Sand's snout, feeling that the wolf was aware of the need for silence. They were dangerously near the clearing before they could see it well. Otah, keeping Sand on a close leash, lay prone and studied the area. Nothing moved. There was not a single human sound. Birds called from the trees and a raven sailed into the clearing and alighted on a log. He stepped off and waddled about seeking anything edible that was left behind. A rabbit hopped into view and sat up to clean its paws. There was every evidence that the people were gone. Sand was becoming nervous, anxious to explore the campsite with all its intriguing smells, but Otah held his collar. "Not yet my friend," he whispered, his eyes continually scanning the area. "If they plan to catch us they will be hiding nearby. We wait!" He was becoming a patient man!

Almost another hour passed before Otah was finally convinced. Mosquitoes and wood ticks had made the wait a torture for both of them. With relief he stood and attempted to relieve the cramps in his legs. Sand stretched too. The wolf had done well and Otah was proud of his friend. Still cautious, they entered the edge of the clearing, avoiding the open pits and earthen piles that dotted the place. He untied the wolf and watched as the animal circled the area, taking in the strange scents which abounded there. Sand's behavior was further proof that they were indeed alone.

No longer fearful, Otah rounded a pile of earth and approached the ashes of the previous night's bonfire. He was shocked at what lay before him. Fourteen blades of the finest flint he had ever seen were positioned in a perfect circle. Inside the shining ring of stone were even more treasures. He gasped at the sight of a pair of double-soled boots of buffalo hide. They had been worn before and were a little too large, but he was overjoyed anyway! Real *boots!* Several blocks of unworked flint lay among the other gifts. A round fox skin bag with a drawstring closure drew the man's eye. He picked it up, marveling at the beautiful workmanship. Opening it he found it full of some sort of ground up brownish material, on top of which was a beautifully carved slate raven. The brown granules had a pungent but not unpleasant odor. Could he eat it? He tried a pinch but spit it out when it burned his tongue. "Oh yes I know that now," he said aloud, "the Mastodon Hunters prized this material and the smoke it made. This could be valuable for trade with them when I have tracked them down." He set the pouch and the carved bird pipe aside and examined the rest of the offerings. A tiny box made of birch bark and decorated with a pattern of quills next caught his eye. No bigger than his palm, it was truly a thing of beauty. "How could these hungry and ragged people have had such wonderful things?" he wondered. The little chest contained only one thing. A shining blue and brown stone the size of his thumb lay within, cradled in a bed of dry moss. A hole had been drilled through the bead. "A perfect gift for Leaf when I find her!" he cried, a tear trickling down his cheek. It was then that the real treasure revealed itself. The finest flint spearhead he had ever seen lay glistening in the sun. Pink and yellow with white streaks that looked like lightning running across the face, it was truly a magnificent blade!

Otah stood and pondered for a moment. Then it became clear to him. These people were *traders!* They must have come for flint to use in trade when they returned to wherever they made their home. They had not yet been able to trade the items they had been so busily preparing. Once their trading was done they would be able to procure better clothes and good food. They had chipped the blades from the flint core stones, as there was no point in packing the heavy stone back to their permanent village. Fragments and bright chips of stone littered the ground. Whatever else he had noticed about these people, Otah had to admit that they were masters at working flint!

One item remained in the circle. It was a clay bowl, not large but well made. Even better, it was filled with some sort of blue and red seeds of a type Otah had never seen. Gingerly he chewed one of the kernels. It was delicious and nourishing, so he ate several more. Sand had found a large piece of half-cooked meat hanging from an abandoned tripod, and was busily devouring it.

At last Otah picked up the sad little bundle the child had been forced to give up. The doll was crudely made, being merely a roll of rabbit skin with sticks for arms and legs, but it had been precious to her. He could not take it. Otah felt like crying as he held the pathetic bundle. Well he remembered one almost like it that Leaf had carried about like a little mother. Quickly selecting a pouch of otter skin that lay on the pile, he put the doll in it. Several paces toward the place where the lodges had stood he laid the bundle down and weighted it with two rocks. "I hope you return soon," he said to the silent clearing. "She may never come back, but I have done all I can for that little one," he thought sadly.

All was well. Otah could not believe his good luck. Enough flint for years, a gift for Leaf, tobac and a pipe to trade, a perfect spear point, and the wonderful boots he was already wearing, but it was long past the time that they should have left.

There was one more thing to do. With Sand's help they soon found the "spirit costume" lying in some bushes high above the quarry and Otah retrieved his robe. Since his pack was too full he rolled it into a tight bundle and secured it under one shoulder. Fear was still stalking him, but even so he took time to snap off several smelly tines from the deer skull. After scattering every part of the costume in the forest he was ready to hurry away. They headed north as once again fortune had smiled on them!

*   *   *

Travel was slow, for spring had definitely arrived, making for muddy and slippery footing. Reluctantly he avoided the easier ways along the streams and traveled paths. The people from the quarries might still try to overtake them to retrieve their valuable goods. Time was taken also in attempting to cover, or at least confuse, their tracks. This was difficult, due to the mud and thick undergrowth, so despite their best efforts even a youngster with little training could have followed them with ease.

Two problems were the hardest to deal with. First, Otah's desire was to hurry. It seemed at times that he could hear his sister calling to him for rescue. He knew that this could not be true but the thought remained anyway. The other problem was more severe. Sand was becoming harder to control. The wolf fought the leash and sometimes had to be threatened with a stick. No longer a pup, Sand was now a fully matured animal whose back, when standing beside his master, was higher than Otah's waist.

Snares had kept them well supplied with food, and the emerging greenery had so added to their diet that both were now in excellent physical shape. Sand was quick to recognize this and appeared to be less dependent upon the man who controlled him. The times in camp after sundown were the worst. Sand would pace the distance of his tether, whining and sniffing the air. Then one night it happened! With his head raised the big wolf let out a truly spine-chilling howl, the first one he had done since their time at the flint quarries, hidden from the people below them. Although the primitive, ancient call was shocking to hear at close range, Otah was not alarmed. Not until . . .

From far off in the forest came an answering call! Immediately Sand threw back his head and prepared to answer the challenge. Otah leaped to his feet and clamped both hands around the wolf's muzzle. The animal struggled a moment, broke free, faced the man and bared his gleaming fangs. The growls and raised ruff said plainly that he was not to be fooled with! Otah backed away, realizing that they were equals now! Slaps or blows from a stick, he knew, would no longer work. Sand would only obey when he felt like doing so. It was even questionable how long he would tolerate the collar and leash. Otah was terrified that he might lose his only friend and companion, but there was nothing he could do about it. The wolf raised his nose and got ready.

Sand's howl was so loud that its echo bounced back at them from the nearby hills. There it was again. Two *answering* calls! They were undoubtedly closer, but still seemed a good distance away. Then there was silence. "I think we will have visitors this night my friend," he said, speaking quietly in an effort to calm the agitated wolf. "You may think these calls are friendly, but I am not so sure. We must prepare for an attack should one come with the darkness!"

Selecting a burning branch from their small fire and dragging the protesting wolf, he soon found what he needed. Two large beech trees growing together would do. He tied the wolf to the trees and started gathering sticks. With his back against the massive tree trunks he began building a new fire. When the flames were large enough to make working possible he began. "I should have done this days ago," he grumbled. He took the gift spearhead from his pack , and using his knife, cut the lashings from what remained of the blade in his father's spear. He slipped the broken fragment from the slot in the shaft and put it in his pack. The new spearhead fit fairly well, but Otah knew that without newly-made fish skin glue the sinew binding would not hold for long. "It must do the job for now," he thought as he wrapped the thin strands around and around the shaft. "We'll do a better job later, eh Sand?" The wolf ignored the voice, standing still and peering into the darkness toward the east.

Two howls, so close it made Otah's hair stand on end! "At least two of them," he whispered. "Sand, I am going to untie you now. There may be fighting and you will need to be free to take part. I hope you will stay with me and not join them but we have been good together for all of this time. *Get ready!*"

If there was anything more sinister and terrifying than the sight of eyes reflected in the firelight, Otah could not think of any. The good news was that so far he could only see two sets of the shining orbs. Otah could not know that the two marauders were brothers born the spring before. Now nearly fully grown, they had been driven out to start a pack of their own. Had the man and his companion been confronted by the usual five to eight pack members they would never have survived.

The two newcomers lay watching the camp. Young and inexperienced, they did not send one animal circling behind the camp. Had they done so, the other could harass and distract until the former could attack. Confused by the fire and the presence of a creature they had never seen before, they continued to watch and wait.

Then Sand challenged! He stayed by his master, as yet unaware that he was no longer tied. Tail up and all fur distended the big wolf moved toward the glowing eyes. Instinct showed him how to take the careful, measured steps that meant *"run or fight now!"*

Otah eased to his feet, his back against the bole of the nearest beech tree. The improvised spear was thrust forward, waiting for the attack. Foolishly the two yearlings charged together. Sand gave a roaring growl and met the first. His big body knocked the smaller wolf off its feet, but it came up snarling and biting. The two of them disappeared in a tangle of snapping, slashing jaws. The second wolf hesitated for just a twinkling, then prepared to attack the man. Head lowered, he came into the firelight, step by menacing step. He was young but strong and quick. Terrified by the uproar from Sand's battle with the first wolf and from the killer gleam in the eyes of the one approaching him, Otah made a stupid mistake. He cocked his arm and *threw the spear!* The wolf dodged it easily, gathered himself and leaped at the man. Otah scrambled behind the trees in time to evade the attack. He circled behind the trees, shouting and waving his arms. Confused, the young wolf backed off a few steps, but did not take his eyes off his enemy. Otah rounded the trees and made a running dive, nearly ending up in the fire. He snatched up a burning branch, not feeling the burn at all. He jammed it in the face of the wolf. Met with what was undoubtedly its first fight without the backing of his pack mates, it turned and dashed away into the night.

Shaking uncontrollably, Otah quickly dropped the fire brand. Blisters were already forming on his fingers and palm but as yet he felt no pain. Growls and snarling still emanated from the bushes beyond the firelight, but they sounded familiar! With hope high, Otah gingerly parted the bushes to allow a little light to show through. Sand lay half across the body of his enemy, jaws still locked on its throat. Otah backed away and leaned against a tree, almost giddy with relief. He let Sand lie where he was as long as the wolf desired.

The fight was *over!*

*   *   *

Otah judged that the possibility of pursuit was probably over. The travelers were still careful to leave as little sign as possible but now they moved northward with more confidence. A warming fire every night made sleeping almost comfortable. The man made sure that the campfires were built on cleared ground under a well leafed out tree so the smoke was dissipated as it trickled upward and away. Hot food, whether small game or venison, tasted wonderful and brought both of them much needed strength.

Sand was allowed to run free most of the time. Although Otah was well aware that his companion might someday fail to return, so far the animal had always rejoined him by nightfall. Sand's bloody muzzle often suggested that he had killed and eaten some small animal. Once the wolf caught up to his master early in the day, which was unusual for him. It was plain that the animal had been in a fight. His coat was matted and two deep scratches arched across one shoulder. Coarse black hair sticking to his bloody lips told the story. Sand had been in a brawl with a black bear! He stayed close to his master the rest of that day and the next. Otah could find no serious wounds, and this time the wolf made no objection to being put on the leash!

Now well north of the flint quarries, Otah decided to prepare a more permanent camp in order to see what was needed to make repairs on his equipment. He set his snares in likely spots along a small creek and built a rough shelter of brush. The skin houses he had seen being used by the people at the quarries were much on his mind, but he had only his sleeping robe and the untanned skin to use. Once again he vowed that once back at his home in the black swamp he would build such a house as soon as he had enough hides to do it. There were fish in the stream near their camp. Now that they no longer needed to flee possible danger from the south there was time to do some fishing. He cleaned a small rabbit bone and broke off a section the size of his little finger. Rubbing it on a sandstone pebble, he smoothed and sharpened both ends. Using his knife, he carved a groove all the way around the center of the bone. It was a long process but he was patient and the result was a fine piece of work.

A section of sinew three paces long was tied around the groove in the small bone gorge he had made. A piece of rabbit liver carefully threaded onto the end of the pointed bone served as bait. After tying one end to a root he threw out his fishing line and left it over night.

It was hardly light enough to see when he hurried to the steam to see if he had caught anything. The line was stretched tight into the stream, its jerking motion assuring Otah that a fish was on the other end! Eagerly he pulled it in, hand over hand. The fish was as long as his arm and fat with roe. He killed it with a rock and began the skinning. Since it was a catfish there were no scales to contend with. As well as the delicious meals to come, the skin was what he needed.

For the first time he selected a lump of the unworked bluish-gray flint left for him by the people at the flint source. Holding it on the ground with one bare foot he struck it carefully with a small river-smoothed stone. He was not yet accomplished at this work but was elated when a thin sliver popped off the edge of the flint core. "There you go, Sand!" he chortled to the watching wolf. "Now you'll see how easily I can skin this fish. Oh, and yes, there will be a good-sized piece of catfish for you as well." Holding the tiny flint blade was difficult without some kind of handle. Otah promised himself that hafting the piece would be his next project, but for now he would make do. Careful to avoid the two poisonous spines just behind the catfish's head, he stripped off the shiny black skin. With a small fire going he placed the clay bowl [another "gift" from the people to the south] in the edge of the fire. The water soon began to boil. The skin he chopped into small pieces and popped into the pot. It would take the rest of the day, but by nightfall the bowl would be half full of a very effective glue. "Now, Sand, my friend, we can repair father's spear in the way it should have been done." Well satisfied with his work, Otah cut a green stick and made ready to cook his catch. The fish was *gone!* Sand was gone too! Off in the bushes he heard eating noises, but by the time he found the wolf only the head and tail were left. Otah could swear the animal was *smiling!*

Two additional days and nights were spent in the camp on the stream bank. Three more fish were taken and both man and animal ate their fill. Otah used glue and sinew to bind the gift spearhead into the end of his father's spear. Heating it slowly over a low fire set the glue until the sharp and shiny blade was secure. He tested it every way he could think of, and it proved to be a fine weapon once again. He still carried the clumsy spear he had made but he had bound it together with his attempt at an atlatl. Several times he almost threw both away but for some reason he could not.

The fresh fish had rejuvenated both companions. Sitting by the fire with Sand nearby, Otah had time to remember. "Leaf," he asked again as he always had, "where *are* you? Do you still live? Are you with Fox of the Mastodon Hunters? Are you happy? Afraid? How can I *find* you?" All the good things and fortunate happenings of the past days slipped away as he thought of his sister. He pulled the little birch bark box from his pack. It had been slightly damaged somewhere in their travels but the blue bead was still inside. He wiped a tear from his cheek as he held the stone toward the fire. It seemed to glow with promise. "I am coming, Leaf! I am *coming!*" he cried, squeezing the smooth stone in his palm.

He packed everything carefully and left the camp, heading northwest again. That they were nearing the swamp was made evident by the absence of hills, even smaller ones. Migrating geese and swans were making their V-shaped flights below the clouds, and many would find nesting sites on sand hills just above the level of swamp water. "Eggs!" Otah told the wolf. "Before long we will be entering the southern edges of the swamp. Nests will be there in plenty, and goose eggs boiled in our new pot will be a welcome change from all this meat!" Sand, no longer hampered by a leash, looked back at his master and loped away, to be gone for two days. The animal would find eggs too but they would not need to be boiled!

Making fire had been a nightly ordeal ever since Otah was no longer afraid to have an evening blaze. It was time to make an improvement on this part of his equipment, so stopping his daily march early, he began preparations. To make a fire wand like the one lost under the river ice some time ago, he needed the hardest wood he could find. From a shag bark hickory he cut a section of limb the length of his arm from wrist to elbow. Again preparing a striking platform from the same flint core he had used for the tiny blade, he struck off a lens-shaped fragment. The flint left for him by the people at the quarries was of exceptional quality. It fractured so precisely that even one as untrained as he could achieve remarkable results. Using an antler tip saved from his "spirit disguise", he chipped a half-circle opening on one end of the stick. The edges of this newly made tool were so sharp it was an easy matter to shave off the bark and further dress the small shaft. The man next cut from a willow sapling a section twice as long as the hickory wand. This he bent in a bow shape by attaching a thin rawhide strip from one end to the other. By twisting the wand into the rawhide he could whip the fire drill back and forth, twirling the wand into the rotten wood fire board. Each of these items, along with generous amounts of dried buffalo dung, was packed carefully for safety in travel. Slowly the life-saving tools and weapons he had lost were being replaced. Otah was happy with his efforts, but more importantly he was proud of his planning and patience!

Only the atlatl remained to be perfected, but it would have to wait until he was home again. With all the flint he now carried it would be possible to finally correct the obvious flaws in the weapon.

*   *   *

The pack with its load of flint and other offerings from the people seemed to grow heavier with every northern mile. Otah and Sand were having no trouble finding food, with goose eggs, edible plants, and the occasional fish easy to get. Therefore he did not need to carry reserves of food. The grain offering was nearly gone, however. It had sustained him well during the critical days of their escape from the workers at the flint deposits. He had the presence of mind to save a handful of the kernels which he meant to use as bait for wild turkeys. Their feathers would provide the fletching for the atlatl darts.

At last indications pointed to the southern boundaries of his beloved Black Swamp. While others might hate the muck, the snakes, and the mosquitoes, to Otah they spoke of home. Raised in this environment he had no trouble negotiating this sometimes dangerous part of the world. Often he and Sand simply traveled on the many fallen logs half buried in the mud. Snakes were everywhere, but Otah was not afraid of them, as almost from the time he had learned to walk his father had showed him how to recognize the ones which meant death. Even little Leaf had learned to tell which were the dangerous ones. Much as he loved this wild land, travel was becoming more difficult. Patience and care were needed lest he lose his precious bundles as he had once before.

Spring rains were a problem for the travelers, as every step had to be carefully negotiated. Wet roots, slippery rocks, and the ever present "shin tangle" lying low to the ground seemed designed to cause a fall. None of these was a problem for Sand, however. Even with his lame back leg, the wolf limped ahead, completely unconcerned. Often he would stop and look back at his master as if to say, "Hurry up, can't you?" Grumbling, Otah would try to increase his pace, which sometimes resulted in a slip or a fall, but nothing could upset the man now!

Every step drew them closer home!

Finally one morning the sunlight revealed a sight he had been longing for. Otah's own river, swollen and swift from the rains, lay before them. Even though impatient to see what had become of his hut, he was not about to do anything foolish, this close to the end of their journey. A raft must be constructed, and this time he would do a decent job, one which would see him safely across. Sand could fend for himself if it refused to set foot on the raft.

It took most of two days to secure the logs well enough to withstand the current. He lashed the pack to his shoulders with Sand's rawhide leash and launched the unwieldy affair into the current. Paddling steadily he nosed the raft slowly toward the northern shore as it literally flew downstream. Progress northward was slow but far to the east the raft finally grounded on a protruding sand bar which led directly to the shore. Otah grabbed a handful of willows and swung himself ashore, pack and all. Sand had paddled across hours before and was leisurely watching what he considered his stupid master's progress. Almost running, Otah burst into the little clearing which held his hut.

They were home!

The house was almost a total disaster again! Wind and rain had scattered the bark covering and his prized bearskin was nowhere to be seen. Dragged off and eaten by coyotes or other animals, the heavy pelt which had kept his family's backs warm for many winters was gone without a trace. Three of the saplings which supported the walls and roof were gnawed in two, showing clearly that porcupines had been at work, savoring anything with a hint of salt or grease. Rain had dribbled in from the smoke hole and several areas of broken bark covering. The floor was thick with mud, and animal droppings, mostly from raccoons, littered the ground.

He sank down on his pack just outside of the opening which once had been the door. Sand spent several moments inspecting the mess but soon left the place, seemingly as disgusted as his master. He limped off a short distance, lay down and fell asleep.

Otah was discouraged, and he was *angry!* He had planned to rest in the hut for a day or two, then set out on the trail of the Mastodon Hunters. Now a decision must be made. Rebuilding the dwelling would take several days. Meat must be secured and dried for his journey, since there was no way to know how much food could be found on the trek, nor how long it would take. "This is the problem with living alone," he sighed. "If my sister or mother were here they could have protected the hut while I was gone." There was no profit in thinking about what might have been, however. It was, as always, up to him and the wolf.

It was possible of course that by now the Clan he sought would be so far away that they could not be found. He tried to make plans, but this time his patience failed him. It seemed that Leaf was calling, and he wanted to *go!*

Otah sat before a small fire that evening, and as his mind began to clear he listed the things that must be done. As always, first was food. Snares must be set, roots dug and set out to dry, fish caught, cleaned and smoked. Then the most important work would be his attempt to rebuild a workable atlatl. The new flint was what he had most needed to complete the weapon, and now he had plenty! It required a straight shaft as long as both arms spread wide, but very slim and smooth, which would be the part to be cast. In the end of this a hole had to be drilled to form a socket for the small fore shafts. These little darts would be pushed into the socket. When an animal was struck the fore shaft would stay in while the spear shaft would fall free for another cast.

Several thin fore shafts with tiny, sharp flint points would finish the weapon. Finally, a turkey must be killed for its stiff feathers. These would be glued along the butt of the slender shaft to provide for true flight when the long arrow-like missile was cast.

Rather than take time to repair the hut, he threw a crude camp together in the clearing and began to work. Snares were placed each evening and checked at dawn. Game was plentiful, and he was kept busy skinning and butchering the small animals he took almost every night. Each day, as soon as he had prepared the meat for drying, he would work on the atlatl. It was hard to be patient and see that each job was done well, since his desire was to hurry toward the east in search of the Clan. His inner voice told him that this would be nothing but disaster. If Leaf had gone to the Other Place, or could not be found, then so be it, but each task correctly accomplished meant he was closer to his plan to search for her.

He had made several sets along a small creek that flowed into the river not far from his camp. Stepping quietly near one of the snares he was delighted to see a big raccoon fighting the loop encircling its head and one foreleg. When the animal saw the hunter, it began to slash and tear at the hated sinew. Otah approached warily, well aware that mature raccoons were strong, and not afraid to fight. Hissing and slavering, it kept a beady eye on the man, but continued its attempt to escape. Otah made the squealing sound on his hand several times, but evidently Sand was nowhere near. With a sudden mighty effort the raccoon ripped the sinew from its head, dashed away to the creek and swam across. Climbing up the far bank it turned for an instant and gave Otah a look of pure hatred before disappearing in the bushes. "Sand, where *are* you?" he groaned. Had the wolf been with him they would have had meat enough for many days.

It was time to re-establish his mastery over the wolf, so that evening he called the animal close to the rough shelter they were now using. "Sand, my friend, you have been given much freedom these past days. Surely you have earned it, but now you must once again submit to the collar and leash. When we find the Mastodon Hunter Clan you will have to be under my control. If you are allowed to run free they will kill you! So.....lie down while I fasten your collar." He carefully encircled the wolf's neck, pulling the hated collar tight under its chin. Sand *attacked!* With bared fangs the animal caught the man's forearm in a powerful grip, but Otah managed to pull free. He backed away a few steps, watching the wolf closely. Otah saw all the usual signs; raised ruff, tail low, and ears laid back. "I had thought this would no longer be necessary, but....." Before it could make its move he brought the heavy rawhide rope smashing across its ears. Roaring like an animal himself, he shouted out, "*Sand! No!*" He raised the rope to strike again but Sand had had enough. The wolf cowered on his back, and with a pathetic whimper of defeat exposed his throat in the "submission posture" that would have been required in a pack. "That is more like it!" Otah growled. He kept the rope high and threatening, but didn't need to strike again. "You have become like a child with too much freedom too soon," he chided, fastening the rope to the collar. "After all it is for your own good, and," he added, "perhaps mine as well. Soon we will be on our way east and it will take both of us to stay alive until we find the Clan." He had expected that such blows would no longer be necessary, but he was still learning about wolves!

*   *   *

Every moment not spent gathering and preparing food saw him chipping at his new blocks of flint. Six slim fore shafts were now completed, the ends of each holding extremely sharp points no larger than a fingernail. The new spear-thrower itself had been a tougher challenge but it too was now complete. So far his traps had not caught a turkey, even though he had baited several snares with the red and blue kernels he had saved. Twice he had found birds caught in the circles of sinew, one a ruffed grouse and the other a crow. Giving up on securing any turkey feathers, he had decided that the stiff wing feathers of the crow might work almost as well.

Nearly a week had passed until the day finally came. Selecting two fore shafts without flint points he positioned the atlatl high behind his right shoulder. The slender shaft lay along the length of the device, kept in place by the hunter's fingers. Holding his breath in excitement he chose a target. A dead stump twenty paces beyond his lean-to would serve. With all his strength he snapped the atlatl forward. The spear hissed through the air and struck the target. Even without a point of flint, the fore shaft sank half its length into the rotten wood. Otah gave a whoop of joy! He fitted another blunt fore shaft into the spear and cast again, but missed this time. The missile ripped through the bushes and disappeared. He had a hard time finding it, but was elated when he finally did. The long arrow-shaped shaft had flown almost forty paces straight and true. "Now," he told the watching wolf, "we are *ready!* We leave in the morning!"

With all his tools and equipment in his back pack and Sand on a long leash, at last they were on their quest. Keeping the river on his right, Otah traveled fast. They used game trails when possible, most of which followed the high ground above the swamp, just as Otah desired. With only slight detours he was able to retrieve his three snares and the turkey trap. All were empty but he was glad. All his energy was focused in one direction. East. . .east. . . east seemed to be a chant in time with his footsteps. "We are *coming* Leaf!" he shouted at the forest, but there was only a faint echo in reply.

Wind and rain had begun by mid-afternoon. Hating the thought of a wet and cold camp, he skirted the river bank for a time, looking for any kind of shelter. He had about given up when he was rewarded by a half-cave cut into the clay bank by the current. He gathered dead beech limbs, choosing only those with the bark still on, and dragged the protesting wolf into the shelter. Cutting away the rough bark left sticks that were nearly dry, and the new fire drill had smoke rolling in only a few minutes. Of course Sand did not like the fire. He huddled against the earthen wall as far from the blaze as he could get. This was fine with Otah. He had learned well about the smell of a wet wolf! Both enjoyed a good night's sleep.

Animal trails were abundant on the hills above the river's flood plain. They made good progress even though the spring rain continued to fall for most of the morning. When Otah finally stopped to dig some jerky from his pack the wolf suddenly moved stiff-legged to the end of his tether and stood growing, his muzzle pointed northward. Otah could see nothing that would cause the wolf to bristle. "What do you see?" he whispered, drawing his newly fashioned weapon from its sling across his shoulder. "You lead the way and we'll see what is bothering you." Sand had no chance to lead out. With a bellow of rage a forest buffalo came charging straight at them! Wolves were their hated enemy. The beast had every intention of goring the wolf, then trampling it to death! Otah moved faster than he ever had. He ripped his end of the leash from his belt in time to allow his companion to dash away, the tether trailing. The huge animal paid no attention to the puny-looking two-legged thing. It wanted the wolf, and wanted it *dead!* Otah dropped his pack, grabbed a low-lying oak limb and scrambled higher. With the wolf out of sight, the buffalo turned its wrath toward the man in the tree. Bellowing and ripping up clods of earth it patrolled angrily back and forth below the tree. Otah was safe enough but where was Sand? His own question was answered soon enough. Far from the cowards the Mastodon Hunter named Fox had claimed about wolves, the animal had circled the buffalo and was planning to attack its back legs. *"No, Sand!* Otah screamed. *"No!"* The wolf paid no attention. His blood was up and he meant to attack, hoping to sever a tendon and cripple the huge animal. At that moment Otah's heart seemed to stop beating. From his perch in the oak he could clearly see the impending death of his companion and friend.

The trailing end of Sand's leash had caught on some bushes!

The wolf was fighting the leash with every muscle in its body but the rawhide held and the collar was choking him. Had it not been for the hated leash, Sand would have continued to circle and attempt to bite at the legs. Now he was hardly able to move at all. The buffalo was a wise old bull which had survived many a wolf attack. This time he would have revenge!

Otah drew his spear and prepared himself. As the bull moved directly beneath his perch he gripped the weapon in both hands and dove on the buffalo. The flint sliced patches of wooly hair from the hump but only grazed the animal's thick hide. Otah sprawled and rolled, his backpack half under his body. The buffalo, further enraged by the smarting scratch on its shoulder, snorted, backed up two paces and lowered its head. He was preparing to charge! The moment's hesitation was all Otah needed. He grabbed the pack and threw it with all his might. Wonder of wonders, the bag caught on one of the animal's horns! Crazy with rage it tossed its huge head in all directions trying to dislodge the pack.

Otah snatched up his spear, ran to the wolf and untangled the leash. Dragging his protesting companion, he raced away into the undergrowth. Sand struggled against the rope, wanting to return to the fight. A last glance over his shoulder showed that the bull had dislodged the pack and was trampling it in fury.

Safe for the moment, Otah and Sand sat and gasped for breath. "You did well my friend, but without the help of several more of your kind you could never have taken a buffalo, even one as old and sick as that one." Keeping the wolf on a close tether he rested until the sun was high. Warily, checking every thicket, they slipped back to the scene of the fight. The buffalo was gone but the pack was a shambles. Taking no chances he snatched it up and hurried away lest the old bull return to kill them. Otah almost felt a moment of sadness for the animal. "He is alone like we are. Probably driven out of the herd to find his own way do you think?" Sand paid no attention.

On a small knoll free of trees and ground cover he finally felt safe enough to stop and assess the damage to his precious bundle. There were two tears, one an obvious puncture hole where a horn had pierced the leather. The other was probably caused by a hoof. Both were of little concern. Otah had become quite good at sewing patches even though he still considered it women's work. The contents of the heavy pouch were another matter however. He shook out the sleeping robe and spread it on the grass. He emptied the rest of the contents on it and examined each item with care. The dried meat was not affected, but two of the brittle fragments of flint were broken. They could be salvaged of course, for flint could always be re-worked into useful articles. The fire kit was intact. The greatest tragedy however had nothing to do with these life-saving items. Otah's heart fell as the little birch bark box tumbled onto the robe. It was ruined! In a panic Otah prodded through the remnants of bark but the blue stone bead was missing. Raising the pack he turned it upside down and shook it. The jewel popped out and fell at his feet. "It's *here*, Leaf!" he shouted aloud as he cradled it in his cupped hands. "Your gift is safe, my sister, and that is more important than anything else!" He repacked the pouch, adjusted the twisted straps and hoisted it to his shoulders. "Sand, there is still some daylight left. We are wasting time! Come on my friend, we must find the Mastodon Hunters and my sister! She will like you, as she always loved all birds and animals. Did you know that? Yes, she will like you." Otah was not so sure that the reverse would be true!

*   *   *

Two days later the travelers had their first encouragement. In a valley rimmed with oak and poplar trees there was much indication that a large camp had indeed occupied the spot. The grass was trampled and several fire rings were in evidence. The lingering smell of smoke caused Sand to sniff and sneeze in disgust. Just outside the camp area Otah was elated to find the evidence he had hoped for. The tusk was three times as long as he was tall, a beautiful thing of gleaming ivory. Closer examination was cause for more celebration. Where the pointed tip had been, there was a flat surface. The marks of a flint saw clearly showed that the Clan had cut many circular discs from the end of the tusk. These would no doubt have been drilled and polished for some important person to wear. "They were here for certain," he told the wolf. It was busy sniffing at all sorts of debris that had been left behind. Unfortunately there were no food scraps or anything else of use to them. The Clan had taken everything away except the tusk. Probably the other one had been carried with them, as the ivory would be of great value in trade. Without doubt some of the tribe would eventually be sent back for the remaining tusk. This was further proof that the ones he sought were not far ahead.

There would be no problem with directions now. Their trail would be easy to see and easy to follow. Otah was too excited to sleep that night. Only his newly acquired patience kept him from attempting to travel in darkness. He tried to make a plan but it was no use, for until they actually caught up with the Clan there was no way to know what would happen. Would they remember him at all? It had been six winters since he and his father had spent a short time with them far to the west. What of Sand? Otah was well aware of the hatred they had for wolves. He even wondered how they would receive *him*. "After all," he thought, "I have very little to trade except the flints, and those I mean to *keep!* Perhaps they will consider me merely another unwanted mouth to feed. And Leaf. If she really is with them would they allow her to leave with her brother? If so, would his sister even *want* to go? Certainly life for her would be easier with the Clan."

All his efforts had been spent on *finding* the Mastodon Hunters. Now that this appeared possible, he was torn by doubts. Again, it was nearly dawn before he slept.

The morning sun raised his spirits somewhat. Although he was still tired he led the wolf out of the clearing, and they followed the very obvious pathway which had been made by the departing Clan. The direction was north, deeper into the Black Swamp. Having spent all his years in and around the water and muck, Otah was undaunted. He loved the swamp and had no fear of it, yet he was constantly aware of the many dangers present in this unique part of his world. The Clan was also familiar with the terrain, which made the companions' journey that much easier.

The Mastodon Hunters' trail led mainly upon the hills and ridges which favored the direction they were traveling. They also knew how to avoid the dangers in the swamp. Otah and Sand hurried along, the trail plain before them. Although he had never had the tracking skills of his father, it was plain to see that he was getting closer to his goal. Tracks were clear in the wet areas, and drag marks showed where the women had pulled their V-shaped travois across the ground.

Otah made a foolish mistake. On one of the small sandy knolls that dotted the expanse he peered ahead. The high ground curved away to the north as far as he could see. "Look, Sand," he told the wolf. "The trail is plain before us. They would have followed those ridges which lie in the shape of the new moon! We can gain ground and save a lot of time by heading straight across the swampy ground. Then we can easily pick up their trail again and be much closer to them. Come on Sand, I'll lead he way!" He tied his new boots around his neck and secured the pack.

The going was easy at first, gravel covered the bottom and both enjoyed the ankle deep water as they headed north by northwest to intercept the far "horn" of the ridges. The depth of the water increased only a little as they traveled, but the gravel soon disappeared. Mud took its place. Sand was having a hard time with the water now up to his belly. The crooked leg bothered the wolf as he tried to maintain the rapid pace set by his master. Several times he stopped and anxiously looked back the way they had come, but Otah jerked on the leash and plunged ahead. The bottom rose at times but as they reached the midpoint of their supposed "short cut", the mud gave way to a foul-smelling dark brown muck. Sand, sometimes almost swimming, could negotiate it because of his four legs and very large feet. The man however, was sinking deeper and deeper with every step. "Come on Sand, we're almost halfway there!" Halfway was a big problem; too far to the ridges and just as far back the way they had come.

The snake lay coiled, floating on some hollow reeds. Otah stopped and yanked the wolf close to his leg. The reptile looked to be as long as two paces. Otah didn't know this type of creature. Although this one did not have the diamond-shaped head, the man could not know if it was poisonous or not. He had little time to ponder. Sand charged through the muck and water, pulling so hard on the leash that Otah was nearly upset. The snake began to swim away but the wolf bit into its middle! With his big head snapping back and forth the wolf whipped the snake so hard its head and tail narrowly missed the man. Its spine broken, the creature was helpless. Sand began eating it, and Otah let him have as much as he wanted before pulling him away. Half of the snake still dangled from the wolf's jaws as they again fought their way northward. The ridges seemed as far away as ever!

Otah's heavy pack and his weapons caused him to sink farther into the slime with every step, but to turn back now was unthinkable. Adding to the man's misery was the cold. His legs and feet were getting numb.

Man and animal struggled along, aching and freezing. When at last they felt firm sand underfoot they hurried onto the ridge and fell exhausted. Never had a fire felt so good! They slept the afternoon away.

Morning brought agony! Mosquitoes had bitten nearly every inch of exposed skin. His eyes were so swollen he could hardly see. With double handfuls of mud he plastered his face and arms. "Do you itch too, my friend?" Sand was whining pitifully, using his front paws to dig at his nose and lips where the insects had attacked him too. Otah threw green leaves on the fire and sat in the smoke.

Discouragement sapped his strength. He was tired. He was hungry, and he *itched!* He turned toward the wolf and spoke. "Sand, are we making a mistake? Is it time to give up on this fool's errand? We could take the high ground again and be back at our home by the river in five or six days. With the atlatl and plenty of fine flint, life would be easy. You would not need to be on a leash. I could have fire and cooked food every day. The river is full of fish and deer are plentiful. Should we give up and go back?"

He'd had enough. There is a limit to what any man can do, even with the best of intentions. "The Mastodon Hunters won't want us," he mumbled, coughing in the heavy smoke. "After all, Leaf may not even be with them. Chief Spotted Hand is old now and may not even remember me. Maybe he has even gone to the Other Place by this time." Otah was trying to convince himself to give up, and it was *working!* "Very well!" he said loudly, "Let's go home!"

Working quickly while trying to stay in the smoke he emptied the contents of his pack on the grass. Everything was a jumble, and he must organize the bundle for better ease in traveling. It did not take long. Sand, sensing a change in his master, stood up and stretched. It appeared that he was ready to quit as well. Otah finished tightening the rawhide bands on the pack and hoisted it to his shoulders. The spears and atlatl rode above his shoulder, ready for instant action should the need arise. He took one last look around; making sure that nothing had been left behind, just as his father had always told him to do.

There it lay, almost hidden in the grass. *The blue stone!* Leaf's gift. Otah smiled a little, gave a long, tired sigh and started walking, heading *north again!*

Traveling the ridges just as the Clan had done, it was becoming clear that the Mastodon Hunters were not far ahead. He moved cautiously now, avoiding the open spaces as much as possible. It would be disaster to happen upon the Clan unexpectedly! Worse would be his discovery by scouts that might very well be watching their back trail.

Food was becoming a problem again. Before much longer they would have to stop traveling long enough to hunt and fish. This would also mean some sort of temporary camp where they could prepare the meat for drying and smoking. Moving more slowly, Otah began to watch for game sign. There was plenty of it, as most of the animals avoided the swamp just as he had. Their trails and runs were ideal for his snares and traps. Sand, perhaps even hungrier than his master, indicated his desire to follow the fresh scent of the animals he would enjoy eating. Otah chose a sandy knoll well away from the swamp and a good distance east of the Clan's trail. Here there was a constant breeze from the west which would carry away the smoke from their fires. Even better, it would help keep the mosquitoes at bay! The camp was a crude affair of saplings and brush, but since the temperatures had warmed considerably as summer approached, keeping warm at night was no longer a problem. Otah hated these delays, but there was no way to avoid them. Without food, and food preserved for travel, they could not go on.

They hunted and trapped for four days, another two days spent skinning, butchering, and drying the meat. Also, Otah had developed a simple fish spear which was quite successful.

Two adult raccoons had been snared, and Sand had killed both after vicious battles which proved these animals were not afraid to fight! Otah had taken a muskrat which had made the mistake of leaving its house of reeds to feed on new grass along the bank. The small pelt was beautiful, but Otah couldn't eat the strong-tasting flesh. Sand had no such problem! Fish were abundant in the clear pools which appeared here and there along the edge of the swamp. The fish taken were mostly eaten immediately. Well supplied and well rested, Otah and Sand resumed their cautious journey. There was no doubt that they would encounter the Clan before much longer.

Patience. . . patience. . . plan. . .

Crouched beside a tiny fire well off the trail, Otah tried to decide what must be done when he finally had the Clan in sight. "We can't just walk up to them, Sand," he whispered. "They would kill you for sure, and if Fox really has my sister, I might be next! I remember all of them well, even though it was many winters ago. They are strong and well organized, and their chief and Holy Man control everything that goes on. Their tools and weapons are of the finest, even better than those made by my father." As usual, Sand paid little attention as he lay far from the fire chewing on a bone. "It's not your problem is it, my friend? I must do all the thinking for both of us. Still life would be dismal without your smelly carcass beside me!" Sand was asleep.

Two more days' travel and their journey was nearly at an end. Smoke had been visible beyond a series of low hills to the east. Sand was nervous and spent much time with lifted nose, testing the breeze. Otah was preparing to make a cold camp that evening when the wolf suddenly stood up and stared into the forest. A low, resonant growl alerted his master. "What do you see, friend?" he whispered, peering into the trees. "That is the same growl you made back at the flint quarries! Does that mean *people?*" He took hold of the wolf's muzzle to keep him quiet. For a moment he thought he saw movement. Sand saw it too and tensed for an attack. Otah pulled the leash up tight, as they were far from ready for a confrontation with the Clan.

He had a plan, a plan which called for patience. This journey with all its hardships and frustrations had taught him that!

Well before dawn the following morning he rose from his sleeping robe, careful to make no noise. He checked Sand's leash to make sure it was tied securely to a small

tree, as Sand would not be allowed along on this part of his plan. Working by the light of

a half moon he boosted his pack into the tree he had selected the night before. Only his

spear and knife would be taken. It could be that he would have to run for his life before

this day was over! He threw two generous strips of meat to the wolf, hoping it would be

enough to keep it quiet, at least until he was out of sight.

It was impossible to travel through the dark undergrowth silently. Several times

he tripped and nearly fell, but by jamming the butt of the spear into the ground he was

able to steady himself. When he finally felt his way to the easier footing of the Clan's

trail the dawn was upon him. After a very short walk he forced himself to hide a few

paces from the marks of the Mastodon Hunters' passing. He lay hidden and watchful

until there was enough light to see well. He raised himself to a crouch and examined

every tree and bush around him. Convinced that he was alone, Otah moved silently and

swiftly through the forest, far from the trail. He was heading for a small hill beyond

which he had seen the smoke from cooking fires. The aroma of roasting meat made his

mouth water, and proved that the Clan was camped just beyond the hill. He moved faster

now, in order to reach the crown before sunup. Taking advantage of every tree and bush

he zigzagged to the crest of the knoll.

The camp was there, just as he had expected, but further away than he had

thought. Also a screen of low-lying bushes was in the way. He did not hesitate, but hand

over hand pulled his thin body into the branches of a tree and lay full length along a thick limb. Leaves and branches hindered his view somewhat but he could certainly see *enough!* It appeared to be a semi-permanent camp, no doubt for the purpose of hunting and fishing. There would also be abundant berries and nuts which the girls and women could gather later in the summer. They would grind these with dried meat and fat to make pemmican.

An old woman emerged from one of the skin-covered houses. Otah could see her clearly. She carried a bowl, undoubtedly heading for water for cooking. She was soon out of sight, and a younger woman appeared but before he could see her clearly she walked behind one of the houses and he could not see her after that. Slowly the camp came alive. Otah was astonished at the talk which flew from one Clansman to another, mostly from the women! Men began to make their leisurely appearance, finding comfortable places to sit in the sunlight. They did no work, but simply watched the women preparing food. When it was ready they still did not stir but waited to be served. Otah was thrilled to see this. How nice it would be to be served in this fashion! These Mastodon Hunters knew how to have a happy life, at least the *men* did!

When it appeared that the men had finished eating they formed a group under a spreading tree. There seemed to be much arguing and head-shaking until they finally appeared to be in agreement. Gathering their weapons and packs they set off toward the swamp. "They are going on a hunt of course," Otah thought. "With the men gone I will be better able to leave this cursed tree limb and get back to my companion. I will need to lead him well away from this area, lest he break free and be seen." Inch by inch he lowered himself, keeping the thick trunk between his body and the camp. At one point he froze, heart pounding, when a little girl wandered near his hiding place. She toddled away at last, never guessing that a stranger was hiding in a tree nearly above her head!

Sand was curled up under the bushes, seemingly content to wait for his master. He had guarded the pack, as Otah knew he would. Nothing would venture near this battle-scarred warrior on purpose!

Otah decided to move their rough camp further back from the Clan's village. He knew the way now, and the same tree would serve well for the further spying he meant to do. After locating a safer spot he set his snares and rested until the sun was low in the sky. Again he made sure the wolf was securely tied and well fed.

Not even his spear accompanied him this time. As the western sky burst forth in a spectacular display of color he lifted himself to his perch on the same limb as before. Leaning forward he carefully stripped off a few leaves which had hindered his view that morning. Several fires could be seen shining among the dwellings, the women tending them. Otah filled his nostrils, hoping for the aroma of roasting meat, but the wind was against him this time. Several children were running about, not helping with any chores, and often simply getting in the way. Otah yearned for companionship, but seeing these people so happy and content was almost his undoing. For one long moment he was overcome by an aching desire to climb down and simply enter the camp. "The wolf," he thought desperately. "If it weren't for Sand I could do just that! My traveling would be over. I could help hunt and find food to pay for my keep. Perhaps Leaf is there somewhere too. Yes, I could do that were it not for my companion." Still undecided, he

began to remember, just as had done several times before. Sand licking and cleansing his

festering arm. Sand running down the wounded deer. The heat from the Sand's shaggy

body keeping him from freezing to death! *"No!* Whatever is to be my fate, it will be with

the best companion I will ever have. The wolf and I are *friends!"* His mind made up, he

slid down from his perch and slipped silently back to his camp.

It was nearly full dark by the time he had checked his snares. One held a grouse,

already dead, but two more were empty. These he left in place for the night and the next

day.

There was no need to examine the final snare! More than fifty paces from it he

knew well enough what it held. The odor of *skunk* lay heavily all over the whole area!

His first idea was to stay completely away from the set. There was no way he could

release the animal [he certainly didn't want to *kill it]* without being sprayed by the most

horrible odor in nature. But to leave the animal caught in the sinew snare would, he

knew, be very dangerous. Suppose one of the hunters or even an inquisitive child should

decide to investigate? The snare would indicate the presence of a stranger in the area. The

Mastodon Hunters would then have no trouble finding his camp. Undoubtedly he would

be considered an enemy which they would enjoy killing! The skunk must be dealt with

soon!

Sand would have made short work of the animal but the commotion might alert

the Clan. It was up to the man, and the light was failing. Working as quickly as he could

while trying not to make noise, glumly he set to work. Using his flint saw he cut a sapling as big around as his spear and very long. This he lashed securely along the butt of the weapon. He now had a "spear" nearly twice as long as before. Holding the pole ahead of him he tried sneaking up on the skunk. It saw him at once, raised its bushy tail and ejected such a stink that Otah was instantly nauseous. Trying to keep from breathing, he extended the pole until the sharp spearhead touched the snare, which parted immediately. Not badly hurt, the skunk ambled arrogantly away. The long pole with its spear point had been a good idea, but it was not long enough. *Otah stank!*

Back at the camp Sand stretched his tether to the limit in order to stay as far as possible from his master. As bad as he knew he smelled, Otah could hardly imagine what the wolf was going through, since the animal's sense of smell was hundreds of times more sensitive than his own! Poor Sand!

The next morning just at dawn found Otah once again secure in the tree. "Maybe I am being *too* cautious," he told himself, but he knew he was not! He watched the camp activity as the sun peeked over the trees. For the first time he saw two men emerge from the largest dwelling. One was dressed in the most beautiful doeskin shirt Otah had ever seen. Perhaps he was their chief? Both men sat down to be served by an old woman. Otah kept watching. Then trouble began! A red jimmy squirrel had come running along a limb just above the one where he lay. The animal saw him then, and immediately set up an angry chatter that echoed all around the area. A little boy of perhaps four summers crawled out of his house, rubbing his eye, and staring sleepily toward the noise that had awakened him. The squirrel kept up its scolding. Otah tried making shooing motions with one hand but this only excited the little creature more than ever. The boy was wide awake now! He dashed into the house and soon emerged, carrying the tiniest atlatl Otah had ever seen. A miniature quiver held several small darts for the device. Panic struck! "He means to try a cast at the red jimmy!" Otah thought. What should he do? The boy had been well trained by someone, perhaps old Chief Spotted Hand. The lad approached cautiously, the spear thrower in position and ready. Otah tried to flatten himself against the limb as the child crept forward.

AAIIIEEEEE! The boy had seen him and was giving the alarm! He then turned and ran back as fast as his fat little legs could carry him. Otah began to work his way behind the tree trunk and slip toward the ground. The boy was shouting and pointing excitedly but the two men were only laughing. Otah was nearly down when one of the men rose reluctantly and followed the excited little boy. Otah was plastered against the far side of the tree, shaking with fear. Twenty paces from the tree the man caught the boy by the hair and pulled him back. Chuckling, the well dressed Clan member held his nose and backed hurriedly away. The boy stamped his foot and raged at both men but they simply laughed all the harder. As soon as their backs were turned, Otah slid on down and crept away as fast as possible.

A skunk may have saved his life!

Safely back at their hidden camp Otah gave half a grouse to the wolf. Trembling with relief, he spoke quietly to his companion. "I believe the time has come, Sand. I was almost caught this morning and would have been had I not smelled so bad! It would be better if we approached them, rather than to allow them to find *us!* Sooner or later their hunting excursions will come this way. Evidence of our presence will be quickly noticed by any careful hunter. Even the women, as they searched for edible plants, could be our undoing. There is no longer a choice. Tomorrow evening if the hunters have returned and have eaten well, we shall pay them a visit. Here is the rest of the bird, so eat it all. This meal may be our last!"

Sleep would not come that night. Sand was restless too, sensing his master's unease. Finally both sat up and watched the moon rise. Sand raised his muzzle and gave a long and powerful howl, but Otah made no effort to silence the animal. The Mastodon Hunters would pay little attention if any were awake. Wolf howls would only be part of a normal night for them. Then from far off across the swamp came an answering call! Sand bristled and pulled hard at his tether, but the man did not let him go.

*   *   *

Otah moved with utmost caution. Every footstep was carefully planned, and wherever possible he trod only on flat stones or dry places. Sand gave no trouble on a short leash. He had eaten well and was content to let the man lead. Each snare was checked and retrieved. Luckily all were empty. He didn't go anywhere near the one which had held the skunk, as it was ruined anyway. All traces of their latest camp had been obliterated, a leafy branch used to sweep away every footprint and paw print. They shared what was left of the dried meat, then crawled into a thick stand of cattails at the very edge of the swamp. The mosquitoes attacked but liberal coatings of mud kept them from biting.

Otah was surprised to find that he had slept through the afternoon, and evening was upon them. *It was time!* He checked Sand's leash and collar once more and they headed north. Otah's pack rode on his back, but he did not unsheathe the spear or the atlatl, as he intended to enter the Clan's camp with open hands. Although protesting the short leash, the wolf stayed close, his broad back brushing Otah's thigh. "If the hunters have been successful there would have been a feast," Otah whispered. "I remember how much they ate when I was with them as a boy."

A keening wail brought the wolf's hair rising. He growled low, but Otah grabbed his snout and hung on. The scream came again as two women burst out of the forest ahead of them. Their gathering baskets forgotten, they dashed away toward the camp. Still holding the wolf's jaws Otah stopped in a small clearing and waited. It didn't take long, as shouts and commotion floated across the forest. Sand was struggling to break free but his master held on with a grip of iron. Two figures, both men, emerged from the undergrowth, each with a spear ready. They moved forward cautiously. Their eyes never left the sight before them; a very mud-covered man dressed in what appeared to be rags, holding a full-grown wolf by the nose! They stopped and spoke rapidly to each other, arms flailing with agitated gestures. The Clansmen came no closer, so Otah simply waited, unmoving. The two shot continuing glances back the way they had come. Otah was very afraid but also puzzled. Why didn't they attack? Then he understood, as many more men appeared and formed up behind the two in front. They still did not proceed, seeming to be almost as frightened as Otah!

"Enough of this!" Otah thought, and drew his spear from its sling. The Mastodon Hunters growled in anger and brandished their own weapons. Otah threw his spear to the ground and extended his bad arm, palm open. The other hand was busy trying to control the wolf, which was ready and eager to do battle. The watching Clan members suddenly parted as another figure approached. Otah recognized him as the finely dressed individual he had seen from the tree. Drawing a beautifully decorated robe tighter around his shoulders this man stood spread-legged and arrogant. He gave a shout. *Otah knew him then!*

It was Fox, or "Kardo" as he now wished to be called.

Otah was surprised that Fox did not seem to remember him. The bigger man stepped closer, but stopped at once when Sand bared his teeth and snarled. Three other Clansmen hurried up to flank their leader. One held a spear, while the other two readied their spear-throwers. Without turning or taking his eyes off the man and his wolf, Kardo reached back and gave a gruff command. A spear thrower was thrust into his hand. He raised the weapon and took careful aim at the snarling animal. He was preparing to throw when Otah jumped in front of the animal. *"No!"* he shouted as Sand fought the leash behind him. "He is mine! I control him! Let him *alone!*"

Confused, the men muttered among themselves, gesturing angrily at Otah and the wolf. The man nearest their leader readied his own atlatl, but his aim was at Otah's chest! Fox turned and shot him a stern look. The man lowered his weapon and his head, proving that the leader was very much in charge here! Handing the borrowed weapon back to its owner, Fox [or "Kardo"] stepped a few paces closer. He suddenly made a face, held his nose and backed quickly away again. By this time Otah had become used to the odor of skunk but the Mastodon Hunters had not! Once again, Otah thanked his stars for the encounter with the skunk. Backing still farther away, the men waited for their leader to tell them what to do. They were amazed when he turned and shouted a command back toward the village. After a short wait an old woman waddled up to the men and stood head down. Kardo pointed at the newcomers and shoved her roughly forward. "EEEE OO OOO O HH H" she screamed when she saw the wolf. He shoved her again, but she refused to take another step. Angrily the leader slapped her across the head. The old woman began to weep piteously, but still didn't approach the man and the animal. Otah recognized her then as the one who had served the men the preceding morning.

Otah knew what he must do. Still holding one hand open and extended he began to drag the wolf back. Two men shouted angrily and took a few steps closer but Otah waved his free hand violently, trying to signal to them that he was not trying to escape. Two more steps took him to the base of a good sized cedar. Stopping the signaling, he knelt and tied Sand's leash to the tree.

Kardo had been watching all of this and seemed satisfied. Again he shouted at the old woman, who was still sitting in the dirt. She rose and started to protest again, but when the leader raised his hand to deliver another blow she began shuffling toward the stranger. Her terror was so great she could scarcely walk, but bit by bit she approached. Another angry shout made her move a little faster. Stopping several paces away, she motioned that the ragged and smelly man should follow her. Otah was relieved at this turn of events, for it seemed that they did not mean to kill him, at least not yet! But what of Sand? It was clear that the Mastodon Hunters were determined and ready to kill his companion. He stopped following the woman and made an appeal for the animal's life. Even without knowing the language, Kardo was quick to grasp the meaning. He gave rapid orders and two men moved a little closer to the animal and sat down, spears ready. Otah effusively thanked the leader, who seemed to understand Otah's intent. He shrugged his shoulders and remained aloof. Apparently Kardo was used to being thanked! Otah tried to indicate that he knew the man, but Kardo quickly turned and hurried away.

At the bank of the small stream that bisected the village the old woman used gestures to indicate that he was to remove all his clothing! Otah did as he was instructed, and at her urging stepped into the shallow water, totally naked. Muttering and complaining, she entered the water herself. Scooping up handfuls of sand and mud she calmly proceeded to vigorously scrub every inch of his filthy and stinking body. A quick glance proved that the Clansmen were taking no chances of an escape. Four of them stood watching, spears ready. One of them had picked up Otah's spear as well, and was critically examining the workmanship. He was obviously impressed.

Otah emerged from his enforced bath with his body red and stinging from the old woman's treatment. He still smelled like a skunk but not nearly so bad. One of the men threw him a remnant of tanned elk skin almost as ragged as the clothes he had been wearing. He wrapped this around his middle. The four men prodded him back to their leader, several times drawing blood from sharp jabs with their spears. Otah pointed at his discarded clothes, but they sneered at such poor garments and left them lying.

Sand had not been harmed but he was still agitated and angry. Otah was not allowed to check on the animal, but it appeared that the wolf was doing well enough for the moment. Kardo gave another command. It was clear that he enjoyed ordering people about. One of the men picked up Otah's pack. Holding it at arm's length to stay as far as possible from the smell of skunk, he threw it at Otah's feet. Kardo pointed to it and spoke a few words. Unsure what was expected of him, Otah knelt and took out the sleeping robe. Fox [as Otah still thought of him] angrily growled a few more words, pointing at the pack again. Otah unrolled the robe and began to empty the contents onto it. The Clansmen gathered around, curious to see what this sorry looking stranger might have with him. The fire-making kit, flake knives, flint saws, and bone knapper tumbled out, but none of these were of particular interest to them. Such things were only what one would expect a traveler to carry with him. But then everything changed! Otah carefully unrolled the rabbit skin pouch that held his supply of flint blades, the ones the people at the flint quarry had left for the "spirit man". Grunts and cries of amazement and appreciation greeted each shining piece as Otah placed it on the robe. While most advanced and sophisticated, they had never seen such quality material or intricate workmanship! There was an intake of breath when the blue bead fell on the robe.

Otah was smiling proudly at them when suddenly Kardo gave the loudest command he had yet uttered. A beautifully decorated pouch of ermine skin, tied around his muscular neck, bounced with every shouted word. Responding to the order, the Clansmen fell on the stranger, knocking him to the ground. In no time they had bound his hands with rawhide thongs and yanked him erect. Another rope was tied around his neck, one man holding the end of it. Now Otah knew how Sand must feel!

They entered the village in a sort of triumphant procession. Women and children stood silently, staring at the half-clothed man with the rope cinched around his neck. They dumped him into a small hut half full of firewood. "How clever," he thought, "they must gather the wood in good weather, then keep it dry in here. But if they are so smart, why am I a prisoner? And why has Fox, or "Kardo", not recognized me? Have I changed that much since we were both boys?"

Kardo appeared in the opening, scowling. In his hands were two of Otah's finest blades. Angrily he shook them at the prisoner and spoke rapidly in the Clansmen's language. Otah could not understand the words nor why he was receiving such treatment. He tried answering, but Kardo silenced him with a cutting motion of one hand. Unsatisfied, the leader stalked off, muttering to himself. At that moment Otah understood! "They think I have *stolen* these pieces!" he gasped. "They think I am a *thief!*"

Time passed slowly. He tried flexing his fingers and moving his arms but his bonds were too tight. There was almost no feeling in his hands. Someone appeared in the opening. It was the old woman who had given him the painful bath. She threw a shirt and leggings inside and began to waddle away. He shouted at her and held out his aching hands. She hesitated a moment, looked all around, then crawled inside. With fingers surprisingly nimble for one of her age, she managed to loosen the thongs enough to let the blood flow once more. He tried to thank her but after fearfully peering in every direction she scuttled away. He was surprised when only a short time later she reappeared, but this time she stayed outside. With a quick, furtive motion she threw him a good sized portion of roasted catfish. Again he started to express his thanks but she hissed an obvious message for his silence. His fingers tingling, he picked the morsel from the dirt and gobbled it as quickly as he could. It seemed that he was not to have any food, but things were looking a little better now. He was still a prisoner but he had a little food and his hands were coming alive again. The rawhide rope around his neck was tight but not tight enough to hinder his breathing. He wondered what, or who, was at the other end of it. Tentatively he gave a yank but the rope was solid. "They have tied me to a tree!" He groaned. "Oh Sand, what have I been doing to you?"

Some time later a small boy could be seen peering into the hut. He stayed well back from the opening, afraid to get too close to the man who had a wolf! Still unable to see, the lad crept closer. When his eyes adjusted to the gloom within he gave an awful shriek and dashed away. As he ran he kept shouting "Cabo!, Cabo!" Otah shifted around until he could see out of the opening. The boy was still shouting that word and pointing toward the hut where Otah lay. He was out of sight for a few moments, then reappeared, dragging Kardo by the hand. The lad was looking very proud. He puffed out his little chest and tried to assume a swagger. Kardo was laughing at the boy but seemed proud as well. He summoned others who were nearby and they all headed for Otah's prison, the child leading the way. Otah scrabbled around until he was out of sight and waited. No one entered but there was much talk and more kindly laughter outside. Otah soon determined what was happening. The boy was the very one who had seen him in the tree. No one had believed him then, but it was plain that he had been right! The boy was now enjoying his well-deserved congratulations!

The story of Otah's capture was all over the village and more than this boy were very curious about him. Otah moved a little. The boy yelled in fright and disappeared. In a short time he was back, holding the hand of a person Otah could not yet see. She bent down and looked in.

It was Leaf!

"Leaf! Is it really you? Don't you know me? I am Otah, *your brother!*"

"But. .. .but. ..you don't look like . . I mean you are . . ."

"Stop!" Otah cried. "I can't understand. Can't you speak in *our* language? You must be talking as the Mastodon Hunters do."

"Yes. . . yes! I can hardly remember. It has been so long! Where have you been. . . I mean. . ," she struggled to find the words from her former tongue.

"Listen," Otah hissed, "I need water. I'm very thirsty. My *wolf!* Have you seen him?"

"Yes, everyone has seen that animal. It is to be killed during the feast of the new moon, three days from now." Her former tongue was coming back to her rapidly. "Why wait so long, Otah? The sooner that ugly beast is dead the better I will like it! It looks just like one of the wolves that killed our mother. I *hate* all wolves!"

"No! *No!*" Otah pleaded. "Let me go and take care of him. He must be thirstier than I and hungrier too. Ask someone, *please!*"

"We are not to approach that beast," she said. "But I will ask Kardo, my husband. He tells everyone he will soon be chief of our Clan, so perhaps he will allow it, but he is a hard man!"

"Try! Try!" he begged. "After my wolf is cared for we can have a long talk. We have much to say to each other, but I cannot until I know that Sand is no longer in danger."

"Sand, is that the name you call that terrible creature? It would be best if it were killed before it bites someone. If that were to happen it would not only be the wolf that would die."

"No! Please ask the man, Kardo is it? I once knew him as 'Fox'. Plead with him. Beg! Do whatever you have to. Sand has saved my life *twice!* We are friends. He doesn't attack me, and without that animal I would not be here. In fact I would surely be in the 'Other Place' right now." Leaf gasped at the mention of the abode of the dead. It was taboo to say those words. "I will try," she said with a frown. "Now I must leave you, my brother. Kardo pretends that we are not children of the same parents. Do not *ever* tell *anyone* that we are!"

"But why. . .?" Leaf was anxious to leave and made no answer. "The boy," Otah whispered, "what of him?"

"His name is Little Kardo, but in secret I call him Little Otah! He is the son of Kardo and me. You are *his uncle!* But you must never tell anyone this either. Especially *this!"*

She stood, looked all around and hurried away, pulling Little Kardo along. Otah was so shocked he could hardly make his mind work.

He had found his sister and a great deal more besides.

Not long after Leaf's visit two burly men reached into the hut and grabbed Otah by the leg. They dragged him outside where Kardo stood waiting, arms folded. The men untied Otah's leash from the tree and yanked him to his feet. They marched him away, heading for the thicket where Sand was tied. Several times they jabbed him with their spears. Such treatment was unnecessary, for Otah was beginning to hope that Leaf had convinced her husband to allow the wolf food and water. He needed no such prodding. Half the village had been watching this activity. They followed along, staying well back from the little procession, Kardo leading the way. Otah knew the place of his companion's imprisonment, and walked faster as they approached. Suddenly an awful thought struck him. Were they only giving the wolf care to keep it alive for entertainment at the feast?

Sand lay under a bush. He was not moving, and his tongue lolled from his mouth as he panted. He sensed them then and came to his feet bristling and snarling. They let go of the rope still around Otah's neck, but left the free end dangling. The Clansmen stopped and stayed well beyond Sand's tether. Another jab told Otah that he was to approach the wolf. "They think Sand will tear me to pieces," he thought. "They will see that we have no fear of one another." Talking softly, he walked forward and knelt down. The wolf whined a greeting that nearly broke the man's heart. Boldly he untied the end of the leash that was tied to the tree. The two men shouted angrily and readied their spears. Kardo gave a curt order and the men backed off. Otah pulled the animal up short and started toward the stream where he'd had a bath. More and more villagers were coming to watch, staying a long way back. Wolves were enemies, and if they could not be avoided they should be killed! Even the youngest among them knew that!

Both man and animal drank from the stream, the watching people gasping in wonder at such a sight. Otah's pack still lay where it had been thrown before. Someone had taken the robe, and of course all the valuables were missing. Pieces of dried meat were scattered about in the dirt, considered worthless by the sophisticated Mastodon Hunters. When they could drink no more Otah led the wolf near the discarded pack and allowed it to snap up such scraps as it could reach. Otah too selected a piece, wiped off the dirt as best he could and started to eat. Some of the villagers began talking and laughing excitedly. They were enjoying the show, but stayed back from the action!

Several commands brought everyone back to the camp. Otah and Sand led the way with more armed men following. They indicated by gestures that the wolf was to be tied up short to a post set near the middle of the village. The earth was well trampled here, and it was obvious that it was the center of many activities. There was no shade, no water, and no food. After making sure of the bonds on his wrists, they began tying Otah to the same post. Angrily he resisted, shoving one hunter reeling backward. The other guard pulled a short club and brought it down hard on Otah's shoulder. Sand growled and leaped up, fighting his collar. Otah calmed the wolf with soothing words and sat down beside it. He did his best to show no fear, but he could not control his trembling. An ugly welt was growing where the club had struck, but that was the least of his troubles. Were they to be killed when the moon was new? Their fear and hatred of wolves was understandable, but what had *he* done? Why was their leader so angry with him? And why had Leaf told him to never let them know that he was her brother? For that matter, where *was* Leaf? Couldn't she be able to save them both?

Otah was very afraid and a little angry. The sun was beating down on the two prisoners and people continued to gather and watch the strange pair. Suddenly Sand gave a yelp. A stone had hit him on the back. Two older boys were laughing and pointing as they gathered more stones and began to throw them. Most of the pebbles missed the target, but when one did strike the wolf he would flinch and bare his teeth. Otah knew that sooner or later he too would be their target. He was not surprised when a rock the size of his fist slammed into his leg. He stood up and shouted angrily at the boys. This was just what they wanted! Grinning and shouting rude remarks, they were preparing to throw again when a laughing voice stopped their fun. Leaf scolded them lightly, but was able to act as if she cared little for the man and wolf tied there in the sun.

Otah felt his anger rising again. How could she act this way to her own brother? He was even further incensed when she picked up a small stone and threw it! She was careful to miss, he noted. She strolled closer, holding Little Kardo by the hand. Otah watched her, not knowing what to make of her actions. She sat down in the shade of a small tree at the edge of the clearing. Taking her son on her lap she astonished her brother by starting to *sing!* How *could she* do such a thing? He remembered very well her little songs when she was a child in happier days back at their hut. Then it dawned on him. The words of her song were in his own language! Little Kardo struggled to get down from her lap but she held him there.

Otah had never listened more carefully than he did now. "How clever she is!" he thought as her soft voice repeated a sing-song refrain.

"Tonight. . this night. . .when the moon is high. . .this night ...

When the child sleeps. . .this night. . .

When Chief Spotted Hand sleeps. . . tonight. .

When the moon is high . . this night. . I will come. .

This night . . I will tell you all. . . this night!"

The song ended, she rose, dusted herself off and strolled away, proving her unconcern to any who might be watching.

It was all he could do to keep from showing his joy. He knew he must not appear to have any more hope than before, lest her ingenious charade be discovered. "Leaf! Oh Leaf," he thought. "You are indeed a clever one! With your help, escape may yet be possible." He rested his head on his knees and tried to sleep.

The sun kept its relentless torment of man and animal.

When evening finally came, two men arrived and dragged him as far from the post as his rope would reach. Keeping a wary eye on the wolf, they removed the bond around their prisoner's neck. Half dragging him, they opened the flap to the wood storage hut and threw him in. Threatening him with a raised club, they tied his hands behind his back, the rawhide having been soaked before its use. There was no chance that the swelling knots could be loosened. Satisfied with their work they left.

*　　　　　　*　　　　　　*

Leaf crept into the wood-house without making a sound. Otah woke at her entrance, but she touched his lips for silence. "Thank you! *Thank you!*" he whispered.

"There is little time my brother. I will talk and you must listen. I have brought you food and a bowl of water." She had to hold the bowl to his lips, as his hands were still securely bound. "Can you free my hands?" he urged.

"I am sorry but my fingers are not strong enough. Wet rawhide must be cut. They would soon discover this and we would both be punished. You must bear it a little longer. In the morning I will plead with our *true* Chief, Spotted Hand. He may allow you some freedom."

"What of Sand?" Otah asked. But once again she touched his lips. "I will do what I can for the wolf as well but even had I permission the animal might attack me. It must suffer a little longer, just as you must. Now I will talk further. Do not interrupt, as our time together must be short. I shall try to tell you all that you need to know."

"Kardo is my husband and the father of my child. I was his first wife, but when he tired of me he took another. Now he seeks a third."

"A third *wife?*" Otah whispered in awe.

"You must not *interrupt!* We must hurry, but I will say this much. He wishes to wed a very young girl of the Clan, but her parents object. Probably he will take her anyway, as he cares little for anyone else's wishes, only his own! She is very pretty, and my very best friend. Perhaps you have noticed her."

I did see a pretty girl this morning. She smiled at me! What's her name?"

"She is Small."

"I could see how little she is, but how is she called?"

"Small! That is her name, *'Small'*. Now you *must* be quiet while I finish telling you what is happening here."

"Perhaps you find it strange that I do not share Kardo's house. That was his choice, but I am glad. He is a cruel man, and as I said, he thinks only of himself. He is good to our son when he feels like it but doesn't do for him the things a father should. A year ago Spotted Hand's sight became so bad he needed someone to care for him. Kardo sent me and Little Kardo to live with the old chief and see to his needs. I am happy there, for Kardo is courting the small one and has no time for me, and very little for his second wife either."

"Now I must quickly tell you what is happening between you and Kardo. He is claiming to be chief, even though it is only Spotted Hand who can name a new chief as his successor. The old chief does not wish to see Kardo rule our Clan, but most of the people are afraid of that braggart and would not oppose him. Believe me, Kardo *does* know you! He attempts to act as if he doesn't but I know that man. He hates and fears you, and his desire is to see you dead! The reason for such hatred is . . ."

A sound outside of the wood hut silenced her instantly. Both sat unmoving to listen. Leaf relaxed slightly when she recognized the stumbling footsteps of the old woman who had scrubbed Otah at the brook. The crone was just outside and seemed to be mumbling crazily to herself. "One must take care. Take care for ears are listening. Eyes are closed in the night, but *ears are awake!* Yes, ears are awake….one must …must take care. *Ears! Ears!*"

The sound of her halting footsteps faded away, but her jabbering continued into the night. To Otah she sounded exactly like one with the mind sickness, but of course he could not understand her language.

"I must go *now!* Leaf hissed. The old one has come to warn us. She hates Kardo and would love to see him get what he deserves. She can be an ally for us. Do not think she is crazy or stupid. She is not! Her brain is as bright as any in our Clan. By pretending to be dense she gains access to all kinds of information that others do not have."

"But you were going to tell me why Kardo hates. . ."

Leaf was gone!

When dawn came the old woman shuffled in with some pemmican and a skin of water. She threw the meat on the dirt floor, but did take time to quickly look at his swollen hands. Clucking her tongue in concern, she held the water skin to his mouth until he had taken all it contained. For an instant her eyes met his in the thin morning light, and Otah was certain he detected there the hint of a twinkle!

Nothing else happened for some time. Otah's hands had stopped hurting. A bad sign! If someone didn't release the rawhide soon he might lose the use of his fingers, two of which, thanks to Sand, were already damaged. He was also concerned for his friend. Still tied to the post, the animal was surely suffering. Otah knew he must act! Kicking the door flap open with one foot he slid into the sunshine. Several Clan members saw him at once. He raised his voice in an angry shout, which brought immediate action. One of the two guards who had been assigned to watch him hurried up and raised his club. Angrily, Otah shouted again, louder than before. The guard was preparing to strike when a quavering but authoritative voice gave a command in the language of the Mastodon Hunters. "Lower that club, Saard! We do not strike men whose hands are tied." The guard did so, but managed to appear offended. He was not used to taking orders from old

Chief Spotted Hand. "How did that half-blind old man know what was going on here?" Saard asked his friend. There was no logical answer.

Thankfully Otah saw the true chief approaching and with him was Leaf and her son. His sister spoke rapidly to Spotted Hand in their language. At another order the other guard knelt behind the prisoner to release his bonds. So swollen were his wrists, the rawhide could not be untied. He cut it away instead. Pain shot through Otah's hands and fingers as he tried to get the blood flowing again. Leaf was concerned and had begun massaging his wrists when Kardo strode up. "What is this?" he bellowed. "Who gave the order to release my prisoner?" Once again, one hand fingered the pouch that lay against his throat.

"It was I, *Chief* Spotted Hand!" the old man answered, staring down Kardo's look of contempt. "I know this young man," he continued. "He is no thief, unlike some whose name I could mention! His goods are to be brought to me immediately! I will keep them safe until they can be returned to him." Of course Otah understood none of these angry words but the expressions and gestures of the two men told him much. Leaf came close. Watching to make sure Kardo was not near, she whispered a brief account of what had happened. Then Spotted Hand spoke again. "Bring the young man to my house. He will live with me for as long as he wishes to remain in our camp." Leaf clapped her hands with joy and quickly interpreted for her brother. Still rubbing and wiggling his tingling fingers, Otah made a quick request. "My wolf is suffering," he pleaded desperately. "Let me go to him!" Leaf relayed the request to the chief, but was surprised at the old man's hesitation. After pondering the situation for several moments he replied. "He says," she interpreted, "that you may see to the animal's needs but that the wolf must be well away from our village by nightfall."

"That would please both Sand and me a great deal!" Otah grumbled as he followed them to the chief's house. The dome-shaped building was larger than most of the others in the village. The dirt floor was packed down and swept clean. Three skin-covered sleeping benches were spaced around he walls. A buffalo robe covered a raised platform that Otah assumed was for the chief alone. Unsure of just what was expected of him, he caught his sister's eye and asked in a soft voice, "Am I allowed to take food and water to the wolf now?" She put the question to the chief. After he had made a lengthy reply she repeated the answer. "You are to have food and water now, then release the wolf and take it a half-day's journey into the forest. Secure the animal there and return to us before dark. No one will bother you."

Otah tore into a slab of roasted meat, unaware that he was eating a portion of mastodon liver. It was the most wonderful food he had ever tasted, but of course he had never had opportunity to taste many different kinds of meat. He drank from a bowl which Leaf handed to him, thankful that though his fingers were still painful, he was able to hold the vessel without dropping it. He was hurrying as fast as he could in order to take care of his companion. He was surprised when Leaf asked a question. "May I help you with the wolf? Is it 'Sand' you call him? Animals and birds seem to like me. Do you remember that? I think I could make friends with that big wolf tied to that tree out there. Let me try." Otah was appalled. "You must never approach that animal!" he warned.

"Yes, I do remember that you seemed to have a certain way with the forest creatures, but believe me this is no *swimming crow* out there!" They both laughed as they remembered her long-ago pet, "crow swims". The chief wanted to know what was so funny, so Leaf began to tell the story. She never finished. Spotted Hand had fallen asleep!

"Did you have a chance to go through my things?" Otah asked.

"Yes, I believe everything of yours was still there." She named each item as he listened intently.

"There should have been one other thing," he said. "Did you find a small blue bead with a hole near the top?"

"No, nothing like that. Maybe it fell out of the hole in the pack. I turned it wrong side out to patch the hole for you, but there was no such bead. Maybe it fell out of the hole before we brought the pack to the chief's house."

Otah tried to control his anger. He remembered seeing the bead on the grass when Kardo first captured him. A suspicious thought began to form in his mind. The bead was not only beautiful, but very valuable as well. An idea of the jewel's possible whereabouts began to grow!

I'll need help releasing the wolf, as my hands are still too numb to deal with the binding. But remember to stay well back until I have him under control. We won't need to take water to him, as I'll lead him to the steam for a drink. If you have meat or fish, however, I can give this to him as we take our half-day's journey."

"Of course," she said, selecting a roasted fish from a birch bark box by her bed.

Sand whined a greeting as they approached, but he kept an eye on the smaller human with his master. The word had spread that something was happening. Nearly everyone was hurrying to the center of the village to see what was going on now. They stood watching from what they considered a safe distance from the tethered wolf. Of course Otah knelt by the animal and patted its head. This brought a chorus of *ooos and ahhhs* from the crowd, as never had such a thing been seen before. This young man from the Black Swamp must be a powerful shaman indeed!

"*Do not release that wolf!*" Kardo's shout caused a stir in the crowd. Leaf told her brother what had been said, but he hardly needed an explanation. Still gently rubbing the animal's neck, Otah stood and faced the glowering man, but Leaf answered for him. "Chief Spotted Hand has ordered that it be led far into the forest, and I am to help release the animal." Kardo made no reply, but stood with head back and arms folded across his chest. Anger seemed to surround him like a dark cloud.

Otah spoke. "I will hold Sand back until you have untied the rope from the post. Do not get closer!" She pretended to not understand, and took a few steps forward.

"I think, my brother, that you do not give enough credit to my gift with animals," Leaf said in the Clan's tongue. Extending her hand, palm down, she stepped slowly up to the wolf, making soothing sounds with her tongue. "*NO!*" Otah shouted, but he was too late. Sand lunged forward, sending Otah sprawling. Leaf leaped back but Sand's fangs had ripped into the calf of her right leg. She screamed and tore herself loose just as Otah grabbed Sand's collar and yanked him back. There was no time for goodbyes. Spear throwers were being readied and Kardo was shouting orders but the crowd was in the way for an attempt at a dart cast. Half running, Otah dragged the animal into the forest and kept going.

Crying in pain, Leaf limped back to the chief's house, where she called for the old woman to come and see to her wounds.

Kardo was striding back and forth before the crowd, using this latest happening as further proof that both the man and his wolf must be destroyed, and most of the Clansmen were quick to agree. The wolf's attack had been just what he needed to further prove that he was right and old Spotted Hand was wrong. Kardo felt confident that very soon now he would be made chief of the Clan, since the name he had given himself, "Kardo", meant *soon* in their language! There was one more thing that he must do. Finding the camp where the man would tie up his wolf would be no problem. Once he knew the place, who knew what might happen some dark night? A dreadful accident could befall both man and animal! No one would ever know what had happened. Only he, *Chief* Kardo, would know the truth, and of course he would never tell!

*   *   *

A simple leaf-covered shelter protected the wolf, and for the time he was content. Otah made the long trip every morning, bringing food. A brook nearby provided for both during the hot summer days. The man still set and checked his snares every day, which kept the wolf in plenty. Most of the time, Otah took his meals with Leaf and the chief.

He was rapidly making friends with the old man but Leaf's son was another matter. He tried to entice the boy by bringing him bright colored stones or other bits of material he thought might interest the lad, but this did not work. Finally one evening when Little Kardo played outside, Leaf explained the situation.

"He is a fine boy, and unlike me, a favorite of his father. As I told you before the man makes much of his son, but pays little attention to his learning. By this time Little Kardo should be able to do some hunting and fishing. Skill in tracking game should be taught, as well as proper use of the spear thrower. Before he lost his sight completely, Spotted Hand had made the boy a miniature atlatl and showed him how to use it. The child loves his father in spite of this lack of training. He can sense that you and Kardo hate each other, which bothers him, but it is not the main reason for his refusal to make friends with you."

"And what *is* the main reason then?"

"He fears that you will take me away when you leave, and he will be without his mother."

"But I have no intention of . . ."

"I know that, but he does not. Perhaps he will change with time. Keep on trying."

Their conversation was suddenly interrupted by a series of shouts from a running hunter who came charging into the village. More shouts erupted from the houses as people rushed outside. "What is going on?" Otah shouted. Leaf did not answer, as she was busy helping Spotted Hand dress himself in his finest clothing. Speaking urgently as she secured his feather hat, she replied that mastodons had been sighted several days' journey to the north! "By the great water" she said as all four emerged from the dwelling.

"The great water?" Otah asked as they hurried the old chief to the center of the village.

"Water! Water as far as one can see on a clear day! And those who know say that no dugout canoe or raft of wood can cross it after paddling for many days!" Otah did not wish to insult his sister so he said nothing, but he didn't believe it.

"I can tell that you think this is a child's story but it is true. Perhaps you will be asked to go on the hunt for the creatures. Then you will see that I speak the truth. The hunters will leave in the morning, as we must have all that these big animals can provide for us. Winter will come sooner than we think."

"But of what use could I possibly be? I have very few weapons, not even a very good atlatl."

"They will use people like you for *decoys!*" she said sadly. "You will need no weapons for that! The job of a decoy is to entice the beasts to charge, then keep ahead of them until they are lured into an area of swamp or quicksand. Once mired in the muck they can be surrounded and killed. It is dangerous work and many have died when forced to do it."

Looking in Otah's direction, the old chief spoke quietly to his young helper. Leaf quickly interpreted for her brother. "My chief wishes for you to go on this hunt. He knows, however that there are some who wish it otherwise. Therefore you are to follow a half-day behind the hunters. Tell no one of this." The entire village was filling the common area by now and Spotted Hand attempted to draw himself up to address them.

"My people," he began, "Mastodons have been located to the north by the big water, just as the Old Woman has predicted. Like many of you I had thought the great animals were all gone, but she dreamed these last ones for us. *She has the gift!* Today and tonight we must prepare. All men and boys must be gone with first light. It is with great sadness that I must stay behind. My presence would only be a hindrance on the trail."

"And who will then be named *leader* of this hunt?" It was Kardo who spoke so rudely to his chief. He stood as he often did with his head back and arms folded across his chest. Spotted Hand turned his blind eyes slowly, and almost seemed to see the haughty young man. He paused for several moments. "*You* will lead," he said quietly, "and Stump will be second in command."

"*Stump?*" Kardo snapped. "Why should he be given authority? He is hardly half as tall as I. He will be a poor leader because he is too kind! One in command, even as second in command, must be strong. Orders must be instantly obeyed, and anyone who differs should feel the sting of a blow! Also, you know that he and I are not friends. He tries to entice the people to disregard my authority! *Mine! Their next chief!*"

Kardo watched with obvious disgust as Leaf led the tottering old man back to his house. "Observe your *chief!*" Kardo said with scathing contempt. He said it loud enough that Spotted Hand and all the villagers could not help but hear.

Otah had watched the meeting take place but stayed in the background, not sure what was expected of him. He was surprised when Leaf caught his eye and motioned him to follow as they entered the chief's lodge. He ambled along until he could duck into the large building without being seen. The chief was seated on his bench, head down and arms hanging, while Leaf was rubbing some sort of concoction on her wounded leg. Sand had bitten deep, but it seemed that no bones were broken. Still the torn flesh was raw and painful. Her brother was stricken with guilt. Had he never brought the wolf into the village she would not need to be dealing with this painful gash. He was about to tell her how sorry he felt when the chief indicated that he wanted to speak. The old man tried to straighten himself and assume some dignity. "Sit here," he said indicating a bobcat skin at his feet as Leaf interpreted. "Go now and return to your wolf friend. Do not return to our village until the sun is well up tomorrow, and the men have left. Come to my house then. I have much to discuss with you. Now go away. I am tired now."

Sand met him with anxious whining and posturing. It was clear that the animal was unhappy with their present arrangement. As they headed toward the brook that flowed nearby, Otah did his best to soothe the wolf. He had brought meat and part of a fish, which they shared, then both drank from the stream. With Sand on a long leash they followed the stream until they found Otah's snares. Once again all were empty so he left them where they were.

"Sand, my friend, we will be traveling very soon, so you must endure this unpleasantness until tomorrow. Then we will once again be free to hunt and track together. We will be following the people you hate, but well back from their trail. What will happen when the hunters find their quarry I don't know, but I promise you that not much longer will we need to be apart. Have you ever seen a mastodon? They are large. *Very large!* Their weight is more than twenty men together. Their great long teeth can crush and kill, and their noses are longer than I am tall. They can *hit* with their long noses too! I saw two of these when I spent a short time with these same Mastodon Hunters. I was but a lad then, but never will I forget the fight that happened when one of the big animals was mired down in the muck."

They sat and rested for a while. Sand was soon asleep, content with a full belly and the sound of his master's voice. Otah wondered what the chief would tell him in the morning. Who could tell what was to become of them?

When the sun rose Otah busied himself taking down Sand's shelter. Leading the wolf along the stream, he was not surprised to find no game in his snares, as several animals had been caught and wolf scent was making others wary. Otah was not too concerned, as it seemed possible that the two of them might be tolerated in the village once the hunters returned. Of course Sand would have to be tied well away from the people, but more and more the wolf seemed to accept being tethered. The man suspected that the animal's crooked and painful hind leg could be part of the reason.

They both ate what remained of the food Leaf had been providing, drank deeply from the brook, and started back.

They traveled slowly as Otah wanted to be sure that Kardo and the rest were well away from the village. There was time to skirt the edges of the Black Swamp. The place held a strange, almost sinister beauty, and Otah never tired of the vistas that were visible from every ridge. Far away to the north and west lay a flat expanse of pools, reeds, and mud flats. Birds of every kind rose crying at their approach. Nests were still filled with eggs, but even Sand spurned these. They were close to hatching, so if broken, their odor alone would be enough to stop both man and beast! Beaver lodges dotted the surface, and Otah made note of these, trying to fix their location in his memory. If ever he was back to this place when the swamp was frozen hard these busy animals would be fair game.

As they neared the village Otah found a shady spot on the bank of a creek. The wolf could get water easily, and having eaten well that morning would probably sleep most of the day, tied up as usual. Otah hiked steadily on until the village was in sight. He stood silently, partly hidden in the trees, and watched the camp. It was soon apparent that the men were indeed gone. He smiled as he noted the women and small children seated comfortably in the shade, enjoying a holiday from the drudgery of their lives. He began singing a nonsense song as he came into the village. He did not wish to frighten them, but even so, several of the women grabbed their little ones and disappeared. Walking slowly and singing away seemed to calm them somewhat, but he noticed each one looked fearfully behind him, watching for the wolf!

Leaf and her son appeared from the chief's house and led Otah quickly to the dwelling. All three slipped inside, closing the door flap behind them. Otah stood still until his eyes had adjusted to the gloom. Spotted Hand was seated on his robe-covered bench, a red fox pelt draped over his skinny shoulders. He was asleep. Leaf motioned for silence and began preparing food for her brother. Whispering did not seem to waken the chief, so they were able to spend a long overdue happy time together.

"How is your leg healing?" he asked. She unwrapped a blood-stained scrap of badger skin and extended her leg. Otah gasped at the sight. An ugly swelling partly hid four deep gashes where Sand's teeth had sunk deep. "Does it give much pain?" he asked, gently probing the area with a finger and thumb. Her quick intake of breath at his touch told him more than words. "I think you must get the poison out!" he whispered urgently. "I had a similar wound from Sand when I captured him. My arm was big and bad. I had to use the spear to lance it! Would you wish for me to treat you in that way too?"

"No! Oh *NO!*" She hissed. "The old woman will be here soon to do what is necessary. She is a healer, but many think her touched and will not allow her to help them. She has promised to come this morning but sometimes she forgets."

Almost at that moment the door flap rustled and the old woman appeared. She paid no attention to either Otah or the chief but began digging through the contents of a small pouch. At the healer's bidding Leaf sat on the floor, her leg propped up on a piece of firewood. "Her name is Geet," his sister stated in Otah's language. Still the old one paid no heed. She mumbled and talked to herself constantly, but neither Leaf nor Otah was fooled by her act. They played along however. Let the crone do as she wished if it made her happy! At last she found what she was rooting around for. Triumphantly her wrinkled hand shot out and stopped almost under Otah's nose. She held a small, twisted bundle of some dark plant material tied up with sinew. Still pushing it at him she made noisy sniffing sounds, clearly indicating that he was to smell the concoction. Otah was elated! He knew that smell! Pushing her aside, he dug into his own pack which Spotted Hand had saved for him. He drew out the decorated pouch left to him by the people at the flint quarries and thrust it into her hands. As soon as it was opened, Geet, the healer, forgot to act crazy. She smiled wide and spoke rapidly to Leaf who translated. "Thank you, young man. You do know how to please an Elder of this Clan!"

"Where is that *wolf?*" They all jumped at the sudden question. Spotted Hand had awakened but had given them no indication of it. Otah assumed that the old chief learned a great deal that he would not have otherwise known by pretending sleep. Casting unseeing eyes toward the healer, he said a word in greeting. She grumbled some sort of unintelligible reply, but both Otah and Leaf caught the knowing look that passed from Geet to the old one. She was a clever conspirator!

"I asked, *where is that wolf?*" This time the chief's voice was surprisingly loud and strong for one of his age.

"Please do not worry, Chief Spotted Hand," Otah answered quickly. "He is tied up well away from the village. No one need fear the animal."

"*I* do not fear that beast," said the chief loudly. "Bring it to me and I will kill it for you. Never should such a cowardly and cruel animal be allowed to live! I have killed *two* wolves in my youth, and would gladly make it three!"

Otah was about to respond in anger but Leaf's hand on his arm stopped him. "Yes, perhaps it is so," he replied instead.

They had nearly forgotten the healer. When they turned to her she was chewing away on an impressive mouthful of the material from Otah's pouch. "*Tobac!*" she muttered, the brown juices running down her chin. She grabbed her old bundle and threw it contemptuously into a corner. Shaking the beautifully decorated pouch in Otah's face she mumbled away, a happy smile on her wrinkled face. The "tobac" Otah had given her was obviously superior to what she was used to chewing. Turning to Leaf, who still sat waiting, she roughly yanked her wounded leg into a shaft of sunlight from the smoke hole. From her sack she selected a thin needle of smoothed bone. After looking it over critically, she spat some juice on it, turned, and without warning drove it deep into the point of infection. Leaf could not suppress a scream of pain, which did not seem to bother Geet at all. Rolling her cud around in her mouth, she spat a gob directly on the bleeding incision she had made. This she patted and probed until it was worked well into the torn flesh. Leaf fell back in a faint, but the healer only gathered up her equipment and prepared to leave. She retrieved the bundle of weeds she had thrown away and thrust them at Otah, meanwhile keeping a tight fist on the little pouch of the good tobac. She had made a good trade!

Leaf became conscious after a few moments, sat up and bound her leg with clean skins, the pain having lessened considerably. Convinced that there was nothing he could do to help his sister, Otah was anxious to hear what Spotted Hand had to tell. He must know why it was that Kardo had such hatred for him. "Chief spotted Hand," he began courteously, "you said earlier that you would tell me why I am so unwelcome in this village. I am anxious to hear what you have to say."

When Leaf had translated, the chief leaned back against the wall and closed his eyes. "I am very tired now," he murmured. "I have been on a hunt of four days without food or rest. Now I must sleep. We will speak again at a later time. Talk to your sister, I will not hear." He closed his eyes and allowed his old head to fall forward on his chest.

Otah said nothing. He had figured out what game the chief was playing! Spotted Hand wanted to know what this young man *really* thought of him. Both he and Geet, the healer, though full of years, were very shrewd! Otah smiled at his sister and began to speak "Do you remember when father and I returned to our hut after the visit to the Mastodon Hunters?" Leaf answered that she did. "Now I wish to learn the Mastodon Hunters' way of speaking. You can translate everything I say into your language." Otah strongly suspected that in this way the wily old chief would hear and remember every word! "Remember Leaf, how our father spoke of Chief Spotted Hand? He told us that never had he met a wiser, more generous, or braver man. Yes, father was very impressed with the Mastodon Hunters' famous chief! I too recall what a great man he was, and still *is!* What a pleasure to even be allowed to *know* such a one!"

A gentle cough and much batting of the eyes made it appear that Spotted Hand had just awakened. He yawned mightily and smiled. "Ah, what a nice sleep," he said, gathering his robes around him. "I am well rested now. What was it again that you desire to know?"

Otah smiled at his sister, safe in the knowledge that the man's blindness made it safe to do so. "I would know all you can tell me of the happenings for which Kardo has hatred in his heart for me, for I knew him when we were boys at your old village. Nothing happened back then to cause this attitude. He treated me badly then but I thought little of it, as I was a stranger and much younger than he."

"I will tell all of it quickly. You must listen with care, then be off to follow our men. Take your wolf with you, but do not allow it to approach the hunters. It would be better if you would let me kill that animal *now!* I may be old, and my skill with the atlatl diminished, but I can still hit a wolf which is tied to a tree!" Without waiting for a reply he continued.

"It is a long story but I will make it a short one." Leaf was hard put to interpret fast enough to keep the chief's words flowing, but her former language was rapidly coming back to her. "Your father was badly injured by a bear, as you will recall. Yes, you should remember that, since it was because *you* lost the atlatl that would have killed the bear! You were a foolish boy then."

Once again Otah felt the nearly-forgotten shame of his long ago carelessness. Having lost their only atlatl, they had been forced to attack the bear with spears. His father's smashed elbow had not healed well, and it was not long until he went to the Other Place. Otah hated to remember it.

"As you will recall," the chief continued, "your father stayed with us until he was well enough to travel. One night, unable to sleep for the pain, he was wandering in the village when he saw Kardo, then called Fox, a young man at the time, enter the Shaman's hut while the medicine man was away on a vision quest. That arrogant and proud young man had stolen the divining bones he knew were kept there! Your father reported this to me at daylight, but by then Kardo had hidden the sacred things. He denied taking them, and even accused your father of being the thief. I suspected the truth but there was nothing I could do. Had proof been available Kardo would have been banished. We Mastodon Hunters despise theft above all other crimes. Do you remember how that braggart treated you when you first arrived here? He called you a thief, hoping the Clan would either have you killed or banished. The fact that you carried such beautiful flints and other goods helped his accusations. Kardo is afraid that your father had told all of this to you before he went to the Other Place. Did he?"

"No, he did not," Otah replied, shaken by such a tale. " I will tell Kardo that I know *nothing* of this as soon as I see him."

"*Never!*" Spotted Hand fairly shouted. "First of all he will not believe you.

Secondly, he will know that I was the one who told you this story. The nights are dark and Kardo has many who obey him. Since he craves the role of chief, he will have me killed. You must say *nothing!* Do you understand?"

Otah promised that he would keep the secret.

Spotted Hand was falling asleep, this time for real. Otah gently shook the man's shoulder. He needed advice on how to handle the danger from Kardo and those who followed the man. "I have nothing to tell you," the chief said sleepily." Go and find our hunters, and take your sister and her son with you."

Leaf gasped in surprise. "But who will see to your needs my chief?" she asked.

"Send the old woman. She will serve me well, as we understand each other! One more thing, Tak-O Tay," he said, using the name by which he had once known Otah. *"Kill that wolf!* Now go away. I am tired."

*   *   *

Otah and Sand led the way. Leaf and her son followed well behind, careful to keep the man and his animal in sight. All were laden with well-provisioned back packs, even Little Kardo, who proudly tramped along, a small bundle secured by a trump line across his forehead. Such travel arrangements were necessary to protect Leaf and her son from the wolf, but conversation therefore was impossible. When evening came and Sand had been securely tied a distance away they made camp. The boy had tired in the afternoon, but despite the pain from her injured leg, Leaf had managed to carry him, as well as both their packs. She was a strong woman, accustomed to hard work.

They talked until the half moon was high in the sky.

Three more days' travel showed that the hunters were not far ahead. Otah was not about to show himself to the Clan, as Kardo would certainly find a reason to harm him.

Patience. . . patience . . .plan. . .

With Leaf's capable help he prepared a camp for her and Little Kardo. Situated on a ridge above the edge of the swamp they would be quite comfortable for as long as Otah might be gone. She and her boy would gather edible greens, fish in the stream that flowed along the base of the ridge, and even set snares for small game. They would hardly need to resort to the preserved food in their packs. Otah was satisfied that they would be safe, but he cautioned them about leaving food scraps near their camp. He further insisted that they keep a fire burning before their shelter; even though the weather was very warm.

"Where are you going? Do you leave us here to be eaten by bears?" Little Kardo showed his hatred for his uncle, making no effort to disguise his feelings. Otah had tried to make friends with the lad during their evenings together but nothing had changed. He was, Otah thought grimly, certainly his father's son!

"You will not be eaten by bears or anything else!" Otah snapped. "You must be a man now, as your mother may need protection. You will be *chief* of this small village." The boy expanded his little chest and folded his arms in such a perfect imitation of his father that both Otah and Leaf burst out laughing. Little Kardo stalked off angrily, but Otah noted that the boy was careful not to go too far from the camp!

"I am sorry that my son will not be friendly toward you," Leaf sighed. "I have spoken to him about you whenever I've had the chance, but he still fears that you will take me away."

"Don't worry," Otah said, "time may make a difference, but at any rate I will not be with you Mastodon Hunters much longer."

"What *do* you intend, my brother? After you meet the hunters will you go again to our village? My husband will try to kill you, just as Chief Spotted Hand warned."

"Truly I don't know," Otah replied sadly. "You heard him give an order about my companion. I cannot kill him. I *cannot!* If I return to the village I would be faced with that order. Still I am beginning to feel I must somehow clear our father's name. *He was no thief!* You know that and I know it. Also your husband has accused me of the same crime, and people are listening to him! One way or another I will need to be in your village again. But now I will find the hunters and see how they proceed. Then I may be able to decide what must be done."

"I see you are being patient and making plans. How well I remember our father telling us to always do that. Be careful! Find the hunters then decide." She and her son prepared for the night.

He adjusted his pack, untied the wolf and set out. The trail was clear and they traveled fast. As usual Sand fought the leash at first but soon settled into the march. They made no foolish attempts at "shortcuts" across the swamp! Traveling the ridge made for a roundabout route, but he had learned his lesson. Game was scarce on their trek, as the Mastodon Hunters' passage had scared them off, but this was of no concern for Otah. They carried sufficient dried food, and furthermore he was anxious to find the Clan.

Late on the third day Sand began to test the breeze, his nose pointed to the sky.

The man did the same and soon detected the smell of smoke. He slowed his pace and drew the wolf close on a short leash. It was apparent to both that the hunters had made camp not far ahead. Wisely, Otah settled himself under a low-lying cedar clump and waited for nightfall. He fed the wolf and chewed a little dried venison himself. Resting in the shade, the wolf soon fell asleep. Otah was unable, but tried to relax and preserve his strength. He was going to need it!

Resting, he wondered what was happening with the men he followed. Why were they in camp? Had the scouts' reports of Mastodons been wrong? An exaggeration? Had the great animals left the area? It seemed strange that the hunters were not moving against their quarry, but he still had much to learn about the methods necessary to kill these dangerous animals.

By now the sun was low in the sky. He tied the wolf's braided rawhide rope to the base of the cedar, secured his spear, and left. He needed enough light to travel quietly until the camp came into view, then he would hide until it was dark enough to approach the camp. Although he had been ordered to join the hunters, he knew Kardo would scorn anything Spotted Hand decreed.

"Am I being too cautious?" he asked himself. "Not at all!" Otah answered his own question. With Kardo in charge of the hunt he *had* to be careful. The danger was real!

He was close! In fact he almost blundered into a guard who was patrolling outside the clearing which held their temporary huts. He was not seen, but in scrambling under some brush he made so much noise that the guard turned and took a cautious step in his direction. Heart hammering, Otah willed his breathing to slow almost to a stop, having no doubt that Kardo had given orders that anyone finding him was to kill him on sight! The guard moved away, but not very far. He was a wise man who knew his job. Something was amiss and he would not let it go. Twilight was welcome as Otah continued to lie in hiding. He was almost convinced the guard was satisfied that there was no danger, when the man came walking purposefully toward Otah's hiding place. Two more steps and he would be found! It was time for action! Otah leaped out of the bushes with his spear at chest level, both hands gripping the weapon as he attacked the silhouette before him. He swung the spear at the shadow, bringing the butt up and forward. It connected hard across the man's cheek. He backed away and fell, his angry shout bringing answers from the camp. Torches were lighted as the hunters responded. Otah slid backward as quietly as he could. When he was several paces into the surrounding forest he had an inspiration. Tipping his head far back, he screamed out the best imitation he could make of the howl of a wolf. All action stopped as the men halted to listen in consternation. It was then that Otah and all the others heard it. From a half hour's journey to the south, Sand's full-throated answer came floating over the swamp!

Otah remained still in the darkness. While he could not understand the excited voices coming from the camp, he could imagine the guard's insistence that he had but narrowly missed death by a gigantic wolf! Perhaps even a *Spirit Wolf!*

Slipping silently away to the south, Otah could only marvel at the way his companion had, unknowingly perhaps, saved his life yet again! With the dawn the hunters would soon find his tracks, and no longer fearing a magic wolf, would be hot on his trail. He must release the wolf and get back to his sister and Little Kardo. Spying on the Clan was no longer an option, and furthermore he was sick of doing it! Now he must rely on Leaf's quick mind to placate the Mastodon Hunters, especially the one he had struck with his spear.

Making no effort at silence he floundered along in the dark forest. In no time he realized that he was completely lost. Clouds had covered the moon, and with no means of determining direction he could not even tell if he was headed the right way. "I had better *plan!*" he told himself. "I didn't use patience and planning when approaching their camp, so that is why I am in this predicament now!" He took two more steps and sank hip-deep in the swamp. Dragging himself to higher ground he sat and thought. Almost as a lightning bolt the answer struck him. Standing tall he threw his head back and howled with all his might. Nothing happened, so he did it again. Still nothing. His voice nearly gone, he tried once more. *There!* Faint but certain came an answering call.

He had wandered far to the east of his camp and the tied-up wolf. Confidence returning, he started out, finally heading in the right direction. Suddenly he slid to a stop as a terrible thought came to him. "What if. . . What *if*. . ." he groaned aloud, "that answer was not from Sand at all? I could be walking directly into a pack of *wild* wolves"! He had no choice however, for the night was far gone and he must get back to the wolf and then to his sister. Stumbling and crashing through the brush, he hurried along as best he was able. The howl cane again, much closer now. He felt sure that he recognized the power of Sand's call.

At last he broke into the small clearing and fell exhausted beside the whining wolf. He would sleep now, but early in the morning be off to meet Leaf and the child. He was sure the Mastodon Hunters would be coming, but following his midnight ramblings would slow them considerably.

The sun was shining in his face when Sand's growls wakened him. The Clan was not far off! With shaking fingers he untied Sand from the tree and ran off. The way was clear to Leaf's camp, and as soon as he smelled smoke form their fire he tied Sand to a tree, threw him some meat, and dashed into their camp.

They were not there!

In a frenzy he examined the tracks which were everywhere. No way could he tell which way they had gone or how long ago. Drinking feverishly from the brook he shouted as loudly as he could. "Leaf! *Leaf!* I'm back. Come quickly, we must run!" the forest stood silent and sinister around him.

About to cry out for his sister again, he was shocked when an atlatl dart sank quivering into a tree only inches from his head! A command stopped him at once. Although he could not understand the words the implication was clear enough. He stood still, waiting. Kardo came striding into Leaf's camp, atlatl poised for another throw. Otah knew of the skill the man had, so any attempt to run would surely mean a dart in his back.

Several more hunters joined Kardo and working quickly, once again bound his hands and shoved him to the ground. Otah noticed that one of them had an ugly bruise on his cheek and one eye was blackened. That one fairly bristled with hate.

Kardo gave quick orders and his men began scouring the area for tracks. Otah knew what they were after. They were searching for wolf tracks! Sand was in danger! Thankfully Otah knew that no such tracks would be found, for he had taken care to keep the animal a good distance away from Leaf's camp. Still it would not take long until they would follow his own back trail straight to his companion.

The bruised Clansman squatted down until his face was a handbreadth from Otah's. He snarled some angry words in their tongue, then without warning smashed a knotted fist into Otah's face. Blood gushed from his flattened nose as the other hunters laughed and applauded. The angry man then drew a leg back for a kick, but a scream stopped him.

It was Leaf! She ran into the clearing, dragging Little Kardo by the hand. Racing up to her husband she rattled off a barrage of angry words. Kardo sneered at her, on his face a scowl of derision. Little Kardo ran to his father and embraced a leg. The man jerked his leg back and sent his son sprawling in the dirt. His eyes followed Leaf as she ran to her stricken brother. While wiping the blood from his face she spoke quickly, asking what he needed and how she could help. She no longer attempted to hide her old language from her husband, sure that he had always known that they were brother and sister anyway.

"My wolf!" he said. "I must release him and get far away before both of us are dead!"

Then Kardo roared an order. Leaf told her brother that her husband was ordering that man and wolf be brought into camp, but kept under control. "But why does he want *that?* What does he plan to do?" Leaf spoke a few sentences to Kardo, who barked an angry reply. She turned to her brother, a stricken look on her face. "What is it? What did he say?" His sister was fighting tears as she relayed the order.

"You and the wolf are to return to the hunting camp. He says he has a special job for you and the animal when they confront the mastodons. Oh Otah, I know what that means. You will be the *decoys!* As I told you before you are to taunt the animals into charging, then keep running ahead to lead them into the swamp where one can be killed."

"Yes, I know how they conduct these hunts. Father and I took part in one when I was a boy. Don't worry about me, as this may be my chance to escape. Sand and I work well together, and have been through some dangerous times. *We will survive!*"

There was no time for further talk. Rapid orders were given, and they were soon ready to depart. Otah was shocked when Kardo indicated that Leaf and Little Kardo were once again to travel with them. This seemed unusual, but there was no time, nor any use to inquire. They untied his hands as Leaf interpreted the rapid orders from her husband. Otah was to bring the wolf, keeping it under control. Two hunters were assigned to watch, but far enough away to be clear of danger from the animal, and Leaf was to stay near to relay any commands. This was good news for Otah, as it might give him a chance to make some plans, since none of the hunters knew the language. Pitifully, Little Kardo did his best to keep up with his father, but all knew he would have to be carried soon, and Leaf was limping again.

*   *   *

There was quite a stir when Otah and Sand came into the Mastodon Hunters' camp. The wolf's fur stood up along his back and he growled constantly, looking from one human to another. Otah kept the wolf on such a short leash that it was practically choking. No one approached closer than ten paces, afraid of the teeth prominently displayed with every snarl. The man and his wolf were banished from the camp, forced to make their own rude shelter many paces away. This suited both well, but not the two guards hunkered down close to keep watch.

Leaf arrived after sunset, bringing food and a skin of water. The guards made no complaint when Otah left the wolf to meet his sister. Brother and sister sat on the ground very near the guards, speaking without fear in their own language.

Leaf told him what was to transpire. The mastodons, three of them, according to old Geet's dreaming, were possibly the very last of the species ever to inhabit the Black Swamp. These great beasts had found an area rich in young cedar trees on which they were browsing contentedly. The hunters were now waiting for favorable winds which might help conceal their approach. Leaf's next remarks were terrifying. "The hunters are talking among themselves, and I listened. They evidently feel that it doesn't matter what I, only a stupid *woman,* have heard! The animals are feeding quite close to a bog, which is exactly what the Clan will use to trap one of them. You and your wolf will be forced to taunt the mastodons into a charge.

"I *know* all this! You have told me before. Not only that, but I even took part in such a hunt while I was still a boy!"

"Then you are going to hear it again! Your life is in danger! You must run ahead of them into the quagmire. If at least one mastodon follows it will soon be floundering in the muck, surrounded, kept from escape, and killed. You and the wolf must cause this to happen just as they plan."

"And what if I *don't?*"

"Then you will be speared, but not to death. You and the wolf will be tied to a stake and tortured with fire. The wolf will be eaten! I *know* this will happen, as I heard them talking!"

"If only Chief Spotted Hand was here," Otah groaned. "He remembers me and the way I helped his Clan in those days long ago. Yes, he would protect *me*, but not the wolf! It is of no concern however, he is not here. It will be up to me to think of some way to stay alive. I am a fast runner. Remember the races we used to run as children? Perhaps I can stay ahead of their charge and still lure the animal into the bog. Surely if I were successful Kardo and the others would be grateful and spare my life."

"You are wrong, my brother. Kardo wants your death. He is expecting the mastodons to do it, but if not, believe me he will take your life himself. Sadly, I can tell that since your arrival in our village he looks suspiciously at *me* as well. He can't understand what we say to each other, and this infuriates him. As father said, we must do some careful planning, and *soon!*"

Anxious to change the painful subject, Otah asked her how Kardo had managed to abduct her.

"You had hardly left on your hunt when Kardo came stalking right into our house. He must have been watching for you to leave. He seemed nice enough at first, and made gestures that he was hungry, so I gave him food and water. He was proud of the little pouch he had tied around his neck, and held it out for me to touch, but never took it off. I was so young then that I thought it was the most beautiful thing I had ever seen. It was beaded all over and of the softest ermine skin. You may have noticed it, because he still wears the thing."

"He acted nervous, jumping up often to open the door flap and look all around. I know now that he was afraid that you might decide to return. All at once he grabbed my arm and jerked me around. I screamed but he only laughed and forced me to prepare a full pack. It was heavy but he made no effort to help. Carrying only his weapons he headed west. I threw the pack down and started to run toward the river, the direction I thought you had taken. He soon caught me and twisted my arm so badly it hurt for days. The moment we left our clearing he pushed me ahead and began using a leafy branch to obliterate our tracks."

"At the Mastodon Hunters' camp he was nice enough at first, although he paid little attention to my needs. Then shortly after our son was born he began to court a second wife. I didn't care! Another woman could help with the work, and he no longer showed any affection for me anyway."

"It was about that time that he ordered me to move into Chief Spotted Hand's house. He told everyone that he did this only to help the chief in his old age. I soon saw that what he really wanted was someone to spy on the chief. He was anxious to know when Spotted Hand was planning to name a new chief, and who it might be."

"So now you know how all of this came to be."

Morning brought a steady east wind. The hunters were up and about at first light but they made no move to begin the hunt, as it appeared that Kardo wanted to make sure the wind remained favorable. Finally satisfied, he ordered the guards to bring Otah and Sand into the camp. He pulled Leaf forward and ordered her to translate his words. Otah tried to look confused, but of course his sister had told him over and over what was expected.

The hunters headed east, but kept the man and the wolf well back from the main hunting party. These two would remain concealed until forced to attract the Mastodons' attention. Otah had done his best to think of some plan, but since nothing had occurred to him, it appeared that he could only do as he was forced and hope that some opportunity might arise at the last minute.

In late afternoon the Clan advanced silently, the sound of the animals' feeding plainly heard. Using hand signals only, Kardo positioned his men in a half-circle west of the animals. With a look of pure hatred he motioned Otah and Sand forward, as nearby hunters made a wide berth around the wolf. It was good that they did!

Kardo gave instructions to Leaf, who passed them on to her brother. The plan was simple enough. A deep bog lay east of the animals, perhaps three hundred paces beyond them. Kardo's cruel smile was not lost on Otah as he eased his way forward, still staying in heavy cover. Sand didn't growl or whine, seeming to sense that these huge creatures would be better left alone. Otah feltthe same way! Rising from a crouch behind a screen of blackberry briars, he had his first good look at the mastodons. It was enough to chill his blood! There were three, two adults and a half-grown calf. Using their tusks and trunks they were calmly crushing down the cedars to get at the tender morsels at the top. Otah recalled his encounter with the forest buffalo. He had thought that animal to be the largest there was. By comparison the mastodons, even the baby, made the buffalo seem small as the fawn of a deer! Although Otah remembered these creatures from his time with the Clan when he was a youth, he had forgotten the sheer size of the animals.

He and his father had lived in the Mastodon Hunters' village for many days. Proudly he recalled how he had alerted the hunters of an unseen second mastodon which could have caused great harm. It was then that Chief Spotted Hand had named him "Tak-o-tay, which meant "flying feet", because his swift running had undoubtedly saved some lives.

Suddenly a fist-sized rock slammed into his back. Kardo had risen from hiding and thrown the stone. Furiously he made gestures that clearly meant that the man and wolf should get moving. Otah gripped his spear and rose. He was not surprised that he had been allowed to carry the weapon, as the Clansmen knew he could do little to use it against their superior numbers.

Sand surprised him by staying close to his master. The tawny sand-colored body actually brushed against the man's leg, and the animal's obvious terror did nothing to assure the man. "A *plan!*" he told himself desperately. "There must be a way to come out of this alive, but what is it?"

Another stone ripped through the leaves, but missed its target. The youngest beast swung his shaggy head in Otah's direction, its short, juvenile tusks pointing directly at him and Sand. An adult, undoubtedly the mother, stopped feeding, and raised her massive trunk. An ear-splitting blast of sound shook the area as she trumpeted an alarm. Otah unhooked Sand's collar, patted the animal's head, and dashed into the open. Sand was running too, instinctively heading toward the youngest animal. Otah was once again earning his name of "flying feet" as he flew past the startled animals. Sand was harassing the smallest animal, nipping at its feet and dodging the flailing trunk. The mother trumpeted again and spun to the defense of her young. Despite their size there was nothing slow about these creatures!

As the man ran for his life the other adult gave chase, fortunately directly toward the bog. In an astonishing leap, Otah sailed over a fallen tree and landed running hard. The mastodon was gaining! There was no way he could reach the pool of muck before it was on him! Gasping and panting he was suddenly shocked to see a sand-colored blur at his heels. The wolf turned with bared teeth and confronted the charging mastodon. The animal whipped its trunk up and out, the end curling around the wolf's middle. With hardly a pause it threw Sand high and away, into the forest. This brief distraction was hardly enough, but Otah was able to gain a short distance ahead. Only one continued to pursue him, the other shielding her young. Otah reached the slippery edge of the bog and plunged in. The bottom provided just enough purchase for a man, but not for the behemoth that followed. As he floundered forward, the bottom became even softer, and he fell. The fall saved his life! As the mastodon sank into the ooze, one tusk just barely grazed the man's shoulder. Finally realizing the danger it was in, the animal forgot the man entirely. It thrashed about, its trunk whirling in every direction, but there was nothing to grasp. It trumpeted savagely, but the other two animals, frightened by the sounds of terror, lumbered away into the forest.

Otah wriggled cautiously away from the struggling animal. The muck clung to his feet and legs, making progress almost impossible, but slowly, very slowly, he was moving out of danger. Finally he was able to push one foot down deep, searching for ground solid enough to support him. Finding none he did the same with the other leg. The worst horror he had ever felt caused an anguished scream. There seemed to be *no* hard bottom. In fact it was as if the bog had no bottom at all!

Quicksand!

Otah's waist was slowly disappearing as he sank deeper into the oozing dark sludge. He screamed again as he saw Kardo come striding toward him. Waving his spear wildly with his one free hand, Otah tried to summon the hunter, but that cruel man stopped well clear of the bog and *laughed!* Otah knew he was about to die. His mind raced crazily as the brackish liquid crawled steadily higher on his body. "What has happened to Sand?" he asked himself desperately. "And where is my sister?" As if to answer that question, Leaf came flying toward him. She had grabbed up Sand's rawhide collar and leash from the spot where her brother had left it. After two agonizingly slow tries she managed to cast one end close enough for Otah to catch and hold. But even pulling with all her strength she made no progress. Sobbing in fear and frustration she implored the hunters to come to her aid, but Kardo roared an order. No one was to help! Things were happening just as he had hoped. In a few more minutes he would no longer need to fear this threat from his past. But ignoring their leader, Stump and another man pushed her aside and grabbed the rope. Even with their combined strength it was all they could do to drag the man free of the quicksand's suction. They left him lying on the bank, shaking and gasping for breath.

There was no more time for Otah's troubles. They would all be needed to finally kill the mastodon and begin the butchering.

Leaf hurried to find clean water. She began washing the smelly goo from his legs and feet. Little Kardo strutted about, his miniature atlatl aimed at the still struggling mastodon. The animal trumpeted again and again, causing much concern for the hunters, as they feared the other beasts might come to its aid. They peered anxiously into the forest where the other two had gone. None returned, so it was time to do the killing, a grisly business, but they were used to it. The mastodon continued thrashing around in the muck but found no footing there. The hunters squatted around the area, well clear of the animal's tusks and trunk, prepared to wait as long as it took for the beast to tire.

Kardo had other ideas. With sharp commands he ordered the hunters to attack before the animal could sink even deeper into the bog. He was right in this, for there was absolutely no way they would be able to drag the monster free of the bog after it was killed. Already it was almost half submerged, but if they acted fast there would be more than enough meat for the coming winter.

Spears and atlatls ready, they ringed the mastodon and prepared to shoot the lethal darts. Little Kardo gave them a chuckle as he readied his tiny missile and made the very first cast. The dart bounced off the mastodon's thick hide, but the hunters cheered as if it had been a killing shot!

The Clan began its necessary work. Their darts plunged deep, but it would take many more to cause the suffering creature's death. By evening the animal was clearly dying. Its trumpeting was pathetically weak and it had stopped trying to get free, but its trunk was still a menace. The hunters were careful to stay clear.

Morning found the huge animal's sides heaving with its effort to breathe. There was no doubt that the darts were doing their work. Left alone the animal would eventually die of blood loss, but it still lived and continued to sink deeper and deeper.

Kardo came striding up, carrying Otah's stabbing spear which he had picked up from the spot where Otqh had dropped it. Otah had slept all night not far from the battle scene, and was still sleeping when the angry would-be chief kicked him hard in the side. Otah jerked awake and scrabbled away from another kick aimed at his head. Leaf hurried up, Little Kardo in tow. Kardo was speaking, his voice harsh and menacing. "He says that you have been chosen to administer the killing blows," Leaf told him. "It must be done immediately, as the beast continues to sink into the mire. Before long it will be impossible to do the butchering."

"And just *who* did the *choosing*, I wonder?" Otah growled with an angry glance at the pompous man. "Both you and Chief Spotted Hand were right. He wants me dead, and unless I miss my guess he may soon get his wish."

Kardo jammed the spear's blade deep into the sandy soil dangerously close to Otah's throat. He gestured angrily at the suffering mastodon and prepared to kick again. Otah scrambled erect and yanked the spear from the ground. For a moment their eyes met in mutual hatred. Otah caressed the beautifully crafted shaft so familiar to him and continued to face his enemy. Kardo quickly stepped back, aware of the murderous look in Otah's eyes. His command brought three hunters running, spears ready to defend the hunt leader. Otah backed off, only with great difficulty controlling his temper. "Ask that brute how I am to do this," he told Leaf, peering nervously at the still living monster. Leaf conferred with Kardo but he refused to answer.

Stimp, second in command on the hunt and no favorite of their arrogant leader, answered instead. "Tell him," the man said calmly, "that there is but one way to do this. To approach through the bog would only mean death in the quicksand. Your brother must leap onto the animal's back and use the spear many times! I am not confident that this can be done without great harm or even death! It is dangerous and foolish but there is nothing I can do to change Kardo's order. He's the hunt master and must be obeyed. I am sorry."

With Leaf translating, Otah shook his head. "What if I refuse this insane proposition?" The hunters did not reply for a long moment, all of them clustered about, watching and waiting. Otah asked again. "What will happen to me if I don't do this? I have no desire to end my life in this quicksand!"

"We will spear you *to death!*" Kardo roared.

After translating, Leaf was weeping softly, afraid to meet her brother's eyes.

There was nothing she could do, as on an expedition like this one she must agree with Stump. She turned away, fairly dragging Little Kardo along. The boy protested violently, as he wanted to see the stranger die!

Without a word Otah circled the bog and its victim. He was hoping for a way to kill the mastodon with little danger to himself, but there was no way! There were two mutually dangerous problems; first the swamp and its quicksand, then the still angrily lashing trunk of the wounded beast.

Patience. . . patience. . . plan. . .

"I'm sorry father," he muttered. "*I* have patience, but these Clansmen have none! Also, I have no plan, none at all!" Suddenly a curious thing happened. Facing almost certain death by one means or another he found himself thinking of old Chief Spotted Hand. Otah almost smiled at the memory. "'Tak-O-Tay' he called me. 'Flying Feet'", he said aloud. The answer to his dilemma was clear at once. Although Kardo and even some of his supporters were shouting insults and urging him to hurry, Otah took his time. Deliberately he removed his shoes and tunic. Stripped to his breach cloth only, he began backing away. At Kardo's shriek, a hunter raced up, threatening the man with a spear. Otah thrust the man aside and backed up another ten paces. Breathing deeply to fill his lungs, he turned to say a last goodbye to his sister, but she was no longer in sight. "I don't blame her," he thought. "Who would want to see her brother drown in the quicksand? Or for that matter, beaten to death by a mastodon's trunk?"

Taking a final deep draught of the fetid swamp air, and clutching his spear, he exhaled and started his run. True to his nickname he did show *"flying feet"*! Although he was unable to hear it, several Clan members broke out in spontaneous cheers. Of course these were silenced abruptly by an angry shout from Kardo.

Almost too fast the edge of the bog appeared. Timing it just right, Otah took one final stride and launched himself straight at the stricken mastodon. To avoid the trunk he had aimed his leap at the very rear part of the exposed back. He landed hard, right on target, but began to slip. At the last second, one foot already in the water, he grabbed the only handhold available. The ridged spine allowed just enough purchase to keep him astride. As he began to slide back again he plunged the spear into the crazed animal's back. It was far from a killing strike, but was not intended to be. Using the spear's handle he worked his way up until he was once again safely perched on the broad back. The mastodon trumpeted weakly and tried to shake the human off its back. Otah held on until the animal finally calmed somewhat, then did what he was ordered to do.

Seven thrusts were needed, each requiring all the man's strength. Only the remarkable keenness of the flint spearhead made it possible for enough penetration to reach the mastodon's vitals. One of these finally severed part of the spine, bringing merciful death soon after.

Exhausted, Otah slumped forward, only keeping his precarious seat by clutching the deeply imbedded spear. The shouting started then! Paying no attention to Kardo's threats, they hurriedly threw a rawhide rope to the successful young man. Unceremoniously they yanked him off the mastodon's back, and hand over hand, three hunters reeled him in so fast that this time the muck couldn't trap him!

*   *   *

A runner was sent to summon the women. They soon arrived and took charge of the meat. The men mostly lay around while the women did the butchering. A precarious bridge of poles had been secured from solid ground to the mastodon's back. While preparing meat was women's work, the men did at times offer to carry an especially large portion, but this was done grudgingly and with ill favor. It was gruesome work. Cutting slabs of the dark red meat was difficult enough at a normal kill, but this animal's carcass was more than half submerged in the bog. Otah was astonished when he saw one of the smaller hunters actually disappear directly into the body cavity! Such delicacies as heart, liver, and lungs were hoisted out with ropes and delivered to the waiting women. The small hunter finally emerged, a bloody but happy mess!

Otah, now considered somewhat of an oddity if not a hero, was free to come and go as he pleased. He and Leaf had spent half a day searching for Sand, but although it was plain to see where it had landed, neither the wolf nor his tracks could be found. Otah was glad that at least the animal's body had not been discovered. Sadly, he was forced to accept his companion's death. So violently had it been thrown, there could be little hope that a major injury hadn't been inflicted. Leaf was secretly relieved.

As the women finished the preliminary work on the meat, plans were made to return to the main village. Many hours of toil awaited them there. The meat must be cut into very thin strips and either cured over many a smoldering fire or hung from racks to dry in the sun. Had the kill been achieved in late autumn their job would have been easier, as then the meat strips need only be hung and protected until frozen. As it was, drying or smoking the flesh was the only way to preserve it for the winter. It was a hard life for women, but the men reminded them that their jobs were more dangerous. The debate was ongoing!

Otah had little to say as they followed the Clan toward the permanent village. He was missing the wolf, but Leaf certainly was *not!* Although he had resigned himself to the possibility that his companion was gone forever, it was still hard to face.

Kardo took advantage of every opportunity to taunt the one he considered his enemy. Of course he carried none of the meat, not even a pack. With a voice loud enough for all the travelers to hear he would say such things as, "Where is your wolf friend, you *thief?*" Or, "You must be happy now, Leaf, my wife. No chance to be bitten *again* by that devil wolf!" The tirade continued off and on all day, as Otah and Leaf did their best to ignore the braggart. Once, they attempted to slow down enough to lag out of hearing behind the others. Kardo soon put a stop to this by issuing a series of harsh orders. They simply had to keep on walking, as Kardo was still in command of the hunt.

Reaching the village at sunset on the third day of the march they were met by the visibly upset Old Woman. Leaf rushed to her. "What is it? What *is it?*" Old Geet garbled a reply, only part of which even Leaf could understand.

"The old one says that Chief Spotted Hand has fallen very ill. She has tried various cures but with little success. I will go to him." Kardo's sneer was evident to any who looked his way. He had not been able to see the stranger dead, but without the old chief's protection it could be easily arranged!

Inside the chief's house with the door flap fastened, Leaf was conversing with the healer. As usual she was much easier to understand away from the other Clansmen. Leaf interpreted as fast as she could. "She says that spotted Hand had ordered her to keep watch and tell him as soon as the hunters returned. She was then to tell everyone that her chief was very ill. It was clear that Geet had an inkling of what the frail but clever old chief was up to, but she refused to say what she thought it was.

At that moment the door flap was thrown open. Rudely, with no consideration of proper respect, Kardo stalked up to Spotted Hand's bench. "I would speak with you!" Kardo growled. The chief was *sleeping!* Kardo tried again. "This stranger," he almost shouted, stabbing a finger at Otah, "is not only a thief, but he. . . he. . ." The old chief slept away, with what appeared to be a half smile on his wrinkled face. Disgustedly, Kardo stomped out, muttering angry threats.

Old Geet was chuckling to herself. Seated on a skin by the wall, she made no effort to get up to offer food. Spotted Hand straightened himself, arranged his robes, and began to speak. He had made a remarkable recovery from his "nap"!

"A clever man!" Otah thought. Leaf prepared food, chewed it thoroughly and handed it to him, but the chief ate very little. He called for water and drank a few sips as Leaf prepared to interpret. "Come near to me," he commanded, and Otah did as he was told. "Have you killed that wolf yet?" His unseeing eyes were facing in Otah's direction. Rather than have to repeat everything, Leaf gave a brief account of the action at the bog. When he fully understood that Sand was gone and probably dead, he seemed satisfied.

Chief Spotted Hand then surprised Otah by reaching one shaking hand toward him. His sister whispered that he should take the proffered hand and hold it. His voice hardly above a whisper, the chief said, "Kardo accuses you. As I told you before, he will kill you if he can. You must *fight him!*"

Otah felt as if he had been kicked in the stomach! Leaf too was shocked by the command. "But he is bigger and stronger than I. There is no way I could win such a contest."

"It will be a fair fight," Spotted Hand continued, unperturbed. "All the village will watch so do not fear. Now hold out your other hand." He whispered some instructions to Leaf, who quickly dug into a bark basket and retrieved a small item. The chief took it from her and dropped it onto Otah's palm.

"What is this?" Otah asked.

"Now close your fingers around it. Do you see how it is shaped to fit your hand? Tell me of its weight."

"For a small stone it is *very heavy!*" Otah replied, hefting the object speculatively.

"It is 'iron stone'" the chief hissed. "Hold it tight in your fist and hit that schemer in the face! *Knock him down! Hit him some more!*" the old chief was shaking in excitement.

Otah was shocked. "But you said a 'fair fight'. This weapon hardly seems fair to me."

"It will be fair," the chief chortled. Kardo will secretly arm himself *too!* I know him well! So if both men have a weapon I would call it fair, wouldn't you?" His toothless gums gleamed as he shook with laughter.

"I don't like this," Leaf told the chief. "My brother is tired, but Kardo is rested, having done hardly any work at the kill site. He makes others do it for him; he even refused to carry a pack."

"I know, I know," the chief replied, still smiling. Tell your brother to have a pack ready and hidden outside of the village. If the fight goes against him he can run. No one could catch young 'flying feet'!"

"My chief," Otah began desperately, "I do not feel this is a fair judgment. I could be *killed!*"

"Shut up! Spotted Hand said mildly. "You will fight, for I have ordered it."

"When will this happen? We have been traveling with full packs. I need time to rest."

"You will fight at sundown. *Today!*" Turning to Leaf who was trying not to cry, he said, "Find the crier. Tell him to announce the combat. Hurry! Now go. I am tired."

Clutching the cleverly formed cylinder of hematite in his fist, Otah stretched out on an elk skin, hoping for a little sleep before he must once again risk his life. The old woman brought food and water, which he forced down, hoping it would provide a little strength. It did not seem to help. "I cannot beat him in combat," Otah thought, "so I must overcome him with guile!" He felt a little better then.

*   *   *

He hated the sun, which lay just above the treetops bordering the Black Swamp to the west. It was time. Leaf and a wide-eyed Little Kardo met him as he emerged from the chief's house, wearing only a breech cloth and a leather vest. He kept his right hand close to his hip, the other held close to his body.

The central clearing was ringed with silent men and women of the Clan. Children clung to their parents, staring at the stranger.

Kardo, of course, had not yet appeared. If he knew anything, it was how to make a dramatic entrance. Then he was there, causing quite a stir. He had oiled his upper body with bear grease, and the beautiful beaded pouch hung securely below his throat. Someone, probably his second wife, had made an elaborate coil of his braided hair, and a wide band of sun metal encircled his upper arm. Without question he looked every bit the warrior. By comparison, Otah appeared small and somehow weak. They each advanced a few steps until they were perhaps four paces apart. Kardo was enjoying this! He showed no fear, but Otah, on the other hand, looked frightened and nervous. He hid his right hand even further behind his back, his fist clenched so tightly that the cords in his wrist stood out. Out of the corner of his eye he saw his sister and Little Kardo watching breathlessly.

Kardo expanded his glistening chest and made an announcement. "This is to be a fair fight," he shouted, turning to face each area of those watching. "This *stranger* has come to us unbidden, with him a Spirit Wolf trained to kill. He had in his pack many flints, some fine tobac, and other valuable things. Obviously he is a *thief!* Furthermore his father, who spent some time with us long ago, was *also a thief!* He it was who stole the divining bones from our old Seer. Banishment is too good for this so-called 'flying feet' one. The wretched animal he called his *'friend'* is no more. Its medicine was as nothing when caught by the mastodon's trunk. Now we will fight, but first I call my two friends to come forward." The crowd stirred in consternation, and there was some discreet whispering. The fight was to be fair, and between two persons only. Kardo should not ask for help in the conflict!

Sensing their disapproval, Kardo simply laughed. "No my people, these two are not to join in the fight. I need no help with this scrawny stranger. No, I ask them to do something for me. For *all* of us! Seize him quickly! Pull his right arm from behind his back. We will see that he is not only a thief, but a coward as well!" Moving closer he told them, "Make him open his hand." Otah struggled for a moment, then held his arm high for all to see. His hand was *empty!* A few people laughed at the confused expression on the bigger man's face. His two friends walked away, angry that they had been made to look foolish.

Suddenly, without waiting for the proper signal to begin the fight, Kardo rushed furiously at Otah. Low down and half concealed in his left fist was a thin flint blade! He smashed into Otah's side, nearly knocking him to the ground. Arrogantly Kardo backed away a step, allowing Otah to regain his footing. Turning to the crowd he started to speak. "Now you will see how I deal with. . ."

Otah slipped the hematite bar from its hiding place in his left armpit, leaped forward and drove his weighted right fist into Kardo's eye. The big man fell backward, badly stunned. Otah was not ashamed, for he remembered Spotted Hand's command. He leaned over and slammed the heavy fist against Kardo's head, just above the ear. The ironstone weight did its job, and Kardo fell unconscious, bleeding profusely.

Otah stood over his foe, trembling noticeably. Pointing at the same two men Kardo had summoned, he motioned for them to come forward. Still without touching the fallen man he indicated that all of the Clan should come closer. Silently they gathered in a close ring around the fighters, so stunned by the turn of events that they had hardly found their voices. With a slow and dramatic gesture, Otah's bare foot turned the fallen man's body onto his back. A sharp intake of many breaths proved that all had seen it. The flint knife fell from Kardo's unconscious fingers. Otah had won, not only the fight, but hearts of the Clan as well!

Still shaking and before the people could leave, Otah called Leaf to his side. Little Kardo paid no attention to his father, who was finally struggling to stand. "Interpret for me," he told her. Facing them all he called out, "Both my father and I have been called *thieves*. Now you will see who the *real* thief is!" Stooping down he picked up Kardo's knife. Shouts of alarm broke out as the sharp blade flicked downward toward Kardo's exposed throat! Leaf screamed, but Otah held up one hand for silence. With a decisive thrust he severed the cord of braided mastodon hair that held Kardo's decorated pouch. He asked Leaf to hold out both hands, then slashed through the soft ermine skin. Into her waiting palms fell four small, highly polished bones decorated with red ochre dots and mysterious curving lines. The people moved back, afraid of the power of the divining bones. A final object then fell free. It was a blue stone perforated for suspension!

Still holding the bones, Leaf rapidly informed the chief of everything that had happened. Even though his sight was gone he had already discerned much of what had gone on by simply standing still and listening. "Take me to the fallen one," he told Leaf.

She led him into the ring of people still surrounding Otah and Kardo. The latter had struggled to his feet, but suddenly fell again, dizzy with pain. Chief Spotted Hand, once more sounding like the strong leader he had once been, made a proclamation. "Kardo, you who would be chief, was it not you who continually spoke of banishment? Did you not tell all who would listen that a thief must not be allowed to remain in our village? Is that not correct?" Kardo, having managed to stand up once again, savagely swiped at the blood still running from below his eye. He said nothing. "You could have *been* chief. I would have appointed you, but greed and arrogance made it plain that you would have been a poor leader. *You are banished!* If morning light finds you here or anywhere nearby, I will send the hunters to take your life! Gather what is yours and go. You may select one wife to accompany you."

"What about my son, Little Kardo?" he asked sullenly.

"The boy will choose at this moment. Turning his blind eyes this way and that, he waited for old Geet to point him in the proper direction. Holding out a palsied hand, he compelled the child to come forward. "Do not be frightened," he said kindly, holding the boy's trembling hand in his own. Little Kardo stared in fear and fascination at the two uneven purplish blemishes on the wrinkled skin. They had been there from birth, and had been the chief's namesake. "Your father must leave our village. He will never return. You must decide now. Do you wish to go away with your father, or would you rather stay with your mother?"

"*Mommyyyy!*" Little Kardo cried. He yanked his small hand free and ran into Leaf's arms.

"I have spoken!" Chief Spotted Hand said. A great fatigue seemed to strike him at that moment. "Give me the spirit bones," he commanded. He then surprised everyone by placing them reverently into the hands of old Geet. An even greater shock was in store for the Clan. The old woman spoke clearly, with no hint of the gibberish to which they were accustomed. Many expressed the thought that "power of the bones" had caused a miracle. The old healer did nothing to dissuade them! With the evil Kardo soon to be gone she no longer needed her deception!

Leaf and Otah smiled secretly at each other. They were sure Geet had been able to speak plainly all along. "Remember, Leaf? Spotted Hand said that he and the healer 'understood each other'"! Otah chuckled.

"Be still!" Geet's angry words shocked the Clan into instant silence. Holding two divining bones aloft in each hand, she began to speak. "The bones are *talking!* I must tell you what they say." Everyone remained silent, afraid of the power the small pieces conveyed. "Each day," she continued, "a generous portion of food, *well chewed food,* must be brought to the chief's house on a clean slab of wood. Chief Spotted Hand and I will eat. Furthermore, every person, young or old, must be always watching for patches of wild mint. It is to be cured and stored, in order that there always be enough to make tea for the chief and myself. Finally, since Leaf will undoubtedly be leaving us soon, a young girl must be chosen as a helper in the chief's house." Several mothers could be seen fearfully drawing their young daughters close. "She will not need to live with us, but must come at dawn. The chosen one may then return to her mother each day when the sun is

high." A soft sigh of relief could be heard throughout the gathering. "After a time, if proven worthy, she will be instructed in the arts of healing, and possibly even be taught the secrets of the divining bones!"

"How will the girl be chosen?" One mother asked timidly.

"The bones will do the choosing, of course!" Geet snapped.

"*AIIAAEEEE!*" The old woman screamed. She gave a heated harangue as the shocked Clan listened in fear. Leaf translated for Otah as fast as she could. "Do not touch the divining bones!" she shrieked. "Bring a clean slab of wood as fast as you can." When a suitable piece was presented she carefully arranged the ivory-colored cubes in a circle, each one touching the next. The onlookers were absolutely silent, creeping forward to see the ritual. "Now," the healer growled, "the chief's house must be thoroughly cleaned, and this is to be done *at once!* I shall require a new cloak of tanned and softened doeskin, with a collar of ermine fastened around the neck." The villagers stood and stared. "Go!" Deet screamed. "All of this must be done before the moon rises."

She looked all around, making eye contact with many, then lowered her voice to just above a whisper. "As I told you, I shall need a helper from now until my days are ended, one who has suffered as I have suffered." She closed her eyes and made strange gestures over the bones until her head fell forward. Everyone watching was breathless with anticipation. Suddenly her eyes popped open. "Lame! Bring Lame to me. Now!"

A small girl of perhaps ten summers was hustled forward, limping and trembling with fright. "Have no fear, little one. You were born with a twisted foot, and many have been cruel to you, as they have been to me. The divining bones have spoken. You will assist me and become a healer." She raised her voice in authority once again. "A hut must be built next to the chief's house, with a doorway in between. All this work is to be completed in three days. Until then the child returns to her mother. Now Chief Spotted Hand and I must retire to the chief's house. Be sure that everything the bones require is done!"

Otah was startled when Leaf, who had interpreted most of this for her brother, suddenly burst out in another coughing fit. He could tell that her coughing was simply another attempt to conceal her laughter. Otah grinned too, marveling at old Geet's very clever way of assuring that she and Spotted Hand would be well cared for in the coming years. Also, she had seen a way to end the sad plight of an unfortunate child. Had the old woman been born a man she would have been a chief long ago!

Kardo and his second wife left in shame well before dawn. The entire village seemed relieved, even those who had pretended to be his friends. "Finally we are free of that cruel man," Leaf said that morning. "We no longer have anything to fear from him!" Otah said nothing, but he was *thinking* a great deal!

"I have learned to know that man," he mused. "He will never allow this insult to go on without revenge! Of that I am sure." He decided then and there that they must be very careful, no matter where they ended up. "He is a coward, but a clever man. There is no enemy more dangerous than a clever coward. Yes, we must be on our guard!"

Two days later they left the village. Otah, Leaf, Little Kardo, Small, and two others made up the group. For Leaf it would be a homecoming.

While Little Kardo was still cool toward his uncle, he did not seem at all upset about his father, for as Leaf had said, Kardo had paid little attention to him anyway. He ran back and forth from the head of the walkers to well behind them. On one occasion he had fallen further behind than he realized. Busy teasing a garter snake with a stick he suddenly realized that the group had gone on ahead and he was all alone. Looking fearfully about, he began to run. Fortunately the rest were soon in sight. Without slowing his pace he grabbed Otah's hand and held on. The man pretended not to notice but he was secretly pleased.

*   *   *

After Kardo's banishment things had begun to happen in the mastodon hunters' village. Chief Spotted Hand was ill, and this time it was real. The old woman cared for him, with help from the newly chosen girl. Coming and going importantly throughout the village, Geet made no attempt to hide the fact that her speech was quite clear. Shrewdly she let all believe that the divining bones had caused the "miracle".

The chief knew that a new leader must soon be chosen. Bickering and factions were already developing among the men, but so far no fighting had erupted. The old man would have to call a meeting of the entire Clan for that evening. Before being fed the soft gruel he could eat, he called Geet to his side. "A new chief must be selected," he whispered. "Which of the young men do you favor?"

"Me? You ask *me?* Who am I to make such a choice? The decision must be yours alone!"

"I *know that!*" he snapped. "I will certainly be the one to make the choice, but I simply wish to know your preference." The old woman grinned, knowing the blind chief could not see her amusement. She allowed several moments to pass, pretending to ponder the matter.

"If it were my decision," she said slowly, "I would choose between these two men." She named both and waited.

"Ah! They are the best. Either would serve our people well. These two are the very ones *I* had in mind!" She waited, again smiling to herself. She waited some more. At last he spoke, as she had known he would. "And. . and. . .of those two fine men. . . uh. . which one of those *two* would you choose? I mean if it *were* up to you, of course."

She fought down the urge to giggle and said the name of Stump. Again Chief Spotted Hand pretended surprise.

"The *very one* I had been considering! Is that not amazing? I will tell the village tonight that Stump is their new chief. By the way, you are to be at my side. Be sure all can see that you carry the divining bones in your hands. You *did* use them to help me choose the new chief didn't you?"

She had not, but assured him that indeed she had. Laughing aloud, she left the chief to announce the meeting. "He is old and sick but he still has his pride," she thought.

She and Spotted Hand certainly did understand each other!

*   *   *

Leaf gave a little cry of happiness when her former home came into view. Otah and the boy hurried inside to see how things had gone while the hut had been empty again. "I cleaned it well before I left," he said proudly. Small and Leaf looked at each other, shaking their heads. There was no way they would spend even one night here until it was *really* clean. Otah grabbed Little Kardo's hand and pulled him outside. "Let them alone for a while," he told the boy, forgetting that neither Little Kardo nor Small could understand his speech. "We might as well begin right now," he sighed. Taking turns, each would point to an object, say its name, then translate. The lad was bright and quick. He seemed to enjoy the game, and at one point ran inside to show the women his new words. Things were starting out well for the five of them.

After a day of rest, all began the work of enlarging their hut. Morning frost on the bushes hurried them along, as there was a great deal to be done before snow fell. While they had packed in a generous amount of mastodon meat, it would not last the winter. Hides must be tanned, pemmican prepared, and fish smoked. Yes, there was much to do!

Chief Spotted Hand had made sure that all Otah's possessions were returned to him, but an even greater surprise was the gift of a fine atlatl and fourteen darts for it. Leaf suspected the weapon had been the chief's own, as she had seen one wrapped in an otter skin behind the old man's bench. Some day when he was a man it would belong to Little Kardo.

Small never seemed to stray far from Otah's side, making him a little nervous as he worked on their new home. He was becoming very fond of the tiny girl and it was obvious that the feeling was mutual. She was a perceptive woman who missed very little of what was going on around her. She and Little Kardo practiced their language skills together, both progressing rapidly.

One thing that Small found troubling was that Otah sometimes seemed unhappy. At times she found him stopped in the middle of a task, staring off across the swamp. Story telling around the fire at night did not seem to interest him much, although he would relate some of his adventures when begged to do so. It was the only time he stopped brooding for a while.

"A story Uncle, *a story!* "

"But I don't know any stories that would interest a fine young hunter like you."

"Oh you *do*, Uncle! Tell us the story of the two buffalos you killed. Please, *tell it!* "

"*Two* buffalos?"

"Yes, don't you remember? You told us before how you threw your pack at one buffalo, then another one, twice as big. . .Oh you know the very story I mean. *Tell us!* " The boy's eyes sparkled in the firelight.

"Ah, I seem to remember now. If you really want me to. . ."

"Tell the story!" Small told him, hiding a big grin behind her hand.

"Very well," Otah sighed. "I was hunting alone without spear or atlatl when. . ."

"No, *No!* " The boy interrupted. "You *had* a spear, remember?"

"I was hunting alone with only a spear when a huge buffalo charged out of the swamp. I was not afraid. No, not at all! I walked right up to the creature and pinched his ear. "Why did you pinch me, you skinny, two-legged thing?" it said. This buffalo could speak my language of course. "I did it because you are a big ugly brute and I intend to finish you with my spear." Then I threw some mud in its eyes and. . . .

"No, Uncle, *No!* The *pack.* You threw your pack!"

"Oh yes, that is exactly what I did. What a memory the boy has! Anyway I threw my pack on its horn. Since then it could only see out of one eye, to the buffalo I only looked half as big. I ran between its legs and was ready to use my spear when the second buffalo came at me. I think I remember that it was a little one, small and weak, so I . . ."

"No, *No uncle!* It was a great big one! Don't you remember?"

The adults, seated in a circle around the low fire were nearly bursting to keep from laughing aloud.

"Yes, you are correct. It *was* big. The biggest buffalo in the Black Swamp. The first buffalo was afraid of the big one and ran away. I jumped on the great big buffalo's back and grabbed its horns. It tried to throw me off, but I held on tight. I rode that animal all the way to the river. If I wanted to go one way I pulled on that horn. If I wanted to go the other way I pulled on the other horn. It was much better than walking!"

This was too much! They all burst out with wild laughter. All that is except Leaf's son. He had fallen asleep.

Small waited until Leaf was alone in the house, then asked a question. "Your brother sometimes seems unhappy. Do you know why? He and your son may not yet actually be friends, but they are learning to like each other a little, so that could not be it. Is it me? Perhaps I should go."

Leaf laughed at the girl. "Yes, he and my son are getting along better. At least Little Kardo has stopped secretly aiming his atlatl at Otah's back! Of one thing I am sure. *You* are not the problem! In fact I expect it will not be long until he decides to build a new hut near this one, but not *too* near! A hut just large enough for two."

Going on with her work of grinding some seeds the two had gathered, Leaf looked off into the distance. "He misses that wolf. It *disgusts* me that he cannot forget that vicious beast! Look, the wound in my leg has barely healed. It bit me, and I'm sure it would have killed me if given the chance. *I'm glad it's dead!*"

"But *is* it?" Small asked. "I saw the big animal throw it into the forest, but I don't think it was found by anyone, dead or not."

"You are right," Leaf answered shortly. "Let's talk of something else now." So the subject was dropped.

A few days later even Little Kardo could tell that something was troubling his uncle. Like a typical five year old he simply used his new language to ask a question. "What is wrong with you Uncle Otah? Why don't you laugh so much anymore? Are you sick?"

"No I am not sick. I will tell you what the trouble is. I miss my companion. He is probably dead, but three times that I know of he saved my life. I owe it to him to at least make a search. How would you like to come along as 'Second in Command'?"

Little Kardo's eyes sparkled for a moment but then he frowned. "I would like to be Second in Command but I don't want to find it. I hate wolfs! That one tried to eat *Mommy!*" Otah smiled and patted the boy on the head. He respected an honest answer, even from a child.

"You are right, Kardo," he said gravely. "I will go alone."

"My name is *Little* Kardo!" the boy exclaimed haughtily.

"No longer! As Second in Command you are not little. You will be called Kardo , after your father." The boy strutted about proudly, and Otah knew he had said the right thing.

When he told the women of his plans to start a search for his lost companion they were not surprised. Small shyly touched his hand and asked that he be careful and come back to them soon. Leaf said nothing, but seemed to pound the grinding stone harder into the flat rock than was really necessary. Words were not needed. She thought he was a fool.

He left early the next morning. The night before the women had prepared his pack and looked over his new boots and well-made clothing, as was their duty. They were still sleeping when he slipped away carrying the spear, the atlatl riding snugly in its case under his left arm. He was better dressed and better armed than he had ever been.

He smiled a little as he strode steadily along the river. "They think I'm just going to wander around all over the swamp, but I'm not. I have a good idea of where to look, and will start my search there." In the eye of his mind he pictured the scene. First the "family trees", then Sand's old den in the dirt bank. His stride lengthened.

He had trouble locating the four trees that Leaf had named so long ago, as they had grown almost as tall as those in the surrounding forest. Finally they appeared, but he circled the clump twice just to make sure they were the right ones. "Next summer," he thought, "I will bring all of them here to see these special trees." Now that he was so close he hesitated. What if the den was empty? Or worse, what if another wolf family had moved in? Wolves that would gladly attack and tear him to pieces!

Patience. . . patience. . . plan. . .

The words from his father brought a smile. "Very well," he thought. "I will find my spot on the hill and watch for a while." Much brush and weeds had overgrown his familiar vantage point. He need not have bothered however, as one brief glance made it plain that the den was not being used. In fact it had obviously been abandoned long ago. If Sand had gone there to recuperate he had left no sign of it. Otah sadly faced the fact that Sand was gone for good.

His hike back to the others was slow. Slow and sad. They asked no questions when he plodded into the clearing that night. It was plain to all that he had not found the wolf.

Life went on. Otah's spirits lightened, and at any rate there was so much work to do there was little time for brooding. Kardo was becoming a true companion. He was quick to learn and had a keen eye for signs of game. Already he had proudly come into camp carrying a fat opossum he had brought down with his miniature weapons. Otah's affection continued to grow.

One morning Otah was watching the boy rub grease into the atlatl. "That is a fine weapon young man. I'll bet your father built that for you didn't he?"

After a pause the boy answered slowly. "No, it was not my father. Chief Spotted Hand made it for me when he could still see a little." This brief statement told Otah much!

A few says later Leaf was becoming concerned about her son. He was often running about, but Otah had given him specific boundaries that he was not to exceed when alone. She called his name but there was no answer, and Otah was off on a two day hunt which heightened her fears. Small stopped her work on a stretched piece of hide and offered to help look for the boy. "Little Kardo!" Leaf shouted angrily, her fears mounting. About to shout again, the boy appeared from a thick clump of downed poplar at the far side of the clearing. "Where have you *been?*" Leaf cried, shaking the boy hard.

"But Mommy, I was not beyond the boundaries Uncle told me."

"Why didn't you come when I called?"

"I was asleep in a nest," he answered.

"Do not lie to me!" Leaf sputtered, shaking him again.

"But it *was* like a nest!" he said, sniffling a little. "Uncle has never seen it either, and it's right under those low trees."

"You will stay in the hut for the rest of the day, my son. Think about the 'nest' you are trying to make me believe in." Hanging his head the lad walked slowly into their house.

"Leaf, *Leaf!* He is only a little boy. Little boys sometimes have big imaginations. He is usually a good little fellow, perhaps you were too hard on him."

"No I'm not!" She retorted. "There are many dangers in the Black Swamp, and anything can happen. He must learn to obey and be honest." Nothing more was said, and the women went back to work while the boy sulked inside.

In early evening Otah returned, carrying a field dressed button buck on his shoulders. He was surprised that Kardo did not come running to see the kill, but Leaf told him of the discipline she had ordered because of the story Kardo had given her. The man entered the house, squinting in the darkness. He had no intention of adding further punishment. In the first place Kardo was not his child, but mainly he didn't believe in the punishment of a man child by a *woman*, mother or not! "What happened today Second in Command?" he asked mildly as he pulled off his muddy boots.

"I found a nest. I *did!* I told them but they said I lied. I did not lie!"

"I believe you," he said quietly. "Tomorrow morning you will lead me to this nest. We will show these bossy women!"

Kardo wriggled forward and crept close to his uncle. "They will see!" The boy stated emphatically, and crawled off to his sleeping mat. Otah chuckled as he found his own bed.

"Second in Command" was up early, being sure to make enough noise to wake the others, especially Otah. The women prepared food, but the boy was too excited to eat much. "You will see," he told the women, his lower lip punched out indignantly. "You will see that I did find a nest. A *big one!*"

Otah took the boy's remarks seriously, as wild boars often scraped together a jumble of brush and leaves that could be called a nest. They were very dangerous animals, always traveling in groups of eight or ten. "Let's go Uncle. Let's go *now!*"

"It is not light enough," Otah laughed. "Who can tell what might be lurking in that big nest you found. Eat your food. We may need your strength." The women smiled secretly as the boy gobbled some meat. Otah certainly knew how to deal with the lad, even though he had no children of his own.

The sun was barely climbing above the trees when Second in Command practically dragged the man from the house. Small looked alarmed when Otah loaded his atlatl. "Are we in danger?" she asked.

"I don't think so," Otah answered. But she noted that he slipped the big axe in his belt and fitted the spear in its cradle over his left shoulder. Both women were becoming more anxious as they watched the man prepare for possible action.

"Sit." He commanded, pushing the boy down on a log. "You are Second in Command. That means you *must* stay directly behind me at all times!"

"Why?" The boy asked.

"Because you are Two and I am *One!*" Satisfied, the youngster moved behind his uncle while they were still in the clearing!

"Otah, I think Little Kardo, I mean Second in Command, should stay here with us. This is beginning to look dangerous."

"He is Second in Command. He goes with me." The lad gave his uncle a look of pure admiration, and moved even closer behind the man. "Point the way we should go," Otah ordered. They marched out, Second nearly bumping the backs of his uncle's legs. Suddenly Otah stopped in his tracks. Second," he said, "where is your atlatl?" Stricken, Second hung his head in shame. "Oh, I see, you were waiting for me to give the order, correct? That was good thinking. Go now and get your weapon. You are an excellent Second in Command." Proudly the little fellow dashed into the house to retrieve the tiny thing. They left the clearing in the direction Second had indicated.

Second was confused. He had been sure he could lead his uncle directly to the spot about which he had told him. Finally, with a shout he pointed triumphantly to a lightning blasted tree. At its base was a thick clump of bushes and brambles. Motioning with his hand, Otah held the boy back and began to circle the area. Second pulled on his uncle's sleeve and pointed back at the tangle of foliage. Otah shook his head and kept circling until he was downwind of the area. For several minutes he stood still and tested the breeze by tilting his head back and sniffing repeatedly. The boy imitated these actions perfectly, although he had no idea why he was doing it. Finally Otah relaxed and spoke aloud. "It is no boar's nest. If it were we would smell the stink! Now you are Number One, and may go ahead to show me the nest."

When they arrived, Second fell to all fours, preparing to enter an opening that much resembled a tunnel through the bushes. Otah stopped him. "Now you must be Number Two again," he told him, taking the lead. The "nest" was lined with soft moss and leaves. Lying prone, they were shocked to be able to see their house and almost the entire camp. Motioning rapidly, Otah backed them out of the tunnel. "Now Second, we run! *Run!*" They pounded into the camp, Otah shouting for the women. "You owe Second an apology all right. He *did* find a nest, a nest made for a *man!* I'm sure we can all guess who has been secretly watching us. I was certain we had not seen the last of him."

"Who?" Second asked.

"Your father." For the first time, Otah wished the Clansmen who had joined them were still here but they had moved on to start their own village.

They made what preparations they could, not knowing if or when an attack might come. Two nights passed without incident, but on the third, just after dawn there was a scream from Leaf, who had left the house to get cooking water. Otah and Small came tumbling out to be confronted by a terrifying sight. Kardo was there, one muscular arm around Leaf's throat. In his right hand was a knife, its flint blade shining in the early light. "Stop or I kill her *right now* rather than later," he growled. Otah and Small stood frozen in the doorway, not knowing what could be done.

There was movement at the edge of the clearing. Kardo's other wife stepped out of the trees and joined her husband, but said nothing. "Where is my son?" Kardo snarled, tightening his grip around Leaf's throat. "When all of you are dead the boy goes with me."

"He is sleeping," Leaf managed to choke out. "Leave him alone. He doesn't want to be with you."

"He will come whether he wants to *or not!* Now you two. Lie down across that log." They did not move. "*Do it,*" he roared, "or I kill this treacherous wife." Turning to his silent companion he gave an order. Handing her a long thin blade from his belt he told her to force Otah and Small to lie across the log as he had ordered them. The poor woman's hands were shaking so hard she managed to drop the knife into the dirt. She scrabbled for the blade in the thin light, but seemed unable to find it. Angrily, Kardo dragged Leaf around until he could kick the weapon to his companion. Strangely, it had been lying in plain sight all the time. The woman picked it up, seemed to stumble, then rose behind her husband.

Kardo's eyes suddenly flashed open wider than any human's could be expected to do. His mouth was gasping as if to scream but not a sound came out. His arm slowly relaxed from Leaf's neck. He shuddered all over, fell face-first in the dirt and did not move. His wife drew the weapon from his back, threw it to the ground, and fell sobbing beside her husband.

Kardo was dead.

"Leaf, go inside. Don't let Second come out. He must not see this. Woman, drag your husband's body out of sight. I will give him a proper burial later today. We must hurry!" He knelt beside Kardo's crying wife. "Who are you?" he asked.

"I am. . . was . . Kardo's second wife." Otah recognized her then. "He was planning to marry Small as well. I am glad he is dead, but. . .what. . but what . . will I do now? I have no one!"

"You have us," Otah said, helping her to her feet. "Undoubtedly we owe our lives to your act of bravery. You may stay with us, or if you prefer I will guide you back to your village. *You* were not banished! Spotted Hand only allowed Kardo to take you with him because the old chief knew that even in banishment a man needs a woman to help him. Now go to the stream and wash yourself. Unless I am mistaken, Second will be hard to keep inside when he wakens."

As Otah expected it was not long before the boy came charging out of the door

229

flap. "What is going on?" he cried. "And who are you?" As the day brightened he recognized the stranger. "Oh, I know you. You are my second mommy. Why are you here? Where is my father?"

"Slow down Second," Otah said, ruffling the boy's thick hair. "Your father was here too but he has left us."

"Will he come back?" Second cried. "I don't want to see him. Will he make me go away with him? *I don't want to!*"

Otah took the boy's hand and sat him on the very log that was to have been their execution site. "Listen very carefully my Second in Command," he began. "Your father has gone far away. Very, very far away, and will never come back. You need not even think about him, as he certainly is not thinking of you. Now hear me! It is not often that a Second in Command has as his Number One an uncle, but, if it is possible, you may at times. . . not *often*, but at times, think of me as a sort of father. Could you do that?"

Second's dark eyes sparkled as he considered the offer. "I think so. Maybe. Not often, but at times!"

"Good!" Said Otah, with a long, tired sigh.

*   *   *

Time passed. The young widow stayed with them after a short visit back to the Clan. To Otah's surprise and delight, three Mastodon Hunters came with her, and asked to join them. Two women, wives of the older Clansmen, came also. Asked why they had chosen to come, the men sadly replied that mastodons could no longer be found anywhere. Their time on earth was ending. "We need to learn new ways," they said. Otah and the others would be happy to teach them.

Their three children added more mouths to feed. Several new houses had to be built and the clearing greatly enlarged. One hut, well built of poles and tanned skin, stood a little way off from the others. It was for Otah and his wife, Small. The pretty young woman proudly wore a beautiful blue bead around her neck. Every time Otah looked at it he felt guilty, but Leaf only smiled knowingly. Her brother had needed to give his bride a wedding gift!

With enough hunters and gatherers, they had food in plenty. Stories around the central fire were greatly enjoyed.

Life was good!

    *   *   *

Two autumns had passed and now Small was caring for their baby daughter. It was too cold and the baby too small for them to accompany Otah on his final fall hunt. He didn't mind this, as a crying baby was not something he enjoyed! Somewhat tired of the camp hubbub, he went alone.

On this occasion he was hunting further east than was his custom. No game had yet been sighted, but this didn't concern him. The air was crisp and clear, and while the swamp was beginning to freeze over it was not yet safe for travel. As always he sought the ridges, moving slowly and silently, his eyes alert for game or tracks.

Stepping from stone to stone, he was crossing a partly frozen brook when he heard a commotion beyond the next ridge. He readied the atlatl, even placing an extra dart in his teeth in case another one was needed. Taking care to avoid any noise he climbed the slight hill and carefully parted the branches of a birch tree.

He counted four wolves circling around and around an oak tree. They had treed something, but could not get at it. Whatever the animal was, it was out of sight in the high branches. Otah was not about to alert the wolves, but thought that if he could fool them into running off he might be able to bring down whatever they had chased up there. He grabbed a dead limb and began to shake it wildly, shouting as loudly as he could and making growling noises. Two of the animals took flight; the other two, partly hidden in the brush, soon did the same. Otah waited for a time to make sure they did not return. Keeping a careful watch, he approached the oak. "Probably a raccoon," he thought, circling the tree and peering upward from various angles.

It was not a raccoon! A very large swamp lynx stared down from its refuge. Otah was not interested in an attempt to bring it down. Lynx meat was exceptionally tough, and of an unpleasant flavor. Even so there had been times when he would have gladly eaten it! Their coats were beautiful but the women had done a great deal of scraping and curing during the past days. He didn't think they would appreciate still another one to deal with. "And," he thought, "I'm certainly not going to do it!"

He stepped away, watching the tawny animal's tufted ears. He was not about to allow the creature to pounce on him from above. Walking backward with his neck craned, he was suddenly shocked as one foot contacted something that moved. He backed off, forgetting the lynx. A very young wolf pup lay curled up at his feet. Pitiful whining sounds came from the little creature. It was as black as night, not even a white whisker to be seen. Otah looked around fearfully, as the mother could be expected at any moment. Hardly thinking, he scooped up the pup and hurried away. He ran then, his weapons and pack bouncing with every step. When he came to the brook he ran straight into the water. Thin ice along the edge scratched his legs but he plunged on. Once he slipped on a moss-covered stone and nearly dropped the animal, but still he ran. Finally feeling relatively safe he sank down on the bank to catch his breath. It was only then that the small creature poked its pointed muzzle from the man's coat. Otah slowly pulled him out, and found that the inside of his jacket was spotted with a few drops of blood! "So that's what happened," he said, using a handful of leaves to clean his clothing. "Let's see where the trouble is." The wolf did not bite. In fact it didn't even growl. "Well you are certainly nothing like Sand! That one bit me hard. My arm still pains me at times. He bit my sister too. But then you are much younger than that wolf. You have not yet learned to hate!"

It was clear what had happened. The lynx must have been lying in wait on a low branch and the cub looked like an easy meal. It had pounced, teeth and claws tearing the tender hide. Evidently the rest of the pack had come to the rescue and soon treed the big cat. When the injured cub proved unable or unwilling to follow when Otah scared them off, they had abandoned it. A cruel practice, but necessary for the good of the pack.

Otah made fire. He kept the animal wrapped in his jacket as it whimpered and cried. "Why am I doing this?" he asked himself. "This animal is hardly more than a baby. Without its mother the thing will surely die. But perhaps if I take him back to our home Leaf could care for him. She has a way with animals and birds. On the other hand, she still limps from a wolf bite! Second stated that he *hated* 'wolfs'! The boy is beginning to like and trust me. Would a baby wolf add to that trust? Perhaps not."

He built up the fire and curled up with the wolf circled against his chest. Otah knew what he must do. It was exactly what its mother would have done. Selecting a bit of venison from his pack he began to chew on it. When it was soft and shredded he drew it out and fed the wolf. Then they both slept.

In the morning Otah surprised himself by heading directly back to the spot where he'd found the wolf cub. "If the pack is anywhere around there I'll just leave the little one on the ground and run for the nearest tree!" He spent half a day trudging back and forth near the place where he'd found the small black wolf., but there was no sign of the wolves. Once he even threw his head back and did his imitation of a wolf howl, but there was no answer. What should he do? He couldn't just leave the injured cub lying there. The lynx, or some other predator would soon make a meal of him. With a tired sigh, once again he tucked the animal under his coat and headed back toward his home.

Nearing the "family trees" he paused to remember all that had happened there over the years. Suddenly the quiet was broken by a loud, sustained wolf howl! Otah scrambled to the bank of the river and stood watching and listening. Far to the west on the other bank, four full grown wolves and two cubs trotted out on the sand. They milled around, nipping playfully at each other and generally showing a happy demeanor. Otah threw his head back and did his best to answer the pack. The pack leader's head snapped up. It peered intently in Otah's direction.

Could it *be?*

The alpha wolf stood statue-like for a long moment then turned and herded the others into the forest. Otah could tell that trotting was not easy for the big wolf. It had a decided limp, apparently caused by a crooked right back leg!

"*Go* Sand, my good friend!" He shouted to the empty forest. "Go far! Lead your pack. *I have your son!*"

Otah was surprised that he felt no great sadness. Although Sand had been a good friend and faithful companion, he reminded himself that Sand was never a pet. That brownish, sand-colored coat belonged in the wilds of the Black Swamp.

Everything was as it should be.

Still somewhat hopeful, he continued to scan the far river bank. Then soft whimpering sounds brought him back to the present, and he began chewing another chunk of venison for the pup.

The same questions as before nagged at him as he plodded homeward. Would they accept the little wolf? Would Leaf hate the animal? What would the newer members of their camp think? Would it even be possible to keep it alive? These and other such concerns troubled him.

Then from, it seemed, the very mists rising from the Black Swamp itself, the words came floating.

Patience. . . patience. . . plan!

THE END